MW01517300

I had the evidence of a motive…now, what was I going to do with it?

We got the sixteen-mm film going and Hughie came upright in his seat as soon as it started. The nude man on the flickering screen rated about twenty. The girl—beautiful and delicate with a round angelic face—couldn't have been more than fifteen. The poor lighting and the deep shadows caused images to appear to flicker in the wavering light, but what the two performers were doing left nothing to imagine.

After a few minutes I told Hughie to turn off the projector. We threaded the second spool and started it up again. A different man, mid-twenties, loomed out of the shaded scene, dallying with the same girl, slightly older in this flickers. The naked nymph in those flickering shadows raised my hackles. No way could anyone mistake Rachel Anne Maddon.

"I'd have to say those two youngsters were almighty active," Hughie said, grinning brightly. "You make the girl?"

I nodded, said nothing. I put the two film reels back in the box, but I had no intention of leaving them in my office. "Hughie, you need to forget you ever saw this."

Dunnum picked up the projector. "Can't say I'll ever forget I saw that. But I can remember that I didn't see it, if anybody asks."

Rachel Anne Maddon is about to become America's next great movie star. Adored by the camera, loved by her public, beautiful Rachel Anne has it all, including a dark secret from her past that threatens to blow up her promising future when her mentor and lover—a man old enough to be her father—turns up dead. Did he fall or was he pushed? Or did the bullet in him do the job? Either way, a homicide investigation will be deadly publicity for Rachel Anne and her family.

Rachel Anne's movie studio switches into high gear to protect her teetering career, but then Neil Brand, the studio's security chief, uncovers a blackmail scheme over illicit sex films that threatens other major motion picture stars. As the heat builds, the rich and powerful scramble to get out from under.

That's when the bodies begin to pile up.

KUDOS for *The Naked Nymph in the Dark Flickers*

In *The Naked Nymph in the Dark Flickers* by Ray Dyson, Neil Brand is once again trying to solve a murder. This time it is the murder of an aging actor/director who knew one secret too many. As Brand seeks to find the killer, more bodies pile up. Are the killers all the same person, or is Hollywood running amuck with random violence? Brand puts his life, career, and his friendship with his old cop partner on the line to find out. The book is well written, the plot strong with plenty of twists and turns. The story takes us back to a time in the 1950s when life was simpler and murder was easier to get away with than it is today. ~ *Taylor Jones, Reviewer*

The Naked Nymph in the Dark Flickers is the story of 1950s Hollywood and actors/actresses who think they can get away with anything, as long as they make money at the box office. In this sequel to *The Ice Cream Blonde*, we are reunited with Neil Brand, ex-cop and now head of security at York Studios. When an elderly actor is found murdered, Neil is called upon to find the killer and protect the studios assets. But as Neil digs for the truth, he uncovers some dark secrets that someone will do anything to keep hidden. As the bodies mount, Neil is faced with some hard choices, but can he live with the consequences? Dyson has crafted a tale that takes you back in time to the era of noir and black-and-white movies, when the Hollywood elite were in a class of their own and could get away with murder—literally. ~ *Regan Murphy, Reviewer*

ACKNOWLEDGEMENTS

Many thanks to my editor, Faith Caminski, and to cover artist Jack Jackson for his wonderful work.

THE
NAKED NYMPH
IN THE
DARK
FLICKERS

Ray Dyson

A Black Opal Books Publication

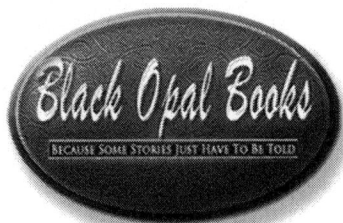

Black Opal Books

BECAUSE SOME STORIES JUST HAVE TO BE TOLD

GENRE: HISTORICAL MYSTERY/CRIME THRILLER

This is a work of fiction. Names, places, characters and incidents are either the product of the author's imagination or are used fictitiously, and any resemblance to any actual persons, living or dead, businesses, organizations, events or locales is entirely coincidental. All trademarks, service marks, registered trademarks, and registered service marks are the property of their respective owners and are used herein for identification purposes only. The publisher does not have any control over or assume any responsibility for author or third-party websites or their contents.

THE NAKED NYMPH IN THE DARK FLICKERS
Copyright © 2016 by Ray Dyson
Cover Design by Jackson Cover Design
All cover art copyright © 2016
All Rights Reserved
Print ISBN: 978-1-626945-35-7

First Publication: OCTOBER 2016

All rights reserved under the International and Pan-American Copyright Conventions. No part of this book may be reproduced or transmitted in any form or by any means, electronic or mechanical, including photocopying, recording, or by any information storage and retrieval system, without permission in writing from the publisher.

WARNING: The unauthorized reproduction or distribution of this copyrighted work is illegal. Criminal copyright infringement, including infringement without monetary gain, is investigated by the FBI and is punishable by up to 5 years in federal prison and a fine of $250,000. Anyone pirating our ebooks will be prosecuted to the fullest extent of the law and may be liable for each individual download resulting therefrom.

ABOUT THE PRINT VERSION: If you purchased a print version of this book without a cover, you should be aware that the book is stolen property. It was reported as "unsold and destroyed" to the publisher, and neither the author nor the publisher has received any payment for this "stripped book."

IF YOU FIND AN EBOOK OR PRINT VERSION OF THIS BOOK BEING SOLD OR SHARED ILLEGALLY, PLEASE REPORT IT TO: lpn@blackopalbooks.com

Published by Black Opal Books **http://www.blackopalbooks.com**

DEDICATION

To Steve, who knew a good thing when he saw it.

To Pamela, whose gams got it started.

CHAPTER 1

Prying earwiggers outside Patricia Metcalf's dressing room stopped jockeying for position and reluctantly edged out of my path when I put an easy shoulder into them. Hangdog stares and muttered oaths greeted me—the wet blanket smothering their fun just as the fun got cracking.

"Careful, Brand," grated a man's voice behind me. "That putz in there has a gun." A murmur of voices backed him up, but nobody moved to stop me.

I squeezed through the lightweight door and firmly closed it behind me, blocking a sea of wide-open eyes struggling for an inside glimpse of the hokum they took for melodrama. The little man who had the floor in the center of the modest room whirled to face me when the door clicked shut. He goofily waved a Smith & Wesson snub-nosed .38 Special in a tight circle, but didn't get around to pointing it at me.

I looked calmly into his reddish eyes and ignored the revolver. "Put the gun down, Cleland. You've lost your audience."

Cleland VanderSaant leaned forward slightly and tried to focus on me. His right arm lowered so that the .38 pointed at the lushly carpeted floor at my feet. A few minutes before one o'clock at the start of a long afternoon and the bimbo already had his buzz on. Some would think the skinny little gink cuddling the S&W J-frame was right on schedule.

"Cut," VanderSaant snarled. His leonine head—much too big for his slight build—rolled back and he looked down his long nose at me. "The director has not enjoined you to enter his scene, and you are not welcome. Kindly remove yourself."

The striking woman sitting regally on the barstool smiled vaguely at me and sadly shook her lovely head. Long diamond earrings caught the light and glinted brightly. Her white cotton robe parted to show a long stretch of delicious gam that she took her time covering. Her vague smile brightened as she watched me watch her.

Beside her, a tall early-twenties bimbo—wearing navy slacks, a light gray shirt, a white sport coat, and a loosely-tied cravat that matched his slacks—leaned against the curved bar for support. An up-and-coming actor billed as Russell Cave, he could have been playing the part of Max Schmeling on the ropes against Max Baer. His taut face told me he found no enjoyment in this odd show.

"Oh, for God's sake, Cleland, will you stop this nonsense?" Patricia Metcalf's amused eyes indicated a loveseat. "Do sit down."

VanderSaant turned fretful eyes on his wife. Patricia Metcalf kept her hands folded in her lap, her waterproof face composed, her eyes hooded. Apparently, her strutting husband had nothing to say that she had not heard before, but something about his scene-chewing performance apparently still entertained her.

Cave started to say something, but apparently forgot his lines. Patricia's lover shaped up as a hot meringue with no substance, just the kind of dessert Patricia Metcalf liked to taste and tease. A few weeks earlier Cave had apparently decided a fiery and not very secret affair with a beautiful and highly popular actress—even if slightly older—would boost his fledgling career. Patricia Metcalf did not dissuade his pursuit of her. That sort of initiative had long since become commonplace in this loose town, for both sexes. It provided a quick means for moving up stardom's rickety ladder if you played your part correctly. It could blow up on you in a hurry if you miscalculated.

"Nonsense?" VanderSaant staggered slightly as he turned to face his wife. "You say this is nonsense? My dearest, nonsense is a woman of your social stature carrying on at your age with this young whelp who is most certainly not worthy of you. It is an insult to our professional status. In short, it is humiliating."

Cave seemed to waver in his role of the effusive, hot-blooded lover. His handsome pan turned the color of a glass of milk beneath his oiled, coal black hair combed straight back, no part. His dark eyes burned holes in VanderSaant.

"Humiliating to whom?" Patricia asked. "To you or to me?"

VanderSaant wiggled the .38. "To both of us, naturally."

"Perhaps I should have married a priest."

"I don't think that is allowed, my dearest."

Patricia had the attention of the room now. With elegant precision, she withdrew a silver cigarette case from her robe pocket, extracted a gasper, and held it expectantly. Cave didn't move.

"Darling." Her voice carried a faint hint of exasperation.

Cave shook his head slightly, as if coming out of a trance. He reached for a small box of matches on the bar, tried to strike one, failed. His hand shook like a scarecrow in a hurricane. I took the matches from him, struck a flame and held it out for Patricia. She took her time, her eyes never leaving mine. She exhaled smoke toward the ceiling, fixed me with a smile that made my tongue burn, turned her attention to her husband. "There are always exceptions, my love."

VanderSaant squared his bony shoulders, the motion leveling the roscoe's barrel and squaring it at my chest.

"Put the gun down, Cleland," I said, stepping closer to him.

The trembling in his hand became more pronounced. He tilted his head again in a practiced pose he had most likely used many times as a stage actor before his career as a leading man dried up and he turned to directing motion pictures.

"One more step, sir, and I will be forced to defend myself. I warn you."

"You will be forced to go to jail if you pull that trigger."

"Do as he says, Cleland." Patricia's purring voice had the tone of a schoolteacher talking to an unruly student. "Sit down and let's talk rationally."

"Rationally? How can a man speak rationally to a woman who insists on taking a mere child into her bed, almost under the very nose of her quietly suffering husband?"

"My dearest." Patricia's light laugh sounded like tinkling wind chimes. "You do not suffer, and if you did, you would not do it quietly."

VanderSaant turned his head to his wife. I reached out and plucked the revolver from his hand. He staggered backward against a loveseat, clutching his chest.

"You dare assault me, you cur. You, sir, are a poltroon of the lowest degradation."

I looked at the gat. "Cleland, this is a prop." I pushed him onto the loveseat. "It won't fire, you know." I dropped the snub-nose on an end table beside an over-stuffed Queen Anne wingback.

VanderSaant's wild eyes still raked me. "I am aware, you buffoon. A great actor cannot perform to his standards without the correct props. But I would not expect a knave of your low standing could appreciate that."

Russell Cave grabbed an ice bucket and pulled a Daniel Boone.

"Sweetheart," Patricia said amiably, addressing Cave without taking her hazel eyes off VanderSaant, "if you find that necessary, please do it in the bathroom."

Cave nearly tripped over a barstool, somehow kept his balance and made a beeline for the bathroom, his reddened face buried in the bucket.

"Somebody tell me what this is about." I looked at Patricia. "Half the ginks who work at this studio are crowded outside your dressing room, getting an earful. Good thing it's Wednesday and Harry isn't here or he'd be screaming his head off by now."

"Precisely why I picked today," VanderSaant said. "I knew the imperial Mr. York was absent and could not interpose his repugnant authority into my concerns. As you also work for him, you no doubt understand how he enjoys running everybody's affairs, how he revels in meddling in matters that are none of his business. I am getting quite fed up with your Mr. York. Sooner or later that bohunk will learn his place."

"Cleland, I don't think Harry's going to have you around long enough for you to teach him anything. All the king's little men won't keep York from hearing about this little crack-up."

"I suppose it was that ridiculous little person who goes by the absurd name of Merly who brought you running."

"That's his job, Cleland."

Cave staggered out of the bathroom. A small white

towel had replaced the ice bucket. He poured a stiff drink from a bottle of brown plaid and sat on a stool at the opposite end of the bar from Patricia, ignoring her. He took a long pull. Something in the scotch stiffened him enough to stare vacantly at VanderSaant.

"I ought to break your neck," Cave growled. A voice coach had likely taught him that tough guy snarl, but hadn't taught him how to make it carry weight.

"You sit there and count your toes," I told him. "I can't do anything about these two, but I have a license to crack open eggs like you."

For a fleeting moment, Cave looked like he might try to brace me, but Patricia's voice pulled him off any thought of trying. "Russell, darling," she said soothingly. "Do sit quiet and try to be a good little boy."

Cave slumped back against the bar. He threw Patricia a helpless look and began studying the dark brown Aurlands on his bare feet.

"Somebody answer my question," I said. "What's this about?"

"It is quite simple, although I do not see that I have to explain it to an underling. This, sir, is between my wife and me." VanderSaant waved a hand toward the bar. "And that…that lowest of boors who dares to shame myself and my wife with his unwelcome advances."

"Darling, unwelcome to you," Patricia purred. A slight glint in her eyes might have been the remnants of love—or maybe nothing more like sympathy—for her husband. "Russell and I have deeply enjoyed each other's company for some time, and you know that."

VanderSaant's right hand circled the air in little flourishes. "Yes, my dearest, but you two began your tawdry little performances when you were a virtual unknown—a nobody—just like that whelp suckling the hind teat at the bar."

Cave bristled and started to say something. I stepped toward him and his eyes retreated to the comfort of his shoes. He took another pull on his drink, draining the glass. A slightly shaking hand reached for the bottle.

VanderSaant sneered. "But now, with startling brevity, thanks to the brilliance of my guiding hand, you are an actress of the first magnitude, my dearest. You are what your adoring public calls a star. You have standing. Yet you persist in continuing this indecorous pursuit of wanton lust with this wastrel and without the scantest regard for your station. It is a pitiful deportment you present to your admirers. It is disgraceful."

"Good god, Cleland, you are not in some stilted old play. You are speaking to your wife on a matter you find important, and I am quite willing to listen to you if only you calm down. I know how much you enjoy creating scenes that display your celebrated temperament, but surely you cannot believe this is an appropriate place."

"Calm down? Calm down, you say." He forced a smile. "How's this for calm? When we first married and you were a rank unknown and you were using me to advance your career, you would—when we retired to our marital bed—perform…shall we say?…unnatural caresses. Then one day you refused. You said, 'I do not have to do that anymore. I am a star.'"

Her head flew up and her nostrils flared. "I am a star."

"Yes, my dearest, you are every inch a star, but that Cave mongrel is still an unknown, a minor player far removed from the pantheon of stars. And it is indecent of you to continue to tryst with such a person. You must realize that as your station rises so must your self-esteem. Do you not see that people will talk injudiciously if you continue to wallow beneath your station? You will be laughed at. It is an unimaginable sin for a great actor to bring laughter upon her person." He pointed a finger at

Cave. "That mongrel is not worth your slightest recognition."

"I have wallowed enough for you, Cleland." Her voice still purred, but now iron tinged it. "Going back a number of years."

"Careful, dearest Patricia, careful. We do not wish to air in public our very dirty laundry for all the intemperate world to witness. That would be unimaginable for both of us."

"In that case, my love, and speaking of dirty laundry, what of that nineteen-year-old nymph you are so publically carrying on with? She is at least as unknown as Russell, although I venture not as pretty."

"She is a beautiful young lady."

"And why, my sweet, do you suppose she is willing to romp so indelicately with a dried up bag of bones such as you?"

VanderSaant clutched his chest again. "Dried up? Bag of bones? You are disingenuous. I am in the full flower of my manhood."

"Yes, darling, you have been telling me that for years."

"And as for the young lady in question, what is a man in his virile prime supposed to do when faced with such charming pulchritude?"

VanderSaant found his feet and began strutting again.

"I am a great actor. I am a great director, and there is much I can teach, and I am supposed to impart that knowledge. I am expected to take a young lady of Miss Maddon's considerable promise under my wing and bring the full flower of her talent to fruition. To do less would be sacrilege to my art. It is demanded of me. It is demanded of all great artists. If I should do less, people would wonder what is wrong with me."

Patricia practically beamed. "Darling, I would expect

nothing less from you. It would be as if you played Falstaff without the boast."

I couldn't wrap my blistered mind around an emaciated runt like VanderSaant playing Willie Shakespeare's obese Falstaff, but I guess Patricia's point dug a little deeper than anywhere I wanted to go.

VanderSaant stretched out both arms, the palms of each hand open to his wife. "Precisely my argument, my dear. It is demanded of me, but what is envisaged for an actress of your status is to carry on her liaisons with men who meet or exceed that stature. To do less is to insult your dignity and your station. It is also an affront to the propriety of your suffering husband. Our peers understand such manners, and I am not censured. But to carry on with this Cave nobody? That is intolerable. It is an insult. I am looked upon with pity. A great artist cannot abide pity. Surely you understand these things."

"Cleland, darling, I understand perfectly." Her hazel eyes twinkled. "Perhaps it is you who has forgotten."

"Oh, yes, my dearest, you would like me to forget some things, wouldn't you?" VanderSaant said. "I forget nothing."

"Perhaps I should remind you that we are no longer living together. You seem to have conveniently forgotten that I have kicked you out. The terms of the agreement we entered into some years past provide me the right to that decision." She smiled deliciously. "So you are now living in some hovel somewhere in the inner city."

"Hovel?" He practically howled the word, casting his cold lamps on me. "Hovel, she says." His eyes returned to his wife. "My dearest, it is a magnificent townhouse at the lovely and elegant Garden of Eden. It is a palace that is worthy of me. Hovel, indeed."

"Is it worthy of the many young ladies you so selflessly take under your wing, so as not to commit sacrilege?"

The little director collapsed onto the love seat, head thrown back, hands covering his face. "We shall no longer discuss that."

"Well, Cleland, I should look forward to seeing your palace sometime." She flashed that sweet smile again. "I should think there is no hurry to do so, as it seems it has now become your permanent address."

VanderSaant jumped sprightly to his feet. I moved quickly to get between Cleland and Patricia, but he had taken a step to his right, turning his back to me. He pointed an outstretched right arm at the closed French door. Sunlight beating against the white chintz curtains outlined vague forms of a number of people straining to hear this curious performance.

"You ungrateful wench," he boomed. "I shall throw myself out the window."

"Cleland," I said, "you're on the ground floor."

He looked at me imperiously, his mouth working like a squirrel cracking an acorn. He slumped back onto the loveseat and thrust his hands deep into his pockets.

"Imagine me, a master of his craft, a titan of the theater, a monarch of the motion pictures, allowing an underling to interpose himself into my affairs. I am sunk to a new low. I should shoot myself and be done with this unmitigated misery."

"Well, you won't do it with this." I picked up the prop gun and dropped it into the side pocket of my jacket. "I've cleaned all the diapers I'm going to clean today." I motioned to Cave. "You come with me. We're leaving these two lovebirds to sort out their peculiar affairs in private."

Cave looked pleadingly at Patricia, who stared at VanderSaant. Cleland's eyes settled despairingly on the French doors.

"I only came in here," I said to VanderSaant, "to keep

you from shooting somebody. I shouldn't have wasted my time. Let's go, Cave."

Cave, clearly reluctant to retreat, faced Patricia and spread his hands in a gesture of total hopelessness.

"Go, darling. I shall see you later at our usual place. Just now you are rather useless to me, and something of an embarrassment."

VanderSaant turned beseeching eyes on his wife. He raised his head again in that practiced, arrogant pose.

"My dearest, this frightful matter seems to have given me a headache. Might I trouble for a tall glass of scotch? And perhaps a bromo?"

CHAPTER 2

The horn blew a little after midnight. Little good ever comes from a phone call that late. I got it just after the second ring, but didn't switch on a light. Alice stirred a little, mumbled something indelicate concerning Alexander Graham Bell's ancestry and pretended to go back to sleep. I didn't make the baritone voice on the line, but the man did not sound at all unhappy to be calling me this late.

"That you, Brand?"

"It might be if you ask nice enough. Who's this?"

"Beck McLain. Remember me? I'm over at the Braebern."

If McLain was waiting for me to break into applause, the horn would be growing out of his ear. "So?"

"So? Listen, Brand, I've got one of your York highhats over here fried to the gills and kicking up a terrible ruckus. You need to come get him. I might have to cuff him around a little to keep him from getting nasty. He won't like that and maybe you won't either."

"Who is it?"

"Some high-hat rummy trying to wake up the entire house. Get slick, Brand. I need you to get him out of the joint before anyone gets wise to him."

"Got a name?"

"I do not."

"Then find a spot to nail him down for the night."

"I could, but it would be best if you get him out of here."

"That bad?" I was waking up to what McLain was telling me.

"Bad enough. Get a wiggle on."

"Okay, on my way. Where do I find you?"

"Tell the night clerk. He'll send you to me."

I hung up the receiver. Alice rolled over. "I don't like these late night calls that send you scurrying. I suppose you are running out on me for some beautiful damsel in distress."

"Yeah, Jean Harlow."

Alice snickered. "Such a sweet girl. Send her my love. But remember whose bed you just crawled out of."

The swanky Braebern Hotel and Resort covered a prime piece of real estate just over the Beverly Hills line. Beck McLain had no business working that place but through a nifty dodge of some sort he had landed a job there as the house detective. I got to know Beck a little from my time with the Los Angeles Police Department, when we were both detectives and light heavies in the force's boxing league.

We fought each other twice and I came out slightly ahead both times, although Beck—no fan of the rules—certainly got in his licks. A top wire man, his taps—legal and otherwise—gave McLain favored status with the brass until his penchant for payoffs—info gleaned in those taps sometimes found its way to the other side—and for disregarding orders inevitably put him out on the street with no pension.

McLain also had a nasty habit of letting a loose tongue run away from him.

I got out of the police business just ahead of him when

a dirty bull named Elmo Jones framed me for taking a bribe and made it stick.

I landed on my feet at York Brothers. McLain squirreled a job as a roaming cinder dick for the Central Pacific, which gave him free rein to roust bindle stiffs jumping the blinds.

He rode that horse hard, until one night he came down on the wrong bruno and got tuned up like a Lincoln V12. The first-rate broderick Beck took meant the CP railroad brass had no more use for him, but someone found enough pity to let him to scope out a soft cushion at the Braebern.

A low-toned dick for a high-toned outfit.

The fiftyish night clerk, dressed in a spiffy maroon uniform with gold trim and shiny brass buttons, leaned against the desk and pointed a manicured finger down a long hallway when I asked for McLain.

"You must be Brand," the clerk droned in a tired voice. "McLain's pulling the paper off the walls. Last door on the right."

His door was open. Benny Goodman's "Moon Glow" floated out of a floor radio. Beck lounged in an easy chair—coatless, his flowery tie open at the neck, his shirt sleeves rolled up to his elbows—his manner smooth as glass, which meant he had seen me coming. And that meant he was playing games with me.

A short bird stretched on a long couch snored gently, his conk pitched to the left, drool bubbling on his lips. I turned up my lip at Cleland VanderSaant and looked at McLain.

"That cake-eater ain't worth rousting me out of bed, Beck."

"Didn't figure." He snapped off the radio. "Doubtful any disturbed guest would make him, but he was setting up a racket with someone guests would know." McLain smiled. He didn't bother to get out of the chair. "Patricia Metcalf."

"She holed up here with a tall, thin, good-looking bimbo with dark, wavy hair, blue eyes, a perfect chin and an empty melon?"

McLain nodded. "Room eight-forty. Who is he?"

"A daisy who teaches Miss Metcalf how to act like a woman."

VanderSaant groaned and stirred on the sagging couch. "No, no," he mumbled. "Hands off—never—film in safe—" I bent over him to hear more of his stutter, but the gink had shut down.

Beck nodded at the suddenly silent VanderSaant. "Who's the hooch fiend, anyway? What's his connection?"

"Metcalf's handcuffs. He thinks his wife's flings should be with pips like Grant or Bill Powell. He finds it humiliating that she likes younger ginks not worthy of her."

"Well, he put up a big enough row about it. Corked like a sailor just out of the brig, and cussing twice as hard. Pounding on the door, yelling like a carnival barker, waking up every guest on the entire floor."

"Any of them see Metcalf?" I asked.

"Don't think so. She got the gink inside her stall and tried to settle him down some, but he was still blowin' hard enough to rattle the walls when I got up there. I quietened him down with a cuff on the chin and hauled his sorry ass down here to let him sleep it off while I got somebody over here."

I sat on the sofa's arm. "How'd you get me?"

"That Metcalf dame gave me Jimmy Gallen's phone number. I got his answering service and the woman said he was out of town. She referred me to your number. Say, ain't that Metcalf dish a swell Sheba?"

I'd have to remember to properly thank Gallen. "Miss Metcalf check out?" I asked.

Beck shook his head. "After I chewed with you, I rang her stall to tell her you were on the way. Far as I know she's still up there."

"She living here?"

"No, but she keeps that place on a monthly basis and has a key to the back entrance." Beck grinned. "That way she's in and out discreetly."

"How much does she pay you to keep your mouth shut?"

"I could resent that, Brand. Where do you get off bracing me like that? Matter of fact, she is generous to a fault. But nobody around here is going to spill anything. We'd just get canned and she'd switch hotels."

"You mean you wouldn't say anything for small potatoes."

"Ain't no need to talk that way, I'm telling you. I'm trying to be on the up-and-up with you, Neil, and all I'm getting is guff."

"You know what you're getting." I pointed to VanderSaant. "Sit on that bird. I'm going up to see Metcalf."

"He'll be here when you get back."

Russell Cave opened the door after my first light tap. The bright red robe opened to his belly button reached the knees of his bare legs. Patricia Metcalf came out of the bathroom, running a brush through her hair, looking daisy-ready for her next close-up. Her robe matched Cave's, although it reached to her toes. Her toenails had been painted blood red, matching her fingernails.

I didn't bother with niceties. "Any of the hotel guests make you when Cleland set up his razzle?" I asked.

She shook her lovely pan. "How is my darling husband?"

"Sleeping if off. I'll take him home. You best dangle. Somebody sees you and puts you with that stink Cleland started, you'll be dodging Lolly and the newspapers." I jerked a thumb at Cave. "This gink stays here until you get dressed and out. I'll get your husband out behind you." I looked at Cave. "You go last, after we've cleared out."

Cave stepped toward me, jutting out his perfect chin. "We will go when we choose, and we will go together. No half-assed phony copper is going to demand anything of us. You will defer to Miss Metcalf."

"Oh, darling. Sit down." She favored me with a movie-star smile. "Russell has so much to learn, but I do enjoy teaching him."

"He's the egg who has a lot to learn," Cave said, glaring at me. "Maybe I should teach him a thing or two about how to treat a lady. Among other things."

"Darling, do sit down. Do be quiet."

Cave glowered at me a bit longer, but it was strictly for effect. I knew ten-year-old newsboys hustling the streets who could take Russell Cave without missing a sale. After a few seconds, he did what we knew he'd do. He sat on the edge of the bed and fumbled with a deck of Luckies. Patricia pressed her full lips together and regarded me without emotion.

"We will do as you say. I trust you will be able to keep this evening's misadventure out of the public eye."

"I'll do my best." I opened the door. "I'll be in the hallway."

CHAPTER 3

I slipped Beck McLain a double sawbuck, which was all I had on me, but promised him more if nothing negative hit the papers. When he needed to keep his very public players out of the very public eye, Harry York could slice his bacon thick. Beck understood that from a few past experiences with Harry's people.

"Any idea how he got here?" I asked.

Beck shook his conk.

"I'll take him home in my boiler," I said. "If he drove, he can come back for his bus when he gets back on his feet."

"Darb. Tell him to come back sober."

VanderSaant twisted on the couch, coughed raggedly and again mumbled something about a film nobody would ever see.

"He's been beating his gums about that all night," McLain said. "Same thing over and over. I got no idea what he's running on about." He looked hard at me. "You?"

"He's a movie director, Beck. Who knows?"

"No wonder why they used to not rent to actors, but why don't they still keep 'em out? My sainted mother used to have a boarding house out on the east side and she'd rent to ex-convicts long before she'd rent to actors.

She had a sign posted outside her place that said no pets, no solicitors and no movie people."

"Your mother was very discerning."

"Still is, but she ain't got that boarding house no more. If she did, I doubt she'd still rent to movie people. You can't drag her to a picture house."

"Like I said."

Beck pointed to VanderSaant. "Well, help me sling this bimbo over my shoulder. Get your heap and pull around to the north entrance. I don't want to haul him out through the main door where somebody might glom him. Don't need clientele seeing me haul out barflies."

I pulled my boiler around to the back door and we folded VanderSaant into the front seat. McLain pulled back and scoured my Chevy with a look on his puss of a man sucking on a sour lemon somebody had salted.

"Didn't figure a man working for Harry York would be hauling his bones around town in a heap like this."

"Beck, you ever get a security gig with Harry, hunt me up and let me see what you're driving. I might get jealous."

"Say, you'll remember me if something opens up there, won't you. Man could find a lot of worse things to do than greeting them fine tomatoes every day."

"I'll keep you in mind, Beck."

The ritzy Garden of Eden covered a square city block about a half-mile off Hollywood Boulevard. The newly constructed dual townhouses, all apparently built from the same blueprint, sat along a short curved street that connected Dogwood Drive to Lodgepole Lane. Narrow alleyways behind each townhouse granted access to the garages and allowed for noninvasive trash pickup. Only a few streetlamps decorated winding sidewalks along the front of the buildings, which loomed eerily in the light of a slice of moon rapidly clouding over. Large, white numbers stood out on the front of each building. Fortunately, Cleland was sober enough to direct me to his front door.

I helped him out of the car and we started up the walk. The air smelled like rain and the wind found new life. A bolt of lightning raised a ruckus with several claps of thunder far off in the distance.

I dug the door key from Cleland's coat pocket. I could barely see the lock in the scant light, but I got the front door open and half-carried, half-dragged VanderSaant inside. I bumped into a heavy piece of furniture that turned out to be an empire chair. I lowered the gink into it and fumbled for the table lamp outlined against the un-shuttered window. I switched the light on, closed the heavy drapes and looked around.

The large room glittered with expensive art deco: a long couch, four easy chairs, a couple of end tables, a big hutch, a marble fireplace against the far wall, and a bar with six high stools in front of a staircase hugging the opposite wall. From where I stood, I could see the tops of three closed doorways on the second floor, but I didn't go up. Lamps of various designs rested on each table and several floor lamps had been arranged about the room. The lamp I had turned on sat on a small desk by the win-dow. The curtains were open at the room's only other window, a bay job on the other side of the front door.

I closed the drapes and went about the downstairs. A formal dining room filled a space to the right, and a doorway to the left took me into the well-appointed kitchen. A yellow-and-green wind-up clock on a stand beside the kitchen door ran a dead heat to be the ugliest thing I have ever seen. A dark green vine-like engraving wound around the clock's light greenish face, with yel-low leaves the color of the hands on the face clutching the clock's edges in a desperate attempt to flee the crime scene.

A swinging door separated the kitchen from the front room. Beyond the kitchen, a small entryway led to the empty garage. I looked for a stopper to keep the swinging door open, couldn't find one. A streetlight along the alley just outside the windows over the sink threw enough light into the kitchen so that I could see my way around. The typical kitchen sported a breakfast nook but nothing unusual.

A hallway just off the kitchen led past a bathroom and ended at a small bedroom, filled with a double bed, one chest, one drawer and a closet half-filled with clothes VanderSaant would not be caught dead in. A framed photo of a young, attractive woman holding a small child watched me from the nightstand beside the bed. A wind-up clock a lot easier to look at than the one in the living room shared the nightstand with the telephone.

I went back to the front room just as VanderSaant lurched from the chair and collapsed on the couch. I went back to the kitchen and got some coffee going. Rain began to lash at the kitchen window. I took the pot and a cup of strong black joe to the couch and set it on the coffee table. I sat on the edge of the couch and slapped VanderSaant lightly across his jaw. It took a while but I finally got the gink awake enough to talk.

A rumble part gurgle, part rasp escaped his lips.

"You aim to throw up?" I asked.

"Sir." His bloodshot eyes examined me the way a gardener would inspect a bug on his prized roses. "I am a gentleman. I am well-versed in holding my liquor."

"Yeah, I can see that." I picked up the cup. "Drink this."

He tasted it, spit it out and snorted. "You uncouth dragoon. You actually expect me to swallow that horrid concoction?"

"You want cream or sugar? Or both?"

"Cream? Sugar? By gad, sir, you are a worthless ruffian. Look behind the bar. I will accept any remedy you uncover."

"Forget it. You've had plenty enough hooch for a while. Why did you go to that hotel tonight? Don't tell me you wanted to catch your wife by surprise. Her little romps can't come as any kind of shock to you."

"Idiot. Poltroon. How is it you do not understand? Any simpleton should comprehend such a straightforward premise. Did you and I not have this discussion earlier today, although under somewhat different circumstances?"

"Bad enough you got the whole of the York lot chewing their gums over this, Cleland, now you've tried to wake up the Braebern's entire clientele. Harry will hear about this tomorrow and he will raise the roof."

"Harry York. Harry York." A flash of pure hatred twisted his pan. "That's all I hear. Well, my unlearned friend, your idol—Mr. Harry York—can insert his entire studio into his anterior regions and I shall not be moved. I am not concerned over the boorish behavior of that man. In short, I am too valuable to that bohunk's rather dubious enterprise."

"You mean your wife is too valuable, Cleland. Your wife's value to Harry York is the only thing that keeps you employed."

"That, you barbarian, is a stain on my character. A slur on my talent. How dare you besmirch my genius. You are an abominable cretin."

"VanderSaant, listen to me. I know it's hard for you, but listen to me. You keep this up and you will harm your wife's career. A career you depend on. Is that what you want? And quit talking like a nineteenth century charlatan."

"I love my wife. I mean her no harm, but she cannot

continue her insulting behavior. That talentless whelp she insists on seeing will be her downfall. Mark my words. She will lose all respect of her peers and an actress must command respect, or all is lost to her. Why can sweet Patricia not appreciate that?"

"Would it help if I talked to her?"

VanderSaant's eyes focused on me. He seemed suddenly sober. "You would do that?"

"Yeah, I can do that. I'll do whatever it takes to keep you from making a public nuisance of yourself."

"A public nuisance? Me, a public nuisance?" He tried to rise from the couch, but his hangover slapped him hard and he dropped back against the cushion. "Me, the most accomplished actor of his time. The finest motion picture director of his time. Me, a public nuisance? You, sir, are an unabashed idiot."

He twisted his head in the direction of the back bedroom. He burped loudly and I was sure he was about to toss his hooch.

"And where is my man, David? I require him at this very moment to rescue me from your hapless ministrations."

"Who's David?" I asked.

"You should be a member of my film crew. Talking to you is an exercise in futility. I just told you. David is my man Friday."

"He your driver?"

"Among the many duties he performs. He also cooks when I require and serves as my butler." VanderSaant screwed his mug into a sneer. "He prevents miscreants such as you from darkening my doorway. Where is he?"

"He drive you to the Braebern tonight?"

VanderSaant's face brightened. "Ah, it comes back to me. Yes. I dismissed him afterward to do as he wished tonight. I expected to devote the evening to my beguiling wife after I chased away that butterfly's boots who is always hanging around her." He scowled at me. "It is now time you departed, you oaf."

"David isn't here. The garage is empty."

"Not here? You may, in that case, see me to my bed. You need not undress me. Simply assist me up the stairs, if you would be so kind. What time is it, anyway?"

The hideous green-and-yellow clock on the stand beside the kitchen door gave out that it was a few minutes before three. Time for all the bent bunnies and their possibly even more pathetic fire extinguishers to be in bed.

I nodded at the clock. "Where did you get that thing?" The question begged to be asked.

"A very dear friend gave that timepiece to me. I keep it as a reminder of her many charms and her consoling spirit. Unfortunately, the dear lady possesses extremely poor taste in her idea of civilized furnishings."

"I don't think poor is the right word."

"It is the only thing about the dear lady that can be construed as poor. In every other way, she is the very essence of feminine charm."

"Time to go to sleep," I said. "Else the Easter bunny won't come."

I helped VanderSaant to the double-landing staircase. A switch at the foot of the steps turned on a row of recessed ceiling lights. A sudden wind slammed the windows, whiplashing a hard rain. Thunder rumbled. VanderSaant jerked at the sound.

"Hark." He resumed that wild-eyed pose I had seen in Patricia Metcalf's dressing room. He pointed at the door and arched a long finger. "Hear that? The rain hammers at my doorstep like an unpaid madam."

I helped him upstairs. His bedroom, the first door on the left, featured a mammoth bed and more art deco furnishings. A door in the back right opened into a large bath with a tub you could swim in. A closet big enough to hold my jalopy filled the right wall, with double doors that opened on overhead tracks.

I left VanderSaant wavering unsteadily on stocking feet, fumbling with his black suspenders. He could fumble with them all night as far as I was concerned.

"Good night, my kind sir, and thank you for your invaluable assistance. And may flights of angels—"

He raised his right hand over his head, wobbled on failing pins, and collapsed face first onto the bed. He had managed to get one suspender off his shoulder.

I went quickly down the stairs and out the front door. I ignored the hard rain on my walk to the Chevy.

CHAPTER 4

Jimmy Gallen held a mug of jet black coffee in his fist when I looked in on him first thing Thursday morning. Lobby cards and one-sheet movie posters covered the walls of his office, which took up the biggest of five rooms in an ancient house on the York lot. The house, now dedicated solely to the publicity department, had served as Harry's offices when he bought the land back in the Dark Ages.

York's top publicity hound, a handsome Irishman in his late thirties, looked like a million dollars in his black pinstripe suit and solid silver tie, a snazzy matching silver mop fashionably arranged in his breast pocket. He smiled gaily when I plopped into the oak chair in front of his cluttered desk. I turned down his offer of a cup of joe.

"Neil, I understand you had an interesting evening."

"Where were you?"

"On my way back from Agua Caliente, only slightly woozy. Carrie and I motored down for the weekend, decided to extend our stay a couple extra days."

"Luck a lady?"

"I wasted some good dough on a lot of hayburners, but the tables were much kinder. My answering service bright and early this morning informed me that Beck McLain had tried to get ahold of me late last night. I

called that palooka first thing and he filled me in on Cleland VanderSaant's garish little sockdollager. I understand you handled it with your usual aplomb. I sent along
by Merly a little expression of our appreciation. I think
McLain will be pleased."

"Jimmy, you owe me twenty bucks."

"You are a piker." He reached into his top right desk
drawer, pulled out a double sawbuck and handed it to me.

"I did all I could do last night," I told him. "Beck did
us a favor on his end."

"He did us a favor knowing we would pay him handsomely for it."

"And seeing as how he could glom no kale on the other end of that deal." I shrugged. "It's in your ballpark
now, Jimmy."

Gallen nodded. Being Harry York's top publicity gink
had its perks, but dealing with the overpaid wayward
dolls and sheiks who filled the studio's talent ranks was
not one of them. But the natty Irishman, who bore a
strong resemblance to the actor Joel McCrea—right down
to the blue eyes—had grown well-versed in the particu-
lars of hiding unwelcome publicity under a very large and
very polluted rug.

"I have been mulling over my options this morning,
Neil."

"First VanderSaant, then his wife. If you can hold off
Harry that long."

Jimmy sighed but didn't lose his smile. "Haven't
heard from Harry yet, but when he gets wired about last
night there will be flames. He doesn't like that bastard
VanderSaant as it is, and he won't tolerate him much
longer, despite Patricia."

"Easiest way for you might be to light a fire under
Russell Cave. I don't see any backbone there, and Harry
could put him under glass with a snap of his fingers. Even

that brainless twit should be bright enough to understand that."

"Good point, Neil, but I think I will start with that pompous ass what overturned last night's apple cart. As a matter of fact, VanderSaant has toppled apple carts all over this studio ever since he's been here. He's supposed to be on the set for that sword picture this morning, although he is late. I'm to be informed the second he steps foot on the lot."

"Why did Harry give that gink that sword and sandal epic? *The Great Crusade* is Harry's baby from the start."

Gallen shook his head. "Who knows? It ain't like Harry to slip-up on something that important. Not just important to the studio but to Harry himself."

"I thought VanderSaant was getting pushed out of A stuff. What with all his overruns and costly tantrums."

"That was Harry's plan, and I think it still is. I'm sure it is, but things change, you know." Jimmy put both elbows on his desk. "Look, VanderSaant's supposed to do a brief interior shot this morning while they set up the big battle scene on the back lot. With the schedule backed up like it is that bum needs to start shooting back there this afternoon. Hugh Dunnum's doing second unit on that. Dunnum's a friend of yours. I was hoping you could see him and tell him to do what he can on the main shots, just in case VanderSaant is a no-show today."

"Nifty. That bimbo might be able to hold his hooch, but he was in bad shape when I left him at three this morning."

Gallen frowned. "If VanderSaant does show, I'll try to grease things with him and protect Dunnum. You know how arrogant and demanding that pissant is. He will rage to the heavens if someone interferes with his work. Especially a second unit jobbie like Dunnum."

"Let him rage to Harry. It's York's jack."

"You raise another point, Neil. Any delay in that picture will cost Harry a hundred dollars a minute. For a man who rages over pennies, that will be intolerable. And Harry's rage is far worse than that of any measly director."

"Settled then. I'll look up Dunnum. Metcalf is working today and you can see her while you wait for VanderSaant to show. And jump on Cave. He's using Metcalf to try to make a name for himself and a threat from Harry should haul him in line. You need to keep this whole thing a neat little pile of clean dirt. You know how Lolly Parsons feels about Harry and if she gets wind of VanderSaant's antics she'll blow it up just to spite him. And then the picture rags will have to smear it all over their front pages."

"You are preaching to the choir. There are things that never change." A huge grin spread his tanned face. "I took this job back in '29 and one of the first things I was asked to do was escort a certain beautiful young doll to a formal studio affair. An elegant affair it was, and the kitten was a gorgeous young twist who suggested we retire to my place for the evening. I was delighted and we passed a lovely night, only the broad woke me at five in the morning getting dolled up. I asked her why she was in such a big hurry and she said, 'Darling, I must leave. I'm getting married today.' Two weeks later, back from her honeymoon, she called to see if I wanted to pick up where we left off. I couldn't dump that dame fast enough, I don't care how much of a looker she was. Now, she's a major star, only for another studio. Thank God. That's a true tale and one of a hundred similar ones and if they ever were made public the Bible-thumping citizens of this God-fearing nation would burn us to the ground just like Sodom and Gomorrah."

"I think you missed your true calling, Jimmy. You

should be writing fire-and-brimstone for Billy Sunday."

"It's certainly the kind of material that would light a holy fire under him, but it wouldn't be as entertaining as this."

"Indeed." I had a sudden thought. "It occurs to me that the only one of the three hurt by this would be Patricia Metcalf. Cleland VanderSaant is just a name in the credits no one knows, and he won't be around long, but she's the shining example of virtuous American womanhood and the public won't take kindly to her shenanigans. Cave is trying to make a name for himself. He might think any publicity that ties him with Patricia Metcalf can only help him. He could come across as the unwitting victim of a shameless vampire. That might play well along back roads."

Gallen grinned broadly. "That Metcalf dame is a shining example of something, all right. She's had more affairs than European governments. There isn't a bimbo in Hollywood she hasn't tried to use for one purpose or the other. And that goes for skirts, too. She's very democratic in that regard. You remember Billy Cass."

It wasn't a question. Cass, an actor of some importance at the now defunct Knightsbridge Studios, filled the part of Patricia Metcalf's first stepping-stone, but his career went up in smoke a few years ago over the killing of producer and director Greg Poulter, the Knightsbridge founder. Patricia's foundering career had just gotten a foothold and the papers never referred to her by name, only as an extra, saving her budding career.

"Maybe we could shoot Russell Cave and pin it on VanderSaant," Gallen said. "That would get rid of both of them, and we could play Patricia Metcalf as the honorable woman trying desperately to save her unspoiled marriage against the unscrupulous advances of a foul and immoral heel. The public would lap that up."

"Roll with it, Jimmy. In the meantime, I'll see Dun-num."

CHAPTER 5

I found Hughie Dunnum in the far reaches of the back lot, filming second unit shots for the Crusade picture, which was turning into something of a crusade itself. Way back here Harry's people and other studios created mayhem in a couple hundred acres of open flatland perfect for large, outdoor action scenes. The field showed up in dozens of movies every year—Westerns, gangster flicks, war movies, period pieces and a host of other Hollywood epics.

A warm sun beat on us with authority and the stuntmen, dressed as brave knights in shining armor—those getting close-ups wearing tin pretending to be steel, others in longshots wearing silver-painted cardboard—no doubt swam in unrelenting sweat. Dunnum heard me out and promised to do what he could to move the picture along, but the prospect of crossing Cleland VanderSaant did not fill him with enthusiasm.

"Last thing I want to do is rile that arrogant bastard. Hard enough to work with him, as it is." Dunnum loosed a long string of tobacco juice into the sandy ground at his feet. "He threatens to fire me and all my crew just about every day."

"Hughie, you used to be a little firmer with fellas who riled you."

I first met Hughie during the Great War. Ten years older than me, he sprang from a Texas ranching family and had once fruitlessly chased the bandit Pancho Villa around the endless Mexican desert as part of John Pershing's horse troop. My twin, Nelson, and I had been in Hughie's AEF unit in France. Dunnum was our top sergeant, tough and hard as Army biscuits, all growls and curses. I can't count the times I saw him sitting despondently by himself after a fight with the Huns, tears on his pan while he tried to compose a letter to a fallen doughboy's kin.

After the war he found work as a cowboy on B Westerns. Before I joined the LAPD I scraped my way into a few pictures with Hughie, getting shot and toppling from horses and stagecoaches and trains in one interchangeable oater after another. I could be a cowboy, an Indian, a soldier, a good guy, a bad guy, and nothing more than furniture, sometimes all of those in the same picture. Once or twice I was a gangster. The locales and eras changed, but never the hamfisted plot. It turned out to be a hard way to make an easy living, risking your neck for two clams a day if you were lucky enough to find the work. I didn't last long, but Hughie was still at it, mixing stunt work with second unit stuff.

"I wasn't responsible for a wife and two kids then," Hughie reminded me. "I got started late in life up that trail, but I been on it too long to backtrack it now. Man in his mid-forties, 'specially in today's social climate, had best hang on to what he's got. This is an easy job and the pay is good and if you want to say I've gone soft, so be it. But I ain't lookin' to feed three mouths by standin' in a bread line so I'll put up with that horse's ass till this mush is in the can. Anyway, we should wrap it up in a couple of weeks, with any kind of luck, and I'll be shut of your Cleland VanderSaant. For good, I hope."

"Jimmy Gallen tells me VanderSaant has seven months left on his contract, and Harry isn't looking to sign him to another."

"Well, then, in seven months I might plant that horse's ass about neck deep. Lot of folks around here will gladly help me."

"You wouldn't need help."

Dunnum laughed. "Hell, we'd be drawin' straws."

"Right now, just do your stuff. Get as much in the can as possible, and if VanderSaant shows up this afternoon step back and haul in your horns. If he doesn't show, keep filming and don't worry about anything. I'll smooth it with Harry. Just sitting around doing nothing this afternoon will cost York thousands. Trust me, Hughie. You'd rather get raked by that pitiful VanderSaant than by Harry York."

Dunnum grinned at me. "Oh, York don't bother me. I can handle working for tough ginks who know what they want and how to get it. I understand Harry York. It's miserable little bastards with sticks up their asses that burn mine."

I made tracks to the glorified broom closet I called an office, tucked into the back corner on the ground floor of the administration building, a big step up from the original offices. The main building—a frosty white, two block long, four-story stucco-and-wood structure—housed the executive offices of Harry's kingdom, along with offices for directors, producers and writers, several projection rooms and rooms for conferences. Audition rooms took up the far end space, along with the talent department. A commissary took up a big chunk in back, and exercise rooms boasted separate showers for men and women. Harry had set up an outdoor conference area on the flat rooftop, allowing him and his top executives to conduct business and still get fresh air.

A painting depicting a motion picture camera took up the top two stories on the left of the building, and on the right, a streamer pretending to be unspooling film bore letters spelling out York Brothers Studio. Older brother Louis had shortened their name from Yorkapich back when they were getting started and did it without asking his brother. Harry didn't like that, but he was in Hollywood scouting studio locations. When Harry found out, it was too late. The legal papers were drawn and the publicity mill was grinding, and it was too expensive to change the name.

The Yorks had divided their budding enterprise into two locations. Harry stayed in Hollywood to handle the creative end of York Brothers Studio. Louis lived in New York, within arm's reach of the big banks. From there, Louis controlled the purse strings.

Too late, Harry realized the money end made Louis the real studio power. The feud that had started between the two brothers began with the founding of the studio in 1916.

Eighteen years later, the studio had sprouted into the largest in Hollywood, and the animosity between the brothers York had grown right along with it.

My cubbyhole was just big enough for my desk, a couple of steel filing cabinets and one chair. A casement window behind the desk let in a little light. A few items scattered over the desktop left plenty of room for my feet. I had no reason to lock the door during the day. It would have been an insult to people like Merly the Mouth, who sat there comfortably draining straight bourbon from a white Dixie cup. A bottle of Kentucky brown I kept in the bottom desk drawer rested on the top edge of the desk, along with Merly's tiny plates.

Merly served the studio as Harry's gopher. Short, rail thin and just a little stooped—with a wide, spongy nose jutting out from an oblong head with oversized ears—his soft, gray eyes twinkled as I walked in.

"Always enjoy comin' to see you."

"Help yourself, Merly."

"A habit I have happily adjusted to."

I settled down in the cracked leather chair behind the desk, leaned back and propped up my dogs. "Six, two and even Harry sent you."

The smile on Merly's long lips moved his ears back. "I could use the kale but you are a poor soul to take advantage of." He tossed off another slug of brown. "Miss Metcalf would like to see you in her dressing room during her lunch break. One o'clock she said."

"A personal invitation or business?"

Merly shrugged. He took another slug that told me he planned to sit there until the cup was empty. The hands of the clock on the wall—hanging beside a calendar bearing a photo of FDR smiling like a saint in the Oval Office—hung at a quarter after twelve.

"Tell her I'll be there."

"Pipe that." We chatted for ten minutes. Finally, Merly drained the cup and set it beside the bottle. "That's prime stuff. Always enjoy comin' to see you."

I grinned. "And you can buy it anywhere these days."

"Why buy it?" Merly went out the door with no farewell.

"Come back anytime," I called to him.

I dropped by the bustling commissary to grab a ham salad sandwich at the counter before heading over to see what Patricia Metcalf wanted. The joint was busy but it was too early in the day to be packed. I saw Russell Cave alone at a table for two in the corner, sitting behind a pot of coffee. He saw me. I smiled and waved. He pushed out his chin, and found something interesting outside the window.

I laughed and drew a couple of stares as I walked out the door, almost running into a couple of fat monks carrying scripts and several Great War doughboys wearing sandals.

Enter any picture star's dressing room and you will always find wardrobe people, makeup artists, family, friends, agents, studio hotshots and their assistants, and a bunch of dewdroppers just hanging around hoping to get noticed.

This time, no gaggle of curious earwiggers crowded her door. Patricia was alone with her maid, whom she promptly waved out the door. She sat at her makeup table—bright light bulbs circling the mirror—demurely dressed as the loveliest nurse in existence.

"I bet people are dying to get into your hospital," I said.

She smiled faintly and allowed that brilliant piece of patter to pass unnoticed. She motioned to an empty chair beside the table.

"I want to thank you for coming." Patricia indicated a white porcelain teapot on a silver tray. Two matching cups waited patiently beside the pot. "Would you care for a cup of tea?" She opened the bottom left drawer and set out a bottle of brown plaid. "I could spice up your noodle juice, if you like."

"Thanks, but I'll pass this time."

She smiled sedately. "Most of the important people around here get drunk at noon, sober up around three and get drunk again about nine."

"It's a game the important people like to play, but I am one of the least important people you will ever meet around here."

"I differ. You were very helpful last night and I appreciate it. I wanted to extend my thanks." She flashed a golden smile. "Thank you."

"I'm going off my trail, here, but what are you going to do about it?"

"Very simple." She poured a cup of hot tea and added a little cream. She tapped the scotch, and put it back in the drawer when I shook my head. "I thought it over thoroughly last night and again this morning and I have decided my estranged husband is correct. I do hate to admit to that. Cleland can often be a frightful bully, quarrelsome and haughty, even cruel. He can be extremely condescending, but he does understand the game. I still love him dearly but he and I have gotten as much out of our relationship as is humanly possible, so I have decided it is best that he and I affectionately part ways."

"I thought you already had."

She sipped her tea. It was apparently all she intended for lunch. She stared thoughtfully into the makeup mirror.

"That was meant to be temporary, but today I believe a permanent arrangement is desirable."

"You seemed to make it clear yesterday the arrangement was permanent."

"You should never trust what a woman says, Mr. Brand. Especially if she is an actress. I will gratefully accept Cleland's last bit of advice, however. I informed Russell this morning that he and I are no longer possible quarries for the gossip rags. Our little fling, I fear, will be much more beneficial to him than to me. I thought you would like to know of that decision, seeing as how you got so callously dragged into it last night."

"How'd Cave take it?"

Patricia patted a strand of hair into place. "Like a child of two, I am sorry to say, but I daresay he will heal with time. Life is usually complicated, often burdensome, and seldom a straight line. Eventually, dear Russell will learn the game and will, I believe, play it adeptly."

"I don't think he's got the legs for it."

"That is unclear. What is clear is that he'll have to do it without my help."

"How about Cleland?"

"I have not had the opportunity to talk with him this morning, but I'm certain he will come around after his usual blowing off."

"He might not make it in today," I told her.

"That bad?"

"I mopped him up last night after you left the Braebern and hauled him home, but he was more than half under."

"Thank you for that."

"I didn't put him to bed."

After another sip she lit a Fatima, watched briefly as the smoke curled upward. "Cleland is as stubborn as a barn mule."

I raised my eyebrows.

"That surprises you?" She laughed lightly. "I grew up on a farm in Nebraska. That part of my official studio bio is true. I know all about mules. Maybe that's why I married Cleland. He's done the sort of thing you witnessed last night many times."

"I'm sure he has."

"He'll pull himself together and come in to work today just like nothing happened."

"You must have seen something in him to marry him. Something besides a stepping-stone for your career. Something besides a hundred and thirty pounds of ego."

"Yes, I did. Cleland might only be a hundred and thirty pounds—" She leaned forward and smiled wickedly. "—but thirty pounds of that is cock."

I couldn't shoo off that answer quickly enough. "So now?"

"Frankly, I had at first considered you to replace the two of them, Cleland and Russell. You have plenty to offer a lady. But the more I thought about it…" Maybe the flush on my pan forced her to smile. "There are many buds to pick from on the delightful cherry tree that is Hollywood. I will take Cleland's advice and search for someone who is at least on the same level branch I am on. Quite possibly a little higher. I will take my time."

"How about Harry York. I hear his wife is amenable."

"I shudder to think of that man sweating on top of me." She smiled sweetly. "However, Harry York could make me a major star for a very long time. And that, Mr. Brand, is something a lady must consider carefully."

CHAPTER 6

After leaving Patricia Metcalf's dressing room, I went straight to Stage Nine, hoping to look in on Cleland VanderSaant's set to see if the gink had made an appearance. My luck ran out. Nattily dressed in black slacks and a gray tweed jacket, a somewhat wobbly VanderSaant loudly berated a group of extras playing foot soldiers in the background of the interior shots for his Crusade picture. I nudged up beside the rotund Ernie Pell, the picture's key grip. Ernie gave me a sullen nod, no smile and no hello.

"How's it going?"

"Ain't." Pell loosed a stream of tobacco juice into a tin can he was holding. "VanderAss is in a foul mood, biting the heads off everybody, bitchin' about everything, insulting the players and the crew and all our ancestors. In short, the crust is normal on a VanderSaant set."

"He close to being done?"

Pell nodded. "Hour or so, if there's no more big blow-up."

"Dunnum and his boys have an exterior all set and ready to go on the back lot."

Pell nodded again. "His Majesty won't let 'em go ahead with that till he gets there."

"Lot of time being wasted today."

"Time is money."

"Heard that once."

"It's all on VanderAss, anyway." Pell let out another stream of tobacco juice, some of it finding the can. "The more he screws up the more he'll make the big boys unhappy, and maybe we won't have to work with him anymore."

I wandered back to Stage Four, where Patricia Metcalf's hospital weepie churned toward its final scene. She was on set, pleading with a doctor who looked like every movie doctor I could name, the camera rolling. Russell Cave, dressed in an intern's uniform, stood in the wings, silently watching, impatiently tapping the fingers of his right hand on the leg of his pants. He recoiled slightly when I stepped up beside him.

"What do you want?" He tried a hard stare but it was more comical than menacing. "Haven't you and Vander-Saant done enough?"

"I hear she sent you packing."

"Patricia didn't mean it. It was too much pressure on her. She'll reconsider and want me back, you can count on that."

The scene ended and the director yelled cut. Lights came on and Merly stepped out of the shadows and whispered to Patricia Metcalf. She stiffened and nodded, then followed Merly out the door. Cave started after her but I grabbed his arm.

"Stay put. Six, two, and even, pal, she's on her way to see Harry York."

"Let go of my arm."

I grinned and squeezed harder, just to see if the gink would take a poke at me. He didn't.

"You and that dame are dissolved, Cave, and the sooner you pipe that the better off you'll be. Fight VanderSaant if you want. Fight me if you think you can, but a struggling twit reaching for the big time doesn't need to get balled up by Harry York."

"That broad's nothing but rubbish, anyway," he said bitterly. He jerked his arm out of my grasp and stalked off.

CHAPTER 7

Betsy Hammerlin accepted my offer of breakfast in the commissary first thing Friday morning. Harry, always on time, found reason to be late to the lot, and Betsy seemed keen to talk to me.

Every commissary at every studio is divided into two sections. A lunch counter on one side is reserved for the unknown actors, the never-weres and the has-beens, along with the stuntmen, extras and the working crew—secretaries, studio cops, carpenters and grips and electricians and all the other workers pictures can't be made without. The other side belonged to the stars and near stars, the executives, producers, directors, writers and agents.

As head of security, I was a glorified studio cop and belonged to the lunch counter. Betsy did not. Tall and lithe, Harry York's striking confidential secretary—a silky brunette with flashy gams that went the distance—sat wherever she wanted. She didn't even have to wait for the glossy redhead who dispensed the menus and decided on the seating based on who you were. The redhead nodded, smiling, and Betsy selected a corner table with a nice view of the lot.

A raven-haired dame who had preceded the redhead had once given Betsy a harsh time, snootily informing her that she and the other mere secretaries belonged in the lunch counter side. Betsy said nothing to no one. She found a table on the other side of the commissary and ate her lunch, chatting with the other secretaries, but when word got back to Harry York the unamused raven-haired doll was quickly out on her lovely ear.

I don't know, maybe Betsy had something on Harry. My take on Betsy Hammerlin put her down as smart, dedicated, and loyal, and the most indispensable of any of us drawing paychecks from Harry. As the only person at York Brothers Studio privy to Harry's every meeting, she knew every minute detail of everyday business. She trusted me and I was the only one she talked to. She told me things she would never tell anyone else because she understood that sometimes Harry York had to be rescued from himself.

Betsy gave a dish of fresh fruit a special glow. She put a slight gleam of orange marmalade on two pieces of toast and took her coffee with a little sugar and a lot of cream. I dug into a plate of ham and eggs and took my joe black and strong.

"Patricia Metcalf was in to see Harry yesterday afternoon," I said. "I'm sure you heard about Wednesday night."

Betsy's wide smile showed brilliant and perfectly lined white teeth. Few broads on Harry's lot rated a more air-tight pan than his confidential secretary.

"That's the reason for breakfast?"

I grinned. "Can you talk about it?"

"Sure. Harry doesn't mind a few people getting wired, the ones who won't spill. I have some discretion in that matter. Harry asked her to his office to talk about her private life, which he claims he is not going to interfere in, and how it is affecting her public persona, which he does have a stake in. He told her to quietly divorce her husband and that he would be willing to pay for it. He told her she must also disassociate herself from Russell Cave, and do it immediately. He assured her that Cave's continued success in the motion picture business would depend completely on her doing as Harry says...excuse me, asks."

"She'd already done that."

Betsy nodded. "Yes, but Harry was blissfully unaware. She fluttered her fake eyelashes, smiled as modestly as her acting talent would allow, and gushed reverently that she would do anything he asked of her, whispered throatily how much she admired and adored him and how it horrified her to think she was letting him down...mush, mush, mush. She was all feminine and soft, roses and charm. Harry practically floated her out of his office. As long as Patricia rids herself of both of those deadweights, she'll have Harry eating out of her hand."

"She might not even mind him sweating."

Betsy gave me a curious look, but before I could say anything, Merly materialized at the table, note in hand.

Hughie Dunnum wanted me to hunt him up right away on Western set Number One. I told Betsy that I smelled a fire and excused myself. I found Dunnum sitting on the top rail of an empty corral just off the Western street. He pulled a stained tobacco pouch from his vest pocket and sliced off a plug of Oceanic with a congress knife. He slipped the chaw into his mouth and the knife and pouch back into the pocket.

"Thought you might want to help me stop a murder," he said, grinning.

"Yours or mine, I'm all for it."

"Cleland VanderSaant's."

"Not so much."

"Way I see it VanderSaant deserves what he gets, but some good men are about to get their butts in a sling."

I shook my head sadly. "Pipe me."

Dunnum unleashed a stream of dark tobacco juice and pointed to his breezer, a fourteen-year-old dark green Nash four-cylinder.

"Hop in."

Age had collapsed the breezer's top and we jumped into the ragged seats. Hughie cranked the motor and took off for the truck gate in the far back end of the lot, which turned out onto a dirt road that twisted toward distant mountains.

He released another spurt of black juice.

"VanderSaant's filming that big fight scene right after lunch," he yelled over the roar of the Nash. With every bump in the road I felt like the Nash's four pistons were inside my head. "It's that sword picture. Lots of riders and lots of horses. Two riders got busted up real bad yesterday afternoon. They told that idiot the stunt he wanted was too dangerous and they needed time to work it out, but VanderSaant said he'd fire 'em all for holdin' up his production. So they did it and it was a disaster and the only thing that bastard did was cuss 'em out for ruining his scene and costing him time. Scab Harron told me some of the boys got together last night over a lot of drinkin' and what was bein' planned for today. I was goin' up to the set to see what I could do. I was prayin' you'd show up 'fore I left."

VanderSaant was particularly tough on stunt riders because he demanded dangerous bits and wanted thrills beyond reason in his action scenes. Invariably, riders got hurt doing those stunts, and when riders were injured and couldn't work they didn't get paid. And no matter how bad their injuries, the immune director would order them dragged off his set and out of the way so he could get on with his important work.

A goose with diarrhea couldn't get noticed on

VanderSaant's Crusades set. The Huns hadn't caused that much trouble in four years of war.

"What'd Scab say?"

"Some of them boys are figurin' to stage an accident this morning. One of them unavoidable tragedies the studios are always telling the press when somethin' bad happens. They figure to start a stampede when Vander-Saant calls for action. That pissant's gonna be standin' right out there in the open to start it, then he figures to run back to his stutter bus soon's it gets goin'. The boys reckon if the horses stampede while that daisy's out in the open he can't reach his truck in time. They can claim it was an accident and who's to be wiser? Might work, but then again, it might not."

"Easier to stop 'em than sort out the mess when it's over."

He nodded and loosed a stream of black juice. Some of it got over the door, some of it did not. "What I thought," he said.

We bounced through the truck gate and bumped down the dirt road, the breezer jumping like Jack Gilbert when Garbo snapped her fingers. Hughie roared through an open gate, a cloud of dust billowing behind the Nash. A quarter-mile down the road, several dozen mounted knights and medieval Saracens lined up facing each other with about a hundred yards of open ground between them. All this circus needed was the call to action. VanderSaant, out in the open between the two groups, shouted instructions through a megaphone. A dark red beret perched rakishly on his head and square-shaped, wire-rim cheaters had slipped to the end of his nose. He looked ridiculous in a long, chocolate-colored jacket, tan jodhpurs and dark brown knee-high riding boots, although nobody reckoned that egomaniac could ride anything wilder than a barstool. The ends of a long, plaid, woolen scarf wrapped around his neck dangled at the top of his boots, adding to his cartoonish look.

"Give this thing all it's got, Hughie. We might be too late."

The Nash swung off the dirt road and bounced into the rough field. For a moment I thought my head had exploded, but it turned out to be the Nash backfiring. A couple hundred yards in front of us, a bunch of chilled-out movie horses frightened by the backfire broke loose from the phony knights and bolted straight for VanderSaant, who had his back turned while he shouted instructions to his fake Saracens.

"Look out," I yelled, but we were too far away for anyone to hear me. "Hughie, sound the horn."

"Ain't got one."

The Nash let out a series of backfires that sounded like heavy artillery cutting loose at St. Mihiel. The breezer's cannon blasts caused the charging horses to break in several directions, bucking and twisting and scaring the bejabbers out of everyone near them. A camera got knocked over and trampled, and a couple of other cameras mounted on a flatbed Ford tottered but didn't fall. Extras dashed madly in every direction, diving behind anything handy. Some threw themselves into the dirt and covered their heads, hoping for the best. In the commotion VanderSaant got back to the safety of his camera truck. The stunt riders cursed loudly trying to corral the horses. Dunnum pulled the Nash to a stop a couple of yards from VanderSaant, and spit out his chaw at the dismayed director's feet.

The livid little director screamed curses at Dunnum in language that made my ears twitch. He started for Hughie, yelling louder as he closed. Hughie's face turned scarlet. He could whip VanderSaant with his little finger so I quickly got between them to keep Dunnum out of trouble.

"Not his fault," I yelled at VanderSaant. I felt my head quiver. "I ordered him here as fast as possible. What's this about two riders getting seriously injured yesterday?"

"You should ask yourself, instead, you insignificant little worm, why the company would hire these incompetents? They ruined my entire scene. All I requested was some undemanding, straightforward stunt riding. Why should I have to put up with such buffoons? Me, who suffers these outrageous slings for his art. Morons, all."

VanderSaant spread his skinny arms to encompass the entire area.

"I am surrounded by inept knaves on this set. Wretched excuses for tradesmen, all of them. It is a monumental labor I undertake, but the result will be my greatest picture ever, despite the failures of these lackeys."

VanderSaant wheeled from me and hurled invective at several nearby assistants. He wanted someone to at least attempt to do a decent piece of work so he personally would not have to correct every little detail. Finally, he turned to me.

"Still here? Good. If you can speak even a modicum of English without falling all over yourself, go back and tell Mr. Harry York that if he does not dismiss all these people who have failed me so grievously in this, my greatest endeavor, then he will forever be without the services of the greatest director the motion picture industry has ever seen. Be sure you tell that bohunk or I will have you fired, too."

VanderSaant stomped away. I stared hard at the gink's retreating back and then looked at Hughie. I had seen that look in his eyes once before—back in the Great War when a Hun had tried to pin him to a tree with a bayonet. The Hun had lousy aim. Hughie did not.

"We might still run him down," Dunnum said.

"Go ahead."

Hughie snorted. He reached under the seat of his Nash and pulled out a worn silver flask. He took a long pull and held it out for me. I joined him. He took another pull, and when I shook my head, he screwed the cap tight and threw it onto the breezer's front seat.

"Reckon it's passed for now. If we get this scene finished today, then the hard work is done and most of the riders will be finished with this insanity. So maybe, just maybe, we'll get through it."

VanderSaant's assistants and the stunt riders hustled to pull the set back together while the great director stood on the boom truck hurling more invective at their lack of cooperation and their overwhelming ineptitude.

Hughie cursed under his breath.

"Guess I'll hang around the rest of the day." He spit out what was left of his cut, reached into his pocket for another plug. "Take my car back to the lot if you want. I'll get a ride in when we wrap today."

"Good luck, Hughie. And seriously, don't kill that moron. He's not worth the heat that will follow."

"I ain't so sure about that."

CHAPTER 8

The telephone woke me early Sunday before the sunshine got its chance. Hughie Dunnum wanted to know if I was up for a polo match over near the Fox lot. He said Will Rogers and some bit players and picture cowboys were taking on a team led by star actor Spencer Tracy and a bunch of stunt riders. After the match was over, Rogers would probably entertain the crowd with a few of his astonishing rope tricks, always a treat. Ought to be fun, Dunnum said. Hughie's idea of fun always meant rough and tumble riding.

Alice begged off, although polo was one of her favorite sports to watch. She had promised to take her mother to church services that morning and she might have been a little miffed that I was not going with them.

Rogers—who had grown up in the saddle on an Oklahoma ranch and had ridden in rodeo shows around the world—led his team to a win, and then made his lariat dance while he told topical jokes to a thrilled crowd. I asked Hughie to have lunch with me but he was heading off with some of his boys. He asked me to come along but I regretfully begged off. I had promised to take Alice to the beach that afternoon.

I stopped for lunch on the way home and picked up the late Sunday morning edition of the *Morning Journal*.

I ordered a hamburger and glanced at the headlines above the fold. The FBI and the Midwest buttons hunting John Dillinger and the Clyde Barrow gang mostly chased their tails. Frank Merriam and Upton Sinclair fought scandalously for the souls of Californians as more and more out-of-luck workers poured into the Land of Honey, most of them living on a government handout that amounted to less than five clams a month.

I flipped over the paper and immediately caught the headline stretched across two columns: *Well-known actor dies in fall*.

A studio mug shot of Cleland VanderSaant—inset into a photo of the outside of his ritzy townhouse—stopped me cold. I scanned the brief story. Deadlines had made it impossible for any reporter to drag up more than the skimpiest details.

A neighbor walking his dog before daylight this morning saw the front door of VanderSaant's townhouse standing open. Curious, he knocked. Getting no answer, he took a step inside, calling out VanderSaant's name. He saw the body on the floor beside a pool of blood and immediately called the bulls. The death was being treated as an accident, pending an autopsy. Cops theorize VanderSaant came home early Saturday morning, possibly inebriated, lost his balance at the top of the stairs and toppled over the railing to his death.

I wolfed down the hamburger and beat it to the Garden of Eden. Rubber-necking gawkers crowded the area and the police meat wagon took up a spot on Dogwood as close as it could get to VanderSaant's front door. Several marked police cars surrounded the meat wagon and blocked the narrow street fifty yards in either direction. Two unmarked plain black Ford sedans grabbed my attention. Those cars would belong to the four homicide dicks huddled at the front door to VanderSaant's place.

Homicide dicks don't show up to ogle accident scenes. A wide area had been cordoned off to keep onlookers at a distance, and I made a bunch of newshawks and a few radio people being held back in a shaded area of the sidewalk directly across from the front of VanderSaant's townhouse.

I drove my nine-year-old Chevy around to Lodgepole and wasn't surprised to see that street barred by more squad cars. I parked a block away and cut across a yard and into the alley that ran behind VanderSaant's place. Several uniformed bulls prowled the alley, but I knew a couple of them from my time on the force. A few years before they would not have been happy to see me, but the sudden demise of Sergeant Elmo Jones had cleared my name from the bribery charge that got me kicked out, and now I was pals again with some of them, especially the ones who knew I worked at York Brothers.

"What's going on?" I asked after half-hearted greetings and sly insults had been exchanged. "Somebody run a light?"

A leathery bull named Clancy McCurdy—short, heavyset and knocking on the door to blissful retirement—shrugged. His red bulb of a nose crinkled. Bright blue eyes glinted. "We hear that a washed-up actor took a plunge out his window, or something like that."

"Naw, Clancy," chimed his longtime partner, another red-haired mulligan named Timothy Flaherty. "Took a header from the second floor and landed in the parlor."

"I saw homicide boys hanging around," I said.

The two Irish cops nodded in shared understanding. Another uniformed cop came down the alley, a young one I didn't make.

"Know anything about homicide moving in, Sammy?" Clancy asked.

Sammy glanced curiously at me, arched his eyebrows at Clancy.

"Go ahead. He's a right enough gee. Used to be one of us."

"Rupe Morton said they started to move the body and found a bullet in him," Sammy said.

Clancy looked at me and smiled. "Hence homicide."

"Who got the call?"

"All I know is that Lieutenant Harless has taken over the scene," Sammy said.

I dug out some movie house passes I always carried with me. "You fellas mind if I look Harless up?"

"He'd prob'ly be glad to see you." Clancy looked at Sammy. "Brand here used to be the lieutenant's partner."

A light came on in Sammy's brown eyes. "Yeah." He nodded. "I've heard of you." He stuck out a hand. "Samuel Barnhart. Glad to meet you."

Clancy eyed the passes in my hand and rubbed his chin. "You know, I've always had a hankerin' to meet that Gemma Layne. Always liked her pictures."

"Come around the studio some time, Clancy. Gemma is a wonderful lady who always enjoys meeting her many fans."

"How about Catherine Holmes?" Timothy asked. He practically panted.

"Her, too." I looked at Sammy.

He shook his head. "Hell, I never heard of either one of 'em. Got anything in there for a Shirley Temple picture?"

Clancy looked at me and then at Sammy. "Who the hell's Shirley Temple?"

CHAPTER 9

ello, Brand." My former LAPD partner, Lieutenant Frank Harless—homicide detective deluxe—might have been glad to see me, hard to say. His dark eyes held no emotion, a common trait among homicide dicks. "That bimbo on the floor one of yours?"

I nodded. We were standing on VanderSaant's front stoop, where a gaunt dick named Arthur Stiles had left me while he rounded up Harless.

"You didn't waste any time," Harless said.

"Didn't expect to find homicide fouling the joint. From what I read this morning this was just an accidental Brodie."

Harless looked across to the cordoned-off news crowd.

"Newspaper boys never get it wrong." He grinned briefly. "Looked like an accident at first. Bimbo a little fried took a hard fall from the top of a staircase. That theory went smash when they started to bag the stiff. Lab boys are in there now. Wire me about our dead orchid. Someone said he was an actor. A big cheese for your buddy Harry York, I'm told."

"VanderSaant thought so. He works for York as a picture director and sometime producer. Been several years since he gave up acting."

"You hustle over here to clean out his place, like with Cutter?"

I grinned. "Mind if I take a look around?"

"Been in there before?"

"Yeah, Thursday morning about two-thirty."

"Why?"

I told Frank about Wednesday night at the Braebern. Harless had launched a homicide investigation and was going to find out about that night and the trouble Vander-Saant stirred up, anyway. He listened with no expression as I spilled. He took no notes but I knew he'd remember it all, right down to the names.

"Okay, Beck McLain I remember. Patricia Metcalf I've seen in pictures. Who's this Russell Cave gink?"

"Tomorrow's Gary Cooper," I said. "If the lights burn bright enough."

"Okay, you can come in. You might see something that doesn't add up. You know better than to touch anything."

"My fingerprints are already in there."

"You know what I mean. Don't move anything and don't try to take anything out with you. Stay away from the stiff. This time, Harry's eggs didn't get here first."

I stood inside the door and looked around the dimly lit room. The heavy drapes at both windows were still closed and most of the light in the room limped in through the kitchen door. Nothing appeared different from Thursday morning, except the ugly wind-up clock had been set on the floor to prop open the swinging kitchen door.

VanderSaant's splattered body huddled in front of the bar, legs splayed, one arm outstretched and the other crumpled under him. He had apparently just missed the bar when he tumbled over the upstairs railing. A large oblong pool of drying blood had spread out from his smashed melon, darkening the hardwood floor for several feet in the direction of the bar. He was fully clothed except for his shoes and suit coat.

Hard-faced buttons surrounded the body, one of them firing away with a Speed Graphic camera. Three others had nothing better to do than look on and make with bad cracks. A bunch of lab boys scurried around the place, trying not to bump into each other.

I pointed to the clock on the floor. "You boys prop open that door?"

"Don't be stupid."

"That clock was on that stand by the kitchen door when I was here Thursday morning. The garage was empty and there was no one in the bedroom down that hallway."

"Someone lived here with him?"

"He had a man Friday, named David something or other. I don't know where David was Thursday. Vander-Saant said he gave his man the night off Wednesday after he drove him to the Braebern. Is there a car in the garage now?"

"No car, nobody in the bedroom. We put out a bulletin on his vehicle. You don't know this David gink's last name?"

I shook my head. "I've never seen him."

"What's he do?"

"Drives, cooks, cleans up the joint, picks up pro skirts for his boss. Who knows what he does to stay fed."

Harless nodded at the stairs. "Let's go."

The staircase creaked slightly beneath our combined weight, but probably not enough that VanderSaant would have heard someone sneaking up the steps. Blotches of dark red trailed from the railing into the bedroom, stopping just short of the bathroom doorway. The bedroom lights were off, but the bathroom was lit up like a train station. His bedroom looked the same as I had seen it Thursday morning. The roomy bath was clean and tidy. A suit coat had been thrown across the unrumpled bed, and a pair of black wingtips took up space on the floor, one of the shoes on its side. A Colt .38 pocket model lay on the floor, partially hidden under the bed.

Harless pulled out a dresser drawer and held up several flimsy and revealing negligees in an assortment of pastels and lengths. He opened the big closet, exposing a row of expensive suits. He took out a lady's pink silk robe and held it up. The initials RAM stood out in gold script stitching over the heart.

"There are more fluffy items here and there," Harless said. "Some more clothing and plenty of things in the bathroom closet a man wouldn't need. I'm guessing they don't belong to his wife. You know any skirts with the initials RAM?"

I had an idea but I shook my head no. Harless was a thorough cop. Some onions he would have to slice on his own.

"What are those other two rooms up here?" I asked.

"Come with me."

The door at the end of the hallway opened into a room about the size of the master bedroom, furnished with a chocolate-colored leather couch, a couple of matching chairs, a few tables, and built-in bookcases holding a set of Britannica encyclopedias, a fat dictionary, several reference books and a bunch of other tomes. A big desk in front of the only window held a typewriter, a telephone and several odds and ends. I looked at the paper in the typewriter. VanderSaant had been rewriting dialogue for the Crusades picture.

The studio portrait of a young, attractive doll in a small silver-framed photo on the corner of the desk looked familiar. I guessed by the style of her clothing the picture had been taken a quarter-century ago.

Harless pointed to the picture. "Know who that dame is?"

"No idea."

"There's a photo of her in the downstairs bedroom, holding a kid. She looks to be about the same age in that photo as in this one."

"The kid?"

Harless ran a thumbnail over his lower lip, shrugged. "One or two, I guess."

"Still don't know her. Anything on the backs of them?"

"We'll look. Nothing seems hinky in here, but we haven't searched it yet. The other room is for storage, full of boxes and things we'll have to go through."

We went back to the landing, stopping just short of the stairs. I pointed to the blotches on the hardwood floor.

"That blood trail tells me a story."

Harless nodded. "My take is VanderSaant was in the bathroom when someone eased up the stairs. You noticed the stairway is solid. VanderSaant came out of the bathroom and took a bullet. He apparently staggered against the bedpost. There's a splotch of blood on it where he might have hit his head. We'll probably never know, the fall squashed most of his melon. At some point, he went for that piece you see on the floor. He stumbled out of the bedroom, maybe trying to reach his assailant, lost his balance and fell over the railing. The fall definitely proved fatal. The coroner will let us know about the gunshot wound, but it is homicide either way."

"No other shells?"

"That gun you saw on the bedroom floor hasn't been fired. Not much by way of any clues. We've gone over everything. The only bullet we turned up is in the stiff's body."

"Caliber?" I asked.

"Small."

"Body was found just after daylight?"

"Yeah, neighbor across the way walking his dog. A Pomeranian. We're asking around, so maybe we'll turn up somebody who heard or saw something. Somebody must've. These places are packed in pretty tight."

"It's a quiet neighborhood, Frank. Sudden bang would turn heads."

"Remind me. When were you here?"

"Late Wednesday, early Thursday."

"Place well lit?"

I shook my head. "No. Sidewalk is lit but not the walks up to the doors. Back alleys are lit pretty well."

Harless nodded. "We're asking around."

"Bedroom lights are off, but not the bathroom."

"A wall switch operates lights above the staircase. It can be switched on at the bottom of the stairs and turned off at the top. My take is VanderSaant turned on the stair lights, turned off all the downstairs lights, then switched off the stair lights from above. He didn't turn on lights in the bedroom, but waited until he got to the bath. Which likely meant he was alone, 'cause he knew his way around in the dark.

"Downstairs was dark and someone unsure of the layout and afraid to turn on lights would need some way to see. Flashlight maybe, but the beam could be seen from upstairs. I'm thinking the clock was set against the kitchen door to hold it open, allowing enough light into the room from the kitchen to see the stairs. Less likely to be seen."

I nodded. "That means the back door. Forced?"

"Nope."

"Somebody with a key who didn't know his way around the place?"

"That's a hunch."

"Or it was unlocked."

"That's another hunch."

"Whoever shot him didn't bother to put the clock back," I pointed out.

"Whoever shot him likely felt an urgent need to dangle."

"And you think VanderSaant staggered out to the railing and fell over."

"We'll know more when the coroner does his work."

I leaned against the railing, solid and slightly higher than my waist. I stood an inch over six feet. VanderSaant couldn't reach that height if he stood on his toes. Harless smiled tightly, watching me. His conk turned over the same thought as mine.

"Sounds like a hunch to me," I said vaguely.

"Got any ideas who might have bumped him?"

"Yeah, most anyone who knew him."

"A sweetheart, eh? Well, I'll talk to McLain and to VanderSaant's wife, and to that actor Russell Cave. Like I said, neighbors might have heard or seen something. We'll find this David gink and see what he has to say."

I shook my head. "David didn't kill VanderSaant."

"Not likely. He didn't need to skulk around if he lived here, but I still want to put a few simple questions to him."

"Where'd the slug hit VanderSaant?"

Harless stared hard. "You know all you need to know about that bullet, Neil. We're keeping that to ourselves, and I'm asking you man-to-man to give me your word you won't spill anything you've glommed here." He held out his hand.

"You asking as a cop or a pal?"

"I'm asking as your partner."

I gripped his hand.

He nodded. His eyes bored into mine. I didn't know if he felt the same, but Frank Harless was the best friend I had. The best man at both my weddings.

"You've seen all you need to here," he told me.

I pulled my pants' pocket inside out. "See, I'm taking nothing with me."

We went down the stairs. The lab boys hadn't finished. A half dozen prowled the room, looking into and under everything they could look into and under. Several clear evidence bags sat in the corner beside an empty police trunk. One of the bags held the pink robe with RAM over the left breast. The .38 pocket model took up another bag. Other bags held the negligees, VanderSaant's suit coat, his shoes, a dark red object that looked like a button, a piece of wood with dried blood on it that likely had been cut off VanderSaant's bed post, and the two photos of the unknown woman. A couple of other bags held indistinguishable items.

Harless walked me outside. The newspaper and radio people hadn't given up, and the crowd around them had doubled in size. The low buzz of indistinct voices sounded like the hum of a small electric motor.

"Give Alice my love," Harless said. "Tell her to write me a letter explaining just how it is she puts up with a gink like you."

CHAPTER 10

J immy Gallen leaned against the front passenger side of my blue Chevy roadster, smoking a Camel, his long legs crossed at the ankles. His khaki chino pants, soft-soled white deck shoes and red sweatshirt with the letters USC stitched in yellow across the chest told me Harry York's always dapper publicity hawk had been in a panic this morning.

Darkening clouds mounted above the green hills to the north, likely bringing in more rain and foreshadowing an evening fog.

"Don't lean against that tin can too hard," I told him.

"Thought this was your bucket. Doesn't Harry pay you enough to upgrade to something a little keener? The least you could do is borrow one of the studio buses. Harry wouldn't kick as long you don't wreck it. The studio owns some pretty fancy boilers, you know."

"Jimmy," I said, "this is the first time I've ever seen you that you weren't dressed like Joe Brooks. Slumming does not befit you."

"Hustled over as soon as I saw the morning rag. Bastards wouldn't let me get near the place, so I circled around looking for a way to sneak in closer and saw your heap. I take it the law let an old crony get inside."

I nodded. "Homicide dicks are all over the place. Frank Harless in charge."

Gallen's eyes narrowed. "Papers said it was an accident."

"Newsboys pushed a point, Jimmy. I got a look around VanderSaant's cave and there might be a problem. Frank took some delight in showing me a couple of things."

"This I don't want to hear, but go ahead and wire me."

"There are a bunch of clothes belonging to a young frail, most of them frilly, see-through stuff. A robe had the initials RAM stitched over the heart."

Gallen sighed loudly, lit a smoke. "I told you it was something I didn't want to hear. Do you think Harless will sit on it? Won't take the newsboys long to figure out who RAM is. Or, God help us, Lolly Parsons."

"I think Frank will sit on it as long as it's the only thing that connects her to VanderSaant. If there are photos, it might be different. I didn't see any, but I had no chance to toss the place. We better hope there are no love letters."

"In my experience, there are always love letters from the skirt. How long you think before they connect a name to RAM?"

"Two, maybe three days. Harless is a smart cookie, Jimmy, but he probably won't go after that angle until he gets the autopsy report. Right now his main mission is to find VanderSaant's missing servant, or whatever he is. David something."

"Lemmert. He does a lot of odd jobs for Cleland." Gallen frowned. "You say he's missing?"

"I don't know. He wasn't there and no car in the garage. It may be this is his day off or maybe he's just out running errands. The buttons certainly want to talk to him. Harless put out a bulletin on VanderSaant's bus."

"I wish she wasn't in the middle of that picture. I'd like to get her out of town for a while. Send her on a world cruise on Harry's dollar."

The initials RAM were stitched all over his forehead. "That's VanderSaant's picture," I said. "Maybe Harry will shut it down for a while and she can dangle."

"Not likely. A shutdown will cost Harry a load of mazuma and that ass VanderSaant has it way over budget already. Most likely, Harry will shove another director in there just to get it finished. It's supposed to wrap at the end of the month, but it's going two weeks over at least. What a mess."

"There's more."

He sighed again, even louder. "Don't tell me."

"It's not as bad."

"What could be worse? Damn it, Neil, she's only nineteen and he's what…forty-five and married to one of our most popular actresses. It gets out she's vamping a married man more than twice her age it will ruin her career."

"I told Harless about VanderSaant's escapade at the Braebern on Wednesday night."

Gallen took a long drag on the gasper. "You had to do that?"

"I had to do that. It's a homicide investigation and he'll learn about Wednesday night quick enough. Since I was there I had to spill. I could keep quiet about those initials and play dumb, but I had to wire him about the Braebern."

"Pipe that. Well, at least we are not trying to cover up a murder this time. I just want to keep little Rachel out of this mess." His light blue eyes stalked me. "Tell me she didn't kill him. Please tell me that."

"Doesn't shake out that way. Trail points to someone who didn't know his way around that townhouse. David lived there and your little bunny had moved in some of her soft stuff."

He ran his lower lip under his front teeth. "I hope you're right. Shacking up with that bum is going to be bad enough for her if it comes out."

"She's got a mother, doesn't she?"

"What do you mean?"

"Maybe the mother doesn't take kindly to her innocent little girl soaking the sheets with an old daddy."

"Neil, her mother's known about that affair ever since it started. She might not like it, I'm sure she doesn't, but she understands these things."

"How about a father?"

"He died in the war. Got roaring drunk on leave one night and fell out a window. There was a first stepfather but he's long out of the picture."

"A first stepfather?"

"Divorced years ago and also out of this."

"You said first stepfather. Is there a second?"

He ground out the half-smoked gasper. "Actually, there's a third. Rachel's mother was on the stage up until a few years ago. Her career never amounted to much, but she kept trying to bolster it by jumping from actor to actor, another rung up the ladder each time."

"Who's the third?"

"An old Shakespeare sot named Leviticus Bible. Don't laugh, it's his real name. His father must have had a quite a sense of humor."

"That name is familiar."

"Used to be a big-time Shakespearian. Got to be sixty-five or seventy now, if he's a day. Strong hooch ended his career six, seven years ago. He shows up in a picture from time to time, still riding on his name, but you can't keep him sober long enough to get more than an hour or so of work out of him. Damn sad. I saw him once on

Broadway, years ago when I worked in New York. He was in a production of *Hamlet*. Critics hailed him as the finest Hamlet of his age."

"So he's still in the picture?"

Gallen nodded. "He and Blanche are by some miracle still married. But don't wrap your conk around the idea Bible killed VanderSaant because of Rachel or for any other reason. He ain't the type. Besides, I doubt he could stay sober long enough."

A squad car rolled by, Clancy McCurdy driving. He gave me a little wave as he passed, pouring on the gas. In a little while he was out of sight.

"Let's just hope nobody connected to York Studio wasted VanderSaant," Gallen said. "The sex and sin angle will give us enough trouble, but maybe I can salvage Rachel's career. I just need a couple of days."

"One more question. Which one of us spills to Harry? He'll need to be wired as soon as one of us can reach him."

"I'll do it. That part of the job is mine. I'll go over to his house as soon as I clean up. He'll have heard by now but VanderSaant's death won't jar him. He'll think it's an accident and all he'll have on his mind is that picture, but I can't let him wait till tomorrow to hear the rest of the story. If I do that, I'll be cleaning out my office."

I grinned. "That leaves me free to spend the rest of the day with my wife. We're going to the beach if it doesn't rain and then I think I'll take her out to dinner."

"Tomorrow won't be eggs in coffee."

"That, Jimmy, is why I'm going to enjoy the rest of this day."

CHAPTER 11

A steady rain cut out our idea of the beach that afternoon. Alice and her mother had stopped for lunch after church, and then Alice took her home. Alice sat idly thumbing through a copy of *Good Housekeeping* when I came in to the living room. She exploded with questions. During lunch with her mother, she had heard the VanderSaant news. She had never met that bimbo, but she had heard me mention him on more than one occasion.

"How deep into this will you get?" Her mouth formed a little O and her eyes searched me for answers after I had told her it was a homicide case.

"It has very little to do with me. There's a bunny on the lot who might get burnt a little but that's Jimmy Gallen's worry. Strictly."

"I hear you, but have you talked to Harry York?"

"I have not," I said.

"He'll call you into his office tomorrow and your tune might change."

"Maybe. Like I said, that's more Jimmy Gallen's worry. How about me and you find a nice, cozy place for a quiet supper tonight?"

She smiled brightly. "I have a new dress I think you'll like."

We passed an enchanted afternoon while the rain lashed our bedroom windows. Afterward, as we lay wrapped around each other, the rain faded away and the fading sun cast a red and pink glow across the darkening sky. I took a shower and put on my best rags. While Alice dressed, I got Hugh Dunnum on the blower. He had heard about VanderSaant and did not take the news very hard.

"How much longer on those second unit shots?" I asked.

"Three days tops to finish them if nobody interferes. I can go twice as fast as our dearly departed 'cause the boys trust me and I know what they can do. They'll need someone else to direct the other stuff."

"Can't you handle the main action shots?"

"Neil, don't lay that on me. It's a big picture and calls for a director who's been around the block and knows his onions."

"At any rate, that's Harry York's problem. Any chance one of your boys finished what they tried to start Friday morning?"

"Whattaya mean?" he asked after a short pause.

"VanderSaant was murdered."

"I thought it was an accident. The papers all say that sap got bent and toppled over his balcony or something."

"All hooey. Homicide dicks were crawling all over his cave when I got there."

Hughie let out a soft whistle. "Not one of my boys, Neil. Ain't a thing I see any of them doing. They let off plenty of steam Friday night and got embalmed sure enough, but that would have gotten 'em over it by Saturday night. Hell's bells, it ain't the first time one of 'em got something stuck in his craw."

"Darb, but get the word out to them, Hughie, and if somebody acted on a grudge you lam him out of town somewhere. The bulls will sooner or later start sniffing around you once they learn you worked for him. You should make sure only fellas who can hit on all six do any talking to them. Pipe that?"

"Most of 'em ain't gonna see no upside in talkin' to the law, but I can cut a few out of the herd. How long you think I got?"

"Couple of days, anyway," I told him.

"Good. We can get most of that stunt work out of the way and I can get most of the boys over to Jim Cody's picture. They get paid each day in folding lettuce and the studio has no record on them, and the flatfeet will be running around in wide circles tryin' to pin 'em down just for a little palaver."

"I'll look you up tomorrow when I get a chance. I'm going to be busy the rest of the night."

CHAPTER 12

I called Betsy Hammerlin first thing Monday morning and told her I needed to see Harry as soon as he could fit me in.

She told me Harry had put me on his list when he hit the door that morning, although several names down, and it would be two or three hours before I could expect to be summoned. I asked her to breakfast but she laughed lightly.

"Neil, I'm having enough trouble just fitting in time to breathe."

I hunted up Dunnum, hard at work with second unit action on the back lot. The bright sky told me Hughie would have a fine day to do his work. He had already scoured his crew over the VanderSaant shooting and was satisfied they were in the clear.

"Ain't the sort of skulkin' thing any of 'em would do, anyway," he said, cutting another plug of Oceanic. "One of 'em has a beef with another, he'd just bust him in the nose and after they wrestled around on the ground a while the matter would be settled and they'd go off and have a beer together."

"They were going to run him over with a herd of horses," I reminded him. "And VanderSaant wasn't the kind you'd wrestle around on the ground and then have a beer with. VanderSaant was the kind who'd run to his lawyer, after he cried his lamps out to Harry."

"Yeah, but that half-assed plot was a group effort, all of 'em in it together to fix his wagon. I don't figure any of 'em for just up and doin' a man, even a fool like VanderSaant. 'Sides, told you they got over it. Took up a collection for them that got hurt doin' stunts for that bastard and this mornin' they're eager to go, workin' hard."

"Wrap it up as soon as you can, Hughie. I'll see Harry this morning and waltz him around a little and try to talk him into letting you finish your part on your own, as long as you can promise two or three days."

Hughie nodded. "Weather holds and nobody gets in my way." He looked skyward. "Gonna have a continuity problem. We got scenes in the can under a sunny sky. Friday we shot under clouds. Today's a third sky."

"We can't let that hold us up. Too costly for Harry's mazuma soul. Most people won't notice, anyway, and if it's too bad maybe the special effects boys can fix it up a little."

"Well, I'll put all that worryin' on your hanger." Hughie grinned at me. "Looks like you're the boss till I hear otherwise."

"Harry's got a lot of top ginks who can step in."

"Well, I ain't seen any of 'em near here but you."

Dunnum was right. I was suddenly the boss, somehow, until Harry York swung his hammer, and Harry might not be happy with some of my decisions. I was going to find out about that pretty quickly. When I got back to my cubbyhole, a note in Merly's scrawl—folded in half and propped on its side—rested against the Philco cathedral-style wooden radio on the corner of my desk. The note told me to hurry to Stage Nine—where interiors for VanderSaant's picture were being filmed—and hunt up Harry.

Leo Collier, as good a picture director as Harry had in his barn, put his talents on display in a scene with the king and his knights, a couple of them a bit too paunchy for my idea of crusading warriors. Collier steered his actors through a long strategy scene—the mail-garbed heroes of the story plotting to take Jerusalem from the heathens—coming across as brisk and confident, impressively so for a man who had obviously just been called in to replace Cleland VanderSaant.

The film crew—as silent and as stern as barrage cannons on Armistice Day—looked on in a half-circle around the brightly lit set. Collier sat in a deck chair to the camera's immediate left, leaning forward, his head cocked slightly, his eyes closed, listening intently to a writer's idea of medieval dialogue. To Leo's left sat Harry York in a similar chair, an unlit stogie the size of a baseball bat in his right hand and a deep frown on his sallow face. The frown meant nothing. Harry York always had a frown on his puss.

The scene ended and Harry said something to Collier, who stiffly nodded as he unfolded his tall, lean frame from the chair, motioning for his actors to stay put. Harry stood and two assistants—Bernie Weintraub and Herm Rosen—hovered beside him. All three men wore plain black suits with plain black ties, but only Harry had a flower on his lapel—a crisp, red rose. He saw me and waved the stogie, ordering me to approach.

"Brand, we have things to talk over. Looks like Collie has this under control." Best director on the lot and Harry didn't even know his name.

"Quick work getting Leo."

"Got lucky." Harry's raspy growl had no friendliness to it. He lifted his stogie and the shorter of his two flunkies quickly produced a match. Harry held up the Cuban and got it going, all the while looking coldly at me. "He was available and ready to take over so we won't lose much time. He wrapped his latest picture a couple of days ago and was just starting to cut it. Someone else can do that." Harry blew a cloud of smoke toward the filler lights. "Be in my office in fifteen minutes."

Harry headed for the exit, the two lackeys trailing close behind. Several voices raised good mornings, but Harry paid no attention. He went out the door the same time a commotion started to my right. Coming onto the set surrounded by makeup, wardrobe and other assistants—wearing a low-cut medieval costume that revealed as much as any censor would allow of her considerable charms—nineteen-year-old Rachel Anne Madden bowed slightly to the polite applause and honored Leo Collier with an entrancing smile that lit up one of the most stunningly beautiful faces on earth.

"Miss Madden." Collier grinned and bowed slightly in return. "You are a trouper. I know Cleland VanderSaant was a dear family friend and valued mentor, and we here extend our deepest condolences to you and your family, and we must tell you how extremely grateful we are to you that you so graciously and professionally decided to carry on with this work."

"Thank you," she said gently, touching a hand to a chain necklace of imitation gold that helped hide her generous breasts from the censor. "Cleland was a cherished friend and I believe the best manner in which to pay tribute is to finish this project, which Cleland considered his masterpiece. I am happy to do so through this trying time. I pray for his soul and pray that each and every one of you"—she swung her right hand in a tight, all-encompassing motion—"will have patience with me. For that I thank you in advance."

"Cut the hooey," I heard someone say softly. I think it was me.

Collier wasted no more time. He set his players and crew to work and I got out of Stage Nine with my breakfast still intact.

CHAPTER 13

Betsy Hammerlin didn't seem particularly happy
when she ushered me into Harry's massive office.
The thick, medium gray carpet had recently been
replaced with thicker medium gray carpet, but otherwise
the place was unchanged since the day I first set foot in it.
Big enough for a tennis match with room left over for a
few side games of shuffleboard, the imposing office
slugged you right between the eyes, just the effect Harry
wanted.

The ceiling reached twelve feet, and the left wall
sported two picture windows running floor to ceiling. Between the wide windows, the marble bust of the Roman
philosopher Marcus Tullius Cicero—resting on a six-foot
high white marble stand designed to look like a miniature
Roman column—glared at me in warning.

Four Queen Anne wingback chairs in supple oxblood
leather sat along the wall opposite Harry's barge-like
desk, and a long sofa to match the chairs graced the wall
on the right. A hundred or so signed photos of big-time
Hollywood stars and directors littered that wall.

In the corner at the end of the wall, Harry's private office door opened to the long hallway. His private bath,
next to the private office door, featured a bathtub big
enough for four. Harry's desk covered a large space on a

buffed mahogany platform about four inches above the rest of the office floor.

A large floor radio five feet high hid a chunk of wall behind the desk, and above that an oil portrait of York blistered anyone who dared look at it.

Harry sat slumped in a big overstuffed swivel chair behind the desk, staring out the open windows. Sunshine beating through the window claimed a little patch of carpeting between the wall and Harry's desk.

Inside Harry's office, it still looked a little stormy. He didn't glance at me when I came in. He had found something of great interest outside the window but I couldn't see anything but bright blue sky with a little silvery tinge to it. He motioned to one of the big chairs in front of his desk, but short of the platform. I sat down and joined him in admiring the sky. We sat there like a couple of jaybirds for a minute or so until Harry finally spoke.

"There must be some gonif around this lot with an office even above mine that put you in charge of things." His left fingers began drumming the desk. "Maybe it was that pissant brother of mine, still trying to rule the roost from back east." His fingers stopped and he turned to look at me. "Maybe you could tell me and ease my contusion."

In the nearly four years I had worked for Harry, his mastery of English had improved but he could still mangle the language.

"I only told Hugh Dunnum to keep working on second unit stuff. Those boys sitting out there doing nothing costs you plenty."

A little smile might have touched the corners of Harry's mouth. "That's the job for the picture's producer."

"VanderSaant was producer and director."

"I don't know what that bum's producing now, but he isn't directing anything. Good thing Lee Collie was available and could step in. That's a man you can put your faith in."

"I think you can count on Dunnum, too."

"You better hope so. It's your ass."

I thought of several things to say, but nothing I needed to say. Harry fiddled around with a cigar for what seemed like ten minutes before he got it going.

"Okay then, we leave that picture to Collie and Dun...whoever." Harry leaned back in his chair. "Tell me the goods about VanderSaant. I understand you did not get there ahead of the police."

"Not even close. I read about it in the morning paper and hustled over there, but the place was lousy with bulls and newsboys."

"Gallen?"

"Just behind me."

"Paper yesterday said accident, but today they're saying he might have been bumped off, and here we are stuck and no bulge."

"Bulls think somebody threw him over that railing. Homicide dicks were crawling over the place when I got there."

York took several puffs before asking. "Why do they think that?"

"They've got their reasons."

"He's just a director, not a star the public thinks is a white knight. That angle won't hurt us. What about his wife? She *is* a star. She a suspect?"

I nodded. "She'll top the list. Spouses always do, especially ones who like to roam off the range. And Patricia Metcalf likes to roam."

"You think she killed him?"

"No."

"Police talk to her yet?"

"I'm sure they have." A pigeon flashed in the sunlight

at the window. "It's been more than twenty-four hours since the bulls found the body."

Harry stared at his alabaster ceiling and sucked hard on his stogie. "I don't like that. I want my people talking nice to the fan rags, and not talking to the police at all."

"That's all right, Harry. I don't think she killed him and I'm pretty sure Frank Harless won't think so, either."

"Who's he?"

"Lieutenant Harless is a top homicide dick who pulled the case. Letting Miss Metcalf talk to him is the best thing you can do. Pushing them off her just makes them more hinky. She's a smart broad who won't easily rattle and the buttons can't get too rough with her."

Harry rolled the cigar across his lips. "Sure of that?"

"They don't rough up popular picture stars. Get a mouthpiece and coach her on what to say."

"Other than that bum's wife, are there any more of my people—well-known people—who can hurt us in this thing?"

"RAM."

"Ram? What do you mean?"

"Rachel Anne Maddon."

Harry's eyes narrowed into slits. His mouth looked like a torn pocket when he pulled out the burning log that passed for a stogie. "She still humping that bum?"

"Not anymore."

Harry cursed loudly and sharply. "I told both of them to stop it. I can't build her up—make her a star—if she can't stay out of the sheets of a married bum old enough to be her father." He looked hard at me. "How do you know this?"

"Bulls found a lot of soft things at VanderSaant's that belonged to a twist, among them a robe with the initials RAM over her left bub."

"That don't mean they belong to someone at this studio."

"VanderSaant worked here and the bulls will start digging. Her name will come up in a heartbeat, and lots of people know the history between them."

Harry pressed his intercom button. Betsy was on the line in a hurry.

"Miss Hammerlin, do I have anyone working for me whose initials are RAM? Other than Rachel Anne Maddon."

"No, sir."

Harry snapped off the intercom, and glowered at me. The stogie found its way to a crystal ashtray the size of a catcher's mitt. He rubbed his chin and stared at the alabaster. "Maybe I could hire someone with those initials."

"That won't fool the bulls, Harry. It'll only make things worse."

"I can get any extra in casting to change her name to suit those initials."

I said nothing. Harry's rapid fingers started drumming the desk top again. "Couldn't you get her things out of there?" he asked at last.

"No. Bulls already found them when I got there."

"What else they find? Risky pictures? Love letters?"

I wanted to shout risqué pictures. I wanted to open his windows and yell the word loud enough for the world to hear. I wanted to skywrite it in big white letters over the studio: Risqué pictures. "I only saw the clothes," I said quietly.

Harry reached for the blower. "Betsy, get me Hobbes on Stage Nine and be quick." He snapped the receiver onto the hook. "You tell them who RAM is?"

"No, but Harless will have figured it out by now."

"Will that copper spill it to the papers? How about the radio? If Lolly Parsons gets wind of this, we'll be crucifixed. That miserable broad hates me, y'know."

"None of those people will hear anything through Harless," I promised, "but he'll wire those initials pretty quick and he won't waste any time looking her up."

"I don't want him talking to—" The horn sounded. Harry held up a hand, said into the receiver, "Hobbes, is Miss Maddon on the set?...Dressing room...her agent there...her mother...that's good, that's good, drag her out of there and get her up to my office right now and don't bring anybody else and don't let anybody talk to her...that's exactively right...wrap her in a rug or something if you have to, get her up the back way and come to my private door...yeah, hurry. What do you think?"

Harry slammed down the mouthpiece, glared at me.

"She's the lead in an important picture gonna cost me nearly a half-million bucks to make. It's eighty percent done, even behind schedule, and it's over budget, and it will cost me another hundred grand if I have to recast and reshoot her part. I'm counting on that picture to be big box, and now this."

He picked up the smoldering cigar and stuffed it in his mouth, then immediately yanked it out and eyeballed me.

"Maybe I should let you take over this studio. You seem to think it's a pancake to run. If I had half a brain, I'd sell out and retire to the beach."

He reached into a desk drawer and dragged out a large bottle of aspirin. He swallowed four pills, using nothing to wash them down.

"I'd offer you a drink, but as you can see I do not keep alcohol in my office. That could turn into a bad habit. Days like this you can get started and won't stop."

He put the aspirin bottle back in his desk. He leaned back and turned to the window. After a while he asked, "Anybody else involved with that bum I need to know about?"

I shook my head. "No."

"Servants?"

"He had a man Friday couldn't be found yesterday. Harless put a bulletin out. He might have VanderSaant's car. Could be he's pinched by now."

Harry waved a hand in disgust. "Might have? Could be? Tell me something useful you know for a fact."

"You can—"

A light tap on Harry's private door stopped me. York nodded at the door. "Open it."

Rachel Anne Maddon stepped past me without looking at me. Titus Hobbes started in but Harry stopped him. "That's okay," he said briskly. "Wait right out there."

I closed the door in Hobbes' bemused face.

Rachel Anne Maddon was still in costume, but the phony gold necklace and other fake jewelry had fled. Being the diffident creature we all knew to be her true self, she had covered her bosom with a dark brown shawl. Her sand-colored hair glistened in the light. She looked briefly at me, flashed a fetching smile that showed perfect, brilliant white teeth, and let her light blue eyes twinkle deliciously.

"My dear Miss Maddon," Harry said charmingly, although he did not bother to rise and come out from behind his desk. "Please sit down."

"I am sorry, Mr. York," she said, her silky voice returning Harry's charm, "but sitting is entirely impossible in this costume. On the set, I have a tilting board to lean on between shots. Please excuse me for not taking this off, but your man said it was urgent and, anyway, I am due on the set momentarily."

"That's fine." He smiled the smile of a doting father. "I'll be brief. Do you recall a conversation you and I had in this office a couple of months ago? I believe Cleland VanderSaant was present when I suggested strongly that the two of you needed to be very, very caustic in your relationship, that your adoring public would not stand for intimacy between you and a married man more than twice your age. Do you remember that conversation?"

Rachel Anne Maddon cast doubtful eyes at me, obviously wondering why I was still present. I didn't know myself why Harry hadn't dismissed me.

"Look at me," Harry said firmly. "I want Mr. Brand to be here. We have a problem we need to mash out, and you need to be truthful with me."

"Mr. York, I assure you Mr. VanderSaant was never any more than a close family friend and I had strictly a working relationship—"

"Some very intimate women's clothing was found in his bedroom. Soft things, Mr. Brand called them, including a robe with your initials on them."

She turned her eyes downward and her shoulders slumped slightly. She found something of overwhelming interest on the spotless carpet. She needed to sit down but she was cinched up tighter than a plow horse.

"Rachel, sweet. I am going to do everything in my power to protect your career, to build you into the star of your destiny, but you are going to have to help me. You are going to have to do exactly as I say. Is that clear?"

The bunny nodded meekly and raised her head. Sorrowful eyes searched for forgiveness. A tear slid down her flushed cheek.

"The first thing I need to know is did you kill him?"

"Preposterous. I loved him dearly."

"Love has never stopped anyone from killing a paramount—"

"Paramour," I said under by breath.

"—it has probably contributed to it in many cases. Again, did you kill him?"

She wiped at the tears. I handed her my pocket mop.

"No, sir. I promise," she said weakly.

Harry's voice remained soft. "Know who did?"

"I have no idea."

"Did you leave anything in his house other than articles of clothes? You know, love letters, or maybe risky pictures that show...you know...cheesecloth?"

"Cheesecake," I said, this time loud enough to be heard. I looked at Rachel. "And Mr. York means risqué pictures. As in 'dirty.'"

She tossed me a sideways glance that could have cut glass. Apparently, the word dirty offended her delicate nature.

Harry looked annoyed. "Cheesecake," he grunted.

Rachel bristled. "Mr. York, I assure you there are no letters and no pictures whatsoever, and especially not of a lurid kind. I do not pose in the altogether."

"Good. Good. How about a diary or anything the police can tie up to you? Such a discovery would be most ungrettable."

She shook her head.

"That's fine," Harry said. "When did you last see him?"

"Friday evening when we finished shooting. I went straight home and stayed there through the weekend. Then Sunday morning I heard..." Her voice trailed off and she again found something fascinating on the floor. She sniffled and wiped her eyes. Harry watched her like a father ready to grab a whipping stick. She gently blew her nose, folded the handkerchief and clutched it tightly in her hand.

"Was someone with you all weekend?"

"Yes, my mother. And my stepfather. Our cook was there all weekend and also our driver and one maid."

"And you didn't leave the house?"

"No, sir."

"Your mother?"

"No, sir."

"Stepfather?"

"No, sir, none of us left the house during the entire weekend."

Harry sighed. "Do you have a family lawyer?"

She nodded. "Mr. Wilf. He handles our finances and—"

"He won't do. I will take care of that for you. The police are going to want to ask you questions. You will not answer anything. You are too upset over the death of such a close family friend who happens to be the man directing you in your first important picture role. All requests by the police will be referred to my lawyer and you will do nothing but shed tears for any policeman or newspaperman or any stranger who approaches you, and you will say nothing. Is that perfectly clear?"

"What do I tell my agent?"

"What do I care?" Harry's voice hardened. "He'll clam up and tell you to do the same with your career at risk."

"Mr. York, I assure you I will do anything, anything at all, to prove myself worthy of your faith in me."

"Good. Good. I have complete trust in your devotion to this studio. Now, you may return to the set. We need to do as much work tonight as we can possibly do. Mr. Collie has assured me he is more than willing to put in as many hours as necessary to finish this picture, and I expect the same of every cast member and the entire crew. Mr. Hobbes will escort you back to Stage Nine. Remember what I told you, my dear. Say anything I don't like and our next talk will be most unpleasant."

He nodded at me and I opened his private door for Rachel. I felt like I should be wearing a doorman's outfit. Hobbes, leaning against the wall, jerked up straight. His eyes raked me with a hundred questions.

"Take her back to the set," I told him and closed the door.

"What do you think?" York asked.

"I don't know how devoted that skirt is to you and the studio, but she is very devoted to saving her career."

"This studio and her career are the same thing, but that is not what I meant."

"I don't like her for killing VanderSaant, but that's just a hunch and I'm not prepared to go any farther than that. Frank Harless is going to take a hard look at her. Even you can't hold the bulls off forever."

Something akin to a sneer crossed his face. "I can try. I hope to God you're right and she didn't kill that bum."

"What do you want me to do? There must be some reason you kept me in here? I didn't need to hear all that hooey."

Harry nodded, motioned for me to sit down. "There is, but not why you think. I did, however, want you to judge what she told me. I don't want you involved in any aspect of the investigation into VanderSaant's death, unless I ask pacifically."

"What about VanderSaant's wife?"

"If Patricia did it I am prepared to sacrifice her. I believe her career has peaked, but we might get some mileage out of this affair if she didn't kill that bum. Neil, I wanted to talk to you about something completely diffident."

Two things had come out of this meeting: Harry had never even called me Mr. Brand, and he certainly had never ever addressed me by my first name.

"VanderSaant's death has no effect on this studio. It means nothing. Personally, it just moves up the turntable. I put that bum under contract to not just direct, but to produce. He's an all right producer but I can pull any half-twit bum off the streets to produce pictures. That's peanuts. As a director, he had skills, but everything that bum touched fell behind schedule, went over budget, and caused endless trouble. That pissant had unlimited facility for pissing off everybody who had to work with him."

Harry took the time to light another stogie. I got interested in the blue sky outside his big window and wondered what it would be like up in the mountains, fishing maybe, or lying naked on an ant hill.

"I let that bum talk me into giving him this Crusades picture and halfway through it I could see it was a big mistake. Now I have the chance to correct it. Lee Collie will fix it up. He's an extinguished director and people like the man and they work hard for him, and his pictures turn out popular and that means they make money."

"Harry, his name is Leo Collier."

York glared at me. "See. See. That's what I like about you. Nobody else in this entire damn studio has any guts. Nobody bothers to correct me. They all just go along and snicker behind my back. We all of us—yes, even me— learn from our mistakes, but how can you learn from your goofs if you don't know you're making them.

"Now, as for VanderSaant, that was a mistake and I admit it. I figured I owed him for…well, never mind that. I should have kicked that bum out of here after his first picture flopped and eaten his contract."

Harry practically beamed. "But now I don't have to lower myself. Just look at how much money I'm saving."

He suddenly frowned. "Does that make me a suspect?" Harry put the emphasis on the last syllable.

"It's a long list," I told him.

"Well, you can count me out. I got lots of ways to handle bums like him. Just between you and me—and anyone else I want to tell—I was taking that bum down a few notches. No more directing A pictures. I was through putting top projects in that bum's hands. I was kicking him down to B stuff and as producer only. He could have been proud. He could've gone around town telling every-body he was the highest paid B producer in the business. Not that bum. He would have raged and ranted and took it out on everybody who worked under him and gotten even more behind time and over budget, and I would've had to take it away from him and look at the mess that would've made and how much dough it would cost. Now I'm out of it with mazuma saved and I didn't have to do anything."

Harry grinned and puffed heartily.

"You didn't tell him what you were going to do?" I asked.

"Not yet. I was going to wait for him to wrap that Cru-sades picture. I did tell his wife, under the slickest confi-dence. I told Patricia she was a top star and couldn't af-ford to be married to some B pictures bum. I told her to annex her marriage and get free of that bum before I took him down a peg or two."

"And Russell Cave?"

"Same for that pissant. From now on, he's a B player and nothing more. Another bum she can't be mixed up with. I told him to stay away from her, and he didn't do it so now he's gonna learn his lesson the hard way. His build-up's over. Sorry thing is, Patricia did those two things I asked, and now it looks like her career's on a dead vine, based on her fan mail. She used to get five or six big sacks a week and now it's down to only two or three. The unfortunate box for her last two pictures ties up my hands, and here comes the death of her still-husband, and if that turns out to be murder, it's just noth-ing but bad publicity all around. She won't go to B's but I'll have to drop her down to third lead, and that means she'll be crying all over me and trying again to get into…well, never mind. I'm getting off the beaten track. Here's what I want from you. I'm starting a B series about a cop and I was gonna give it to that bum Vander-Saant as sort of a going away present. Because of his salary, I was putting him on it as both producer and director. Okay, I've got another director for it, Teddy Laurence." Harry shook a finger at me. "I got that name right. An up-and-comer. He's done solid work for me on several minor A pictures and he'll be perfect for this series. You'll like him. I'm also giving you a good exec, Eban Browner."

"Giving me? What—"

"From right this minute, you are producing my new *Inspector Cooper* detective series. Congratulations."

I almost fell out of the chair. "Craziest idea I ever heard. I just run security for your studio. I don't know anything about making pictures."

"No producer in the history of this town knew anything about making motion pictures until they started doing it. Nothing to it, if you got a head on your shoulders, and you do. Listen to me, Neil. In the almost four years you've been with this studio you've done solid work. That Cutter mess was the berries. It could have blown up in our faces and put us out on our ears but it didn't, and a lot of that was because of you. I would like to award you for that and this is how I do it. I can't pay a security bum that much, that would be ridiculous, people would laugh at me, but I can pay a producer that much. That bum VanderSaant was collecting three thousand clams a week to produce and direct. You'll only produce a B series, but that'll be worth five hundred to start and I'll boost that each picture if they turn out okay, which I'm sure they will or why would I be doing this?"

"Excuse me for saying so, but I think the inmates have taken over the asylum. Merly could do this better than me."

"Listen to me. The best producer I ever worked with, back when I was starting this studio, was a tie salesman the day I hired him. He was like you. A smart cookie who knew how to solve problems and that's what a producer does, he solves problems. That thing you did with Dunnum was exactly what I needed done. Keep the ball rolling. Don't let people sit around chewing their gums, costing me more money."

Harry got up from behind his desk and perched himself on the corner of the barge. The look on his face was the friendliest I had ever seen Harry look. He put his cigar on the big crystal ashtray and nodded at me.

"You'll be perfect for this cop series. You used to be one. I want this series to be honest, real, tough. I don't want asthmatics. You know? Those bums that think pictures ought to be full of smart-ass messages. Make the stories real, make them move, excite people. Do it in three reels and bring them in on schedule and on budget. You have the feel for it, to help the director and the writers and the players. It's a B picture, sure, but I think you're just the bum to put some pop into it. Those damned Warners don't have a monopoly on crime stories, even if they think they do. And the mazuma's way better and you're, what?, thirty-six now and got a wife. You gotta think of your future."

I could jaw with Harry all day about this, but the bottom line was that I was going home to Alice to tell her we had just either hit the upper income bracket or the soup kitchens. It seemed an easy choice, even if I didn't have a clue what I was getting into.

"If I'm the producer, I want Hugh Dunnum to direct for me."

"No. You get Teddy Laurence. I'm also starting a new B Western series, and I want Dunnum for that. His work on that Crusades picture is solid. VanderSaant tried to take all the credit for the second unit action stuff, but I know who really did it.

"Now, I need someone to replace you. A solid bum I can trust to keep an eye on things around here and protect my people. A bum who will hand me the straight goods and won't back off. In short, a bum just like you. Got any ideas?"

I had a bad idea. Just the way to get started on my new job. "Beck McLain." I said.

"Never heard of him."

"Used to be bull, got bounced just like me. Took a job as a cinder dick and when that didn't work out he got on at the Braebern as house dick."

A light flicked on in Harry's brain. "You trust him?"

I trusted a lot of things about Beck McLain, and none of them were right for the job as Harry York's top security gink. I had wanted to grill McLain since Vander-Saant's death, but I had no bulge. I knew Beck well enough to know this offered me a good way inside him.

"He's smart enough." Okay, that was something of a forthright answer. "He's honest enough. He knows when to clam." Two out and out lies. "He's gotten used to protecting your people from themselves." Again, something of a truth.

"What's a cinder dick?"

"Railroad cop."

"And they say I can't speak English. Okay, you call him. If he wants the job, have him call Miss Hammerlin and set up an interview. Beck what?"

"McLain."

Harry nodded. "Now, Miss Hammerlin will show you your new office. It's on the second floor. It used to belong to VanderSaant. I'll get some people in there to clean it out and then they can bring up whatever you want from your office."

"Can't do that. If the coroner rules his death was not an accident, homicide dicks will want to go through his office."

"That you do not have to worry about. This is my studio. You get out of here and let me get to work. I need to call the district attorney. The time has come for us to talk about many things, and it ain't about cabbage." He grinned smugly. "That's from one of my pictures. Funny, the things you remember."

CHAPTER 14

My new office held down a spacious spot on the second floor of Harry's big white administration building. Large windows overlooked Sunset Boulevard, and a long, chocolate leather sofa took the place of the battered steel file cabinets that had tried dismally to make my previous office feel worthy. I sunk into the sofa and propped my feet on a handy leather-covered ottoman and replayed my just-finished conversation with Alice.

She quickly got over her initial shock and her nimble mind churned out a shopping list that included updated wardrobes, a new car or two, and a bigger, ritzier place to live. I might as well let her at it, even though the odds were I'd be a one-picture producer.

"Well, Brand, I see you got to the top of one little mountain." Eban Browner laughed and wiped his wire-rimmed cheaters with a silk handkerchief. He paused inside my door and looked around, distaste twisting his florid features. VanderSaant had furnished his office with a lot of gaudy do-dads, although nothing as garish as the yellow-and-green wind-up clock gathering dust in his townhouse.

"I got lost somewhere along the way," I told him.

Browner looked like a man whose nose had been

jammed into rotten fish. "You don't plan to keep this tacky junk, do you?"

"Only until the bulls come."

"Cops? What do cops have to do with it?"

"They'll want to search the place."

"Oh, I see." He nodded solemnly. "Yes, I guess they will."

"I'm surprised they haven't been here yet. Not like them."

"Maybe Harry put the kibosh on it."

I shook my head. "No. He wanted to, but I told him it would be best to let them in and get it over with."

"So be it. I just dropped in to see if I could be of any assistance."

"I'm sure you can."

"I know how you feel, Brand. I was there once myself. You weigh your newfound good fortune against pleasing Harry York, and wonder if you're sunk."

"How do you please Harry?"

Eban grinned. "You make money for him. Your job title might have changed, Neil, but it's basically the same thing you've been doing, keeping deadbeats in line. Only in this case, most of the deadbeats are better paid."

"So am I."

"Know what I was doing when the hand of Harry York reached down into the muck and pulled me into the sunshine of his being?" Browner waved a manicured hand. "I was selling real estate in Florida. You remember the great land boom about ten years ago? I was one of those fast-talking sales swindlers out to make a fast buck, and going way faster than the law allowed. I was going to get filthy rich in two weeks, the devil be damned. Harry came down there on his vacation and my eyes lit up. I was going to sell him a big chunk of worthless property, showing him putrid piles of rubbish, parading him through stinking swamps thick with mosquitos the size of bats, telling him this would soon be the home of a new El Dorado. To shorten a tired story, the whole thing went bust but Harry liked my spiel, my enthusiasm, my zest. He hired me to be a picture producer and a couple of years ago moved me up to an executive spot. I had not a clue what I was doing when I started but I got lucky with a couple of pictures that turned big box office numbers and I was suddenly the fair-haired child at York pictures."

"I know nothing about making motion pictures."

"You don't have to. Being a producer is mostly about solving problems, just like in any business, be it real estate, selling shoes or making ball bearings. In this business, a problem is mostly solved by throwing money at it."

Browner smiled. "You've been around here long enough to be acquainted with that supreme method of business."

"I have seen some brain-dead mushrooms blossom and move up around this place." I returned Eban's grin. "Present company excluded"

"Don't be so sure," he said. "Keep this in mind, Neil. You want to hire people with some imagination, but not too much. Too much imagination gives them a glorified air that they know more than you do. If a writer argues over his perfect script—and writers are arrogant in that endeavor—increase his salary. He will understand he is being paid more money to hew the line, not to write better. He knows he is smarter than you and the fact that you have just given him more money increases that belief. He may rage to his friends or he may writhe in silence. Either way, he will give you what you want.

"It's the same with directors, only different. The more skillful the director, the more trouble he will cause. You want a director just good enough to give you what you want on film without gaining the dreadful idea that he is an artiste. An aesthetic."

I laughed. "Harry said he didn't want any aesthetics."

Eban shook his head. "Harry didn't say aesthetics."

"Harry said asthmatics."

"That's our esteemed leader, okay. But he's right, Neil. Trust me, artistes are to be avoided. They will want to take your Harry-approved film—clichéd and banal as it might be, knowing the lower in class it is, the more audiences will slop it up—and turn it into a pile of shiny rubbish that will cause the public's collective nose to wrinkle.

"Remember, writers and directors can be sinister fellows, and they will think the same of you. Picture-making is a team effort that requires give-and-take, but you have the final say. Just be sure you know exactly what Harry wants and if you give him that you will advance to the highest regions of Mount York."

Browner droned on about matters I needed to know, some mundane, some exotic. I would produce this B cop series and he would serve as exec, helping me put together the basic crew that would churn out the entire string. After that, I was pretty much on my own and without much input from him, except his name would always get credit, alone on the screen just before my name as producer, with the director's name alone on the last title.

"You got a small budget, so protect it," he told me. "Whatever you do, be on time and on budget. Remember this, always shoot the money. Any crew member can tell you what that means. Make your pictures as lousy as it takes to make money. Quality can be a rumor. As long as you make money for Harry, he'll leave you alone. Make him enough money and he'll be even happier with you. If he doesn't have to keep looking over your shoulder, he'll figure you're doing a swell job, and the next thing you know you'll be an exec."

After a couple of hours of gum-chewing, Browner left my office, and my secretary sidled in, a worried look on her pretty face. Short and slender, with a body that curved like a mountain road, Virginia Lodge had been kept in place after VanderSaant's death. I expected, from the wary look on her face when we first met, that she had spent a great deal of time fending off Cleland's pawing advances, and was sizing me up in that regard. She had been his personal secretary for nearly two years and knew her way around the business and I anticipated she would be of great value as I stumbled along.

"There is a policeman to see you," she said in a voice slightly above a whisper. "He says his name is Lieutenant Harless."

"Shoo him in, sweetheart."

I had to listen to a half-dozen cracks about my new position, which Frank had only heard about when he stopped at my former cubbyhole and saw two brawny men gathering my stuff. When he ran dry of wit, he made himself comfortable on the sofa and got around to brass tacks.

"I came here to search VanderSaant's office. I got a feeling just by looking at it that you haven't changed anything."

I shook my head no. "I knew you'd be here. Up until a couple of hours ago I didn't know I'd be in here. You talk to VanderSaant's wife? Russell Cave?"

Harless nodded. "Both of 'em." He wasn't going to say any more.

"Find out about RAM?"

"Rachel Anne Maddon. I think you knew that when I first asked."

"Talk to her yet?"

"Not yet. Can't find her, but we will. Thought I'd go through this office while my boys hunt her down."

"Talking to her won't be easy, Frank. Harry called the DA a little while ago."

His eyes narrowed. "That in itself is hinky and don't look good."

"She's a hot property and Harry wants her protected. I have to think if she killed him—and I seriously doubt it—that she would have cleaned out her stuff from his place that night. My wire on her is she's just smart enough to know to do that."

"Maybe. Maybe she didn't get the chance. I still want to talk to her."

"Find Lemmert yet?"

"VanderSaant's man Friday?" Frank's head moved a little, side to side. "No. He's proving oddly elusive, but we're learning some things about him. Sooner or later, he'll turn up like a dirty penny. The names Charlotte or David mean anything to you?"

"I might know a couple twists named Charlotte."

"Those two names were on the back of the two photos in VanderSaant's place. The one of the frail read Charlotte, 1907. The other one, Charlotte and David, 1912. The photographer's stamp put them in New York. The kid looked to be about one, which puts him around twenty, twenty-one now. That's about the same age we put VanderSaant's butler."

"More reason you want him. Any dope on Charlotte?"

"Not yet, but we got New York boys digging around. I'm betting we get some sort of wire on our Charlotte Doe before long."

"In the meantime?"

"In the meantime, Neil, I'm going through this palace you stumbled into with a fine-toothed comb, and I'm doing it without your help. Is any of this stuff yours?"

I shook my head. "Feel free to take anything. I'll be in the commissary, if you want me."

I told Virginia to call me as soon as Harless finished his work, and went out my private door. In the hallway, the two men who had brought my stuff up from my former office waited patiently beside a large wooden box with rope handles, piled with junk. They had wasted their time. Merly could have brought up what few things I wanted to keep. I pointed out a couple items and said to leave them in my office when the man inside it was done and to throw away the rest. I dug a key I had found in VanderSaant's desk from my pocket and dropped it into a box containing pens and ink I wanted to keep.

"If you come across a bottle of bourbon somewhere in that box, don't worry, it's empty," I said and started down the hallway. The sound of the box being searched followed.

"By golly, you're right," a voice called from behind me.

CHAPTER 15

Harry brought in Beck McLain to talk about running security for York Brothers Studio. Harry told me to sit in on the interview. Beck showed up in a burgundy plaid jacket, baggy dark brown trousers, and a slightly frayed red-and-black tie dotted with white geometric figures. The jacket had three buttons on each sleeve, but the left sleeve was shy a button and had a slight tear at the cuff. I met him at the main gate and walked him up to Harry's asylum. Beck offered his hand to Harry, but York did not stand and did not move from behind his barge. He nodded at the two chairs in front of his desk and we plopped into them.

McLain rubbernecked Harry's office with unrestrained awe. Harry's hooded eyes wired me in plain language. He fired questions at Beck while I sat quietly. I wanted to jump in over a couple of things McLain said during his interview, but I remembered to sit quietly and listen. Harry threw me a curious look a couple of times, and when his dog-and-pony show was over he instructed me to escort McLain to the front gate.

"Come on back up here when you're done," Harry told me. "We have things about your picture to get to today."

McLain stuck out his hand but Harry had swiveled toward the big picture window and was ignoring us while he lit a stogie. I grasped Beck's arm and guided him to the door, which Betsy magically opened.

I took McLain to my former office. He might have thought about ditching the York gig when he saw the shabbiness of the cubbyhole. He shook his head in dismay at the cramped space, with the scarred desk, ancient chair and battered filing cabinets. Even the portrait of FDR on the calendar couldn't make him smile. He perched uneasily on the edge of the desk, now vacant except for the phone and the four-blade GE fan. He fished a deck of Raleighs from his pocket and lit up with a match from a book stamped by a strip joint downtown, a dump not far from the main police clubhouse.

"How long did you stay in this dump?" he wanted to know. "Not exactly what I had in mind as an image of York Brothers."

"About three years. Don't let it get to you. You'll spend most of your time wandering the lot, ogling the good-looking skirts."

He grinned. "Lots of them, I bet."

"No more than a couple hundred. You'll like the musicals. Lots of dancing dames showing long, shapely gams in short skirts."

Beck's smile became more of a leer. "Brand, that way you punch the bag makes me think I'm going to like this job just ducky."

"Hands off the talent if you want it to last."

"The high-hats won't like it?"

"The high-hats will have staked out their share. A smart twist trying to build up a career won't see much future in vamping the security gink."

"Pipe that. A fella can still look though. I bet there's one or two he could pick off with the right line."

I tried to match his leer. "You got something there. Ready for me to show you the ropes?"

"Sure. Why don't we start with these filing cabinets? Looks to me like they came over on the Mayflower. What's in 'em I need to know about?"

"You'll find schedules for the studio cops in the top left drawer. The other drawers are just taking up space."

"Cop schedules?"

"Tells you which guards are at what gates and when, and who are roaming the lot, keeping an eye on things other than the tomatoes."

"Any artsy pictures in those drawers?"

"Sorry," I said easily.

"All the air-tight broads around here and you got empty filing cabinets? Guess you took all the good stuff with you."

"Fella gets his chance. Especially with all those young frails out to get noticed."

McLain's smile widened and his eyes crinkled. "Yeah, I just bet. Big stars today weren't always big, y'know."

I grinned wider, too, just like Beck. "They all started small. Most of them did whatever it took to make it in this business."

"Tell you what. I'll get my own little file going and after I've settled into the job and we get to know each other better maybe we can hold a little swap meet."

"Anybody in mind?"

"I was hoping there might be some stuff of Patricia Metcalf."

"Why her?"

"Just a hunch that come to me. Won't surprise me none if that VanderSaant gink had some nice photos of that saucy tomato, and I don't mean Sunday-go-to-church nice." He spread his hands. "Just a hunch."

"Why?"

He grinned. "A good house dick keeps his eyes and ears open, and his mouth closed until it matters what he says. With those two, I heard and saw a lot."

McLain looked at me curiously a few seconds, sucking on his lower lip.

"Brand, as a house dick I'd keep this to myself. My loyalty belonged to the hotel and to its guests. Now that I'm here and loyal to this studio, I can wire you about some things I glommed. Patricia Metcalf skated around with a lot of bimbos in that suite she kept. A lot of 'em I made, but most I didn't. Once or twice a big name star would sidle in, and VanderSaant never caused trouble on those nights."

"Other nights?"

"Other nights he could raise holy hell. Don't know how that gink could get so bent and not pass out. That shrimp could hold his liquor. I'll give him that."

"That shrimp had a lot of practice, Beck. How many nights did you have to take him down?"

"Two or three every month. I always kept quiet and respectful about it."

"Over the bimbos his wife was with?"

"Yeah, his beefs with them were the same as the night you had to come over. He'd cuss her out for bringing up ginks with no names and no decency. Said they wouldn't respect her privacy. Said they'd blab it all over town. It would harm her career. Unworthy of the honor of being with her, I believe he called it."

"Didn't she ever tell him where to get off?" I asked.

"Darb, but the big blowup came that night with Cave. She told VanderSaant she'd already kicked him out of her life and when she finished that picture she was doing, she was headed for Reno to get rid of him permanently. Told him she was going to marry Cave."

"How'd he take that?"

"Like a kick in the teeth. He told her she couldn't do that. Said not to forget he had the goods on her."

"Say what the goods were?"

He shook his head. "But Russell Cave was in the room during all this, and maybe neither one of them wanted him to know."

"Where were you?"

"Just outside the door. VanderSaant was half under and yelling loud enough to wake the dead. Folks started gathering in the hallway."

"So you busted it up."

"Had to." McLain ground out the Raleigh, lit another. "Sure, I wanted to hear more, but it was time I had to step in. I didn't want anyone calling the desk. That happens and things start to get out of hand."

"They did anyway."

"Yeah. VanderSaant kept getting more and more pissed over that Cave bimbo seeing his wife. That night I called you VanderSaant was at his worst, and I figured if something didn't put an end to it soon, there'd be serious trouble."

"VanderSaant have a room there, too?"

"No, but that Cave fella was there several times with Miss Metcalf, and a couple of times with a young, silky frail who didn't want to be seen."

"Make her?"

Beck coolly blew smoke toward the ceiling. "No. Cave wanted a key to the back door just like Miss Metcalf, so he could slip the frail in and out. I told him we don't hand out keys to just anyone who asks. Miss Metcalf and a couple of other big names I could drop got keys for reasons you can wire easy enough, but dewdroppers like Cave don't get their own keys. He tried to get tough and raise a dust-up, but that gink ain't a thing but striped candy."

"The others work for York?"

"York and other studios."

"Okay, Beck. Tell me about Cave and his little trollop."

"By damn, she was a swell-looking twist. About five two or three with a chassis that'd make a eunuch drool. Skin like cream and light blue lamps that cut through you so hard you wanted to slap her. Light brown hair and lips you couldn't taste long enough. Hard to breathe just standing next to her."

"How many times did you see her?"

"Twice. Both times Cave came to me and slipped me some kale to let the doll face in through the back and slip her up to his room so nobody'd see her."

"Did anyone see her?" I asked.

"Me and some of the hotel staff. That's all.

"How long would she stay?"

McLain blew a smoke ring. "Can't rightly say, but the bellboys told me she always slipped out before daylight."

"Cave registered?"

"Yeah."

"But not her."

Beck grinned. "Not her."

"That was a favor to Cave?"

"To Cave and to the twist."

"And no one knew her name?"

"No, but we sure wanted to."

"Yeah," I said. "I bet you did."

"Had to figure her for somebody on the way up. Dame that swell? Figured sooner or later we'd pin a name to her."

I nodded. "Who else at York kept rooms there?"

McLain fidgeted a little and looked unsure. "Now, Neil, maybe I've said a little too much here. I wouldn't wanna rat on others, y'know. We both of us know how the game is played, and you've done all right for yourself."

The cool look in his eyes told me clearly what he expected, but my hand stayed away from my pocket.

"I have. We'll talk that over later when we get down to the straight goods."

We chewed our gums a little longer and I walked McLain to his car. The heavy air carried humidity unusual for mid-April even though the afternoon sun hid behind a bank of gray clouds coming in over the Palisades.

Five hot meringue chorus dolls walked by, giggling among themselves. McLain's eyes stalked them and his tongue moistened greedy lips. He finally got his peepers back to me and the leer on his face disappeared.

"Thanks for putting in a word for me, Brand. I think it went well with Harry York." The leer returned. "Gonna sure be swell working here."

"Take care. Harry will be in touch."

Beck McLain rolled off the lot and I hustled up to Harry's office.

"Tell me again who that bum was?" Harry did not ask gently. He stood at the window, rocking silently back and forth on his tiny plates, scowling at the dark clouds building directly over his kingdom.

"A bum you don't want to hire."

"Damn straight. Wire me."

"McLain used to be a cop. I knew him when I was on the force. He got bounced for a few naughty things, chiefly, I think, an inability to keep his yap closed. Latched on with the railroad, and took to strong-arming hoboes. Got hold of the wrong gink one night and woke up a couple days later hooked up to hospital sheets and wrapped to his ears. Railroad had no more use for him and he glommed that job at the Braebern."

"I have heard that some of my people frequent that hotel."

I nodded. "It's ritzy. It's safe. And it's private."

"And this McLain bum knows this?"

"He does, and not a good idea."

"I believe I know why," Harry grunted.

"Beck McLain would bleed his mother for a buck. Anybody with secrets at the Braebern needs to be careful."

"And you brought him to me for what reason?"

"McLain wasn't going to tell me anything he knew." I stared at Cicero's marble mug. "At least, not without a lot of grease I wasn't going to feed him and you didn't need to. I figured a job offer here, especially after he got to ogle a few skirts, would loosen his gums. He'd want to spill and get in solid."

"Did he?"

I forced my eyes off Cicero and back to Harry. "He did."

"Are some of my people over a hoop on this?"

"Not so far. McLain is working on setting his hooks into Patricia Metcalf and Rachel Anne Maddon. And then there's Russell Cave."

"What about that goombah?"

"He's been seen at the Braebern with Metcalf and with Maddon."

Harry slammed his fist into his right palm three times, cursing loudly with each smack. He returned to his desk and pushed the intercom button.

"Miss Hammerlin, send Miss Metcalf up here immediately. If her agent's with her, he can come up too, but nobody else."

He turned burning eyes on me.

"Okay, then. I'll see that McLain bum gets tossed out on his ear. It would do him well to remember who he's trying to deal over. As for Miss Maddon, we will have to take a long look at her after this picture, and what a waste of money that could be. As for that bastard Cave, I've got a special treaty for him. That bum's been warned about both those dames, and he's continued to defy me."

The burning eyes glowered at me, began to simmer.

"Damn it all, Brand, you are of a curtain one sneaky son-of-a-bitch. No wonder I wanted to make you a producer." He sat down, his face a mask. "Just remember, I can be one sneaky son-of-a-bitch myself."

CHAPTER 16

York's newest picture producer buckled down to work. Long hours trying to learn the ropes turned into longer hours. I dealt with myriad specialists in every phase of filmmaking from backlighting to casting calls, from camera angles to continuity. I learned on the go and there was a lot to learn. I meticulously put a crew together. Teddy Laurence came aboard as the director and I pretty much gave him free rein to pick his crew, from assistant director to cameramen, from key grips to gophers. I called Eban Browner a dozen times a day the first week, systematically whittling those calls down until Eban took to calling me to make sure all was copacetic in my little foreign world. He seemed pleased with my progress.

Through Eban, Harry presented me with a list of screenwriters and told me to choose one for the initial *Inspector Cooper* picture. They were all first-timers, with not a script credit to their names, all eager and low-paid, as befitted my skimpy budget.

"Shoot the money," Browner had advised me, and I repeated that to Laurence, who nodded knowingly and smiled distantly.

We picked our lead actor from another list Harry provided. A middle-aged contract player named Eric

Dunne—a seasoned veteran of nearly a hundred A, minor A and B pictures—tested exactly the way I envisioned the dauntless Inspector Cooper. The rest of the cast fell into place easily, except the role of Elly Martin, the perky newspaper doll trying to get her big break from a hard-nosed city editor by getting the scoop on the murder the intrepid inspector would solve in the final reel. We screen-tested several unknown players with little acting credits but none of them entirely fit the bill.

Then one afternoon in my office—watching the slender, vivacious Virginia Lodge perform her duties—it hit me. Virginia Lodge was the perfect Elly Martin. She looked aghast when I told her I wanted to test her, but she let me talk her into it. The screen test showed promise, but Teddy and Eban told me I would have a hard sell with Harry. They were wrong, sort of.

I went into York's office and demanded Rachel Anne Maddon for the Elly Martin role. Harry laughed, snorted, yelled and cursed loudly, but when his ranting finally ended I said meekly that if I couldn't get Miss Maddon I had a young bunny in mind who was perfect for the part, and I had a test ready and if he saw it he would like her as much as I did. Harry gave in and watched the test, weighed Rachel Anne against Virginia, and decided that since Miss Lodge was only going to cost him one hundred clams a week, then okay. After all, her screen time would only amount to about twenty minutes.

"It's your ass, anyway," Harry groused.

He told me my eye for talent impressed him. I figured he was more impressed by my eye for saving scratch.

I dropped in on Theo Stein, one of Harry's top writers. Alone in his office, he lay flat on his back on a sofa, his long legs dangling over the arm, his nose in a thick book. Theo grimaced and made guttural noises as he read. He laid the open book across his chest when he saw me and fished around for a gasper. He tapped the book.

"Harry bought this property and now I'm supposed to turn it into a mess of hot fireworks. There's hardly anything in this that'll get past the censor, so I don't know if Harry is kidding himself or me."

"Tough deal?"

"Naw." Theo stuck an unlit gasper in his mouth. "I can write this pap in a week. Keep the title and a few character names and make up everything else. Boy meets girl. They fall passionately in love. Trouble intervenes. They finally get together in the last reel. All I got to do is find a way to keep 'em from jumping into the sack in the second reel."

"You know, Theo, I have heard of innocent women who keep themselves chaste until after their wedding day. Some men, too."

Theo's face brightened. "Really? You might have something there. I think I can work with that. Good idea, thanks. You might make a producer yet."

"Just think what I can learn from a genius like you."

"Your humble genius had a nightmare last night, Neil. Dreamed I was stranded on an isolated island with the two most beautiful women in the world. Two stunning creatures who could skin any man with a smile and a wink."

"That's a nightmare?"

"Turns out I was a woman, too. Marie Dressler. " He lit the cigarette and clasped his hands behind his head. "I'm going to work that into a script some way."

I told Theo why I had stopped in. He recommended a young fellow who had recently joined the York ranks as a lowly two-fifty-a-week hack. Robert Gain Gibbon—painfully thin and slightly stooped, with thinning hair prematurely gray—had been an ace newspaper reporter in Boston before Hollywood's golden but perverted finger beckoned. I had a quick interview with Gibbon in my office and quickly hired him to write the first *Inspector Cooper,* with an option for the second. He had a quick mind, a great ear for dialogue and a perturbing habit of wearing his wire-rim, bottle-thick glasses on the tip of his long nose when he typed. He wrote quickly and churned out a tricky plot, easily adapting my suggestions on police procedure and how the buttons operated, along with his knowledge of the newspaper game.

I thought we were off to a strong start. Then Eban called and told me Teddy Laurence was no longer available. Harry had screened the pre-cut version of Teddy's minor A picture and decided Laurence was too good to waste on me. From now on, Teddy Laurence was a director of A pictures and I would have to look elsewhere. I asked again for Hughie Dunnum, but he was hard at work on York's new B Western series, and I was left scanning a lengthy list for another director. I thought about trying the Maddon ploy and asking for Leo Collier—Harry might not remember his name—but I decided that would be going to the mountain once too often. I ended up with young Eddie Southworth, who had just wrapped a thirteen-chapter serial that had done well at the box. Teddy Laurence told me Eddie was a good choice.

Southworth and I hit it off immediately and locked up the deal over lunch in a private room in the studio commissary. I told Southworth I had a writer in place but he could put the rest of the crew together, and that his serial team would be darb.

Eddie set off to work and I went back to my office. Virginia had gone to lunch and Patricia Metcalf had let herself in.

She arranged her luscious body on my couch in a pose straight out of a Gustav Klimt painting. Her black evening gown showed more cleavage than the Hays Office knew existed, and she had hiked the gown up far beyond her knees to expose a delicious stretch of shapely gam. She flashed a lascivious smile that crinkled her eyes, and flicked her tongue across her bottom lip.

"I thought I would drop by and offer my congratulations on your new position," she purred. "I am very pleased for you." Her eyes danced around the newly-spruced room. "Not only are you prettier than Cleland, you have better taste in furnishings."

"I'm happy to hear you didn't decorate for him."

"Cleland's office was his alone, but enough about him. It would seem I have arrived at a very propitious time. I had hoped we would be alone."

I sat down behind my desk. I liked the idea of having it between us. "Your congratulations are gratefully accepted."

She tapped a spot on the couch. "If you came over here, my sweet, I could congratulate you more intimately."

"A simple thank you is intimate enough."

"You have been very kind to me. I would like to repay the favor, especially now that we appear to be on a more even social footing. I can offer you some very nice benefits that Harry York cannot."

"Consider the favor repaid, sister. I was just doing my job."

She swung her feet to the floor and sat up, her back a little rigid. She began putting on her shoes, which had been artfully arranged in front of the couch. The look on her pan had turned a little less friendly.

"I know what you were doing, but now your job has changed. It seems your social standing has risen to a level nearly equal to mine. A picture producer. A well-known actress. That seems to fulfill all the necessary requirements, according to the principles my late husband espoused. I propose an assignation that would make him proud."

"I'm a married man."

"I am proposing nothing that would interfere with your duties as a married man. Our little tête-á-tête would have nothing to do with your marriage. Our peers would see it as only natural and it would be accepted for exactly what it is. Two people expressing their mutual appreciation for each other."

"Our peers have a strange and often indelicate sense of duty. As much as I appreciate the offer, you should go and shake some other apple tree."

"Say, you aren't a three-letter man, are you?" Her mouth worked a little as she thought about it. "Even if you are married. A lot of marriages in this town are just for show."

I didn't say anything. Patricia kept staring at me. "No, I guess not, but you are certainly rough on a girl's ego."

"My wife's ego seems to be just fine."

"Ahhh, my pet, I did not come here to discuss your wife. I am not giving up on you. I think perhaps with some further enticement you will come around."

She stood and came to my desk, flipping her hips in an exaggerated walk that almost had me laughing. She leaned over the desk and gave me a look down the front of her dress that went all the way to Naples.

"I think the boy does have a sense of humor somewhere under that staid exterior. You are a tough nut to crack, Neil Brand, but I am on a mission. I am going to enjoy the journey. It will be almost as much fun as the arrival."

Patricia was gone then, laughter trailing behind her like one of the Sirens luring a sailor to his doom. I sat motionless several seconds, staring at the door.

A few moments later, someone came in the front office. The intercom on my desk buzzed.

"Can I get you anything?" Virginia asked.

"Yeah, some cotton for my ears."

"Sorry, I'm fresh out. Boll weevils, you know."

"Okay, sit tight. I'm off to Alabama to get some. If
anyone calls or drops in, take messages and tell them I'll
get back to them in a couple of weeks."

I switched off the intercom before Virginia could reply
and went out quickly through my private door. I was beginning to feel like Harry York, and that wasn't good.

I had taken up a daily habit of wandering around the
studio lot, looking in on productions being shot on various sound stages or in the numerous neighborhoods built
around the massive York property—exteriors that doubled for everything from medieval times to Westerns to
modern-day and even the future, or somebody's idea of
the future—trying to get familiar with what was going on
in front of the camera. Running security, I had often
dropped in on these sets but those visits were mostly to
check out what was going on behind the cameras. Now, I
was trying to learn the business from the other side.

In front of the auditions room I ran into the writer Erle
Stanley Gardner, leaning on the front fender of a sleek
Mercedes-Benz roadster, its polished black paint sparkling in the sunshine. Gardner was talking to one of Harry's top executives, Benny Irving. I knew Irving had been
handling discussions with Gardner over bringing the Perry Mason character onto the silver screen, working hard
against the building competition from Warner Brothers.
Gardner's Perry Mason books were top sellers, and if
York Brothers got a property that hot I would not be
above putting in my pitch to produce the series. Benny
shook hands with Gardner and disappeared into the administration building.

Gardner climbed into the roadster, but I got to him before he fired the motor.

"You get a deal?" I asked after I had introduced myself.

"Didn't pan out. The offer Warners made me suits me better, but the door here is still open if I change my mind."

"Nice car. Mercedes isn't it?"

"Like it? I'll sell it to you. I'm planning on getting a new one as soon as I sign the picture deal with Warners. A little present to myself."

The idea struck me hard, and the thought of ridding myself of my old Chevy caused me no pain. We settled on a price, and Gardner said he'd give me a ring when he was ready to sell. We shook hands and he rolled off the lot.

I made a beeline to Harry's office. The big man was willing to give me a couple of minutes, no more. Betsy held open the heavy door to the inner sanctum. Harry stood by the big picture window, sunlight making his face glow. He took a puff on his ever-present stogie. His left hand held something that looked like a screenplay.

"You got troubles with that picture, see Eban."

"I want to buy a car to replace that old Chevy of mine."

"So? Buy a car. Buy a good one. I don't like high-end people who work for me driving around in rusty jalopies. Bad image for my studio."

"I need a loan."

"How much?"

I told him and he nodded his head, still looking out the window as if he had never before seen California sunshine. "Okay. I'll take it out of your salary. Half every payday."

"In that case, double my salary and you'll get paid back in half the time."

"Done. Now get out of here. I got a lot of work to do."

I left smiling, wondering if every studio mogul in Hollywood ran his business in such a twisted fashion.

CHAPTER 17

A couple of days before we started production on *Inspector Cooper* Harold Murphy dropped into my office carrying a large, scarred wooden box by its thick rubber handles. A strong padlock kept the lid in place. Harold—a tall, lanky, redheaded lad in his mid-twenties—worked in the props department.

"Mr. Brand," he said, somewhat timidly, "we didn't know what to do with this so we thought we ought to bring it up to you. It belonged to Mr. VanderSaant and he asked us to store it for him where it couldn't be spotted, but now that—"

"What's in it?"

"Bunch of this and that, I guess. Some old picture scripts mostly, and some film, but there's also a lock box that don't seem to have a key."

"Leave it on that chair in the corner, if you would. I'll see what's in there when I get a chance. Got a key for that padlock?"

He shook his head. "Mr. VanderSaant didn't leave us a key. If you want, I can tell somebody in carpentry to come up and cut it open."

"I'll let you know."

Harold nodded. "Mr. Trilby just thought you ought to have it, you being the one who replaced Mr. Vander-

Saant. We figured whatever's inside is mostly worthless. We didn't know who else to give it to, but we didn't just want to pitch it."

I stared at the box, growing curious.

Harold started to leave, stopped by the door. "Mr. Brand, do you remember Mary Kamenshek down in wardrobe?"

"Of course I do. How is she?"

"Oh, she's just wonderful. I mean…well, she and I are getting married and, well, we wanted to make sure we invited you. Mr. Brand, you did a mighty nice thing for her a while back and we can never forget it."

"How is she dealing with her sister's death? Thing like that was a hard blow for a bunny like her to take."

"She misses Winnie terribly, but she's slowly learned to deal with it and she's moving on. She's looking forward to…you know…starting a family. That will certainly help her put away the pain of her sister's passing."

"When's the wedding date?"

"We haven't set it yet, but you'll be among the first to know."

I got Harold out of my office and tackled the mysterious box without hesitation. I dug out the box holding pens and ink and picked up the key I had found in VanderSaant's desk. No surprise when it snapped the padlock open.

Harold was right, it was mostly worthless stuff, except for two things. A sheaf of receipts rubber-banded together showed VanderSaant had been paying rent on a cottage on Marathon Street, not far from the Paramount lot. The last receipt told me the rent was paid through the end of May. A sturdy, metal lockbox—about a foot square and about four inches high—drew my attention. Breaking into it would not be a problem. All I needed was the right tools.

I took it down to the carpenter's shop, borrowed a strong chisel and heavy hammer, and the box surrendered speedily to my tender caresses. Inside were two spools of sixteen-mm film and nothing else. All sixteen-mm film was acetate, which meant it was safe to expose. I hotfooted it back to my office and slowly reeled out one of the spools against the bright light of my desk lamp. I didn't have to spool out much, less than a foot, to see it was a stag flickers with a man and woman, both naked, shabbily filmed in poor lighting. I spooled the film to the start, put it back in the box and locked the box in my bottom right desk drawer. I buzzed my secretary, Rose, a somewhat doughy bug-eyed Betty who had replaced Virginia. She came into my office, carrying a memo from Eddie Southworth.

I took it from her hand but didn't look at it. "Do I need to answer this?

She shook her head. "Just says cameras will start rolling in the morning."

"See if you can get Hugh Dunnum on the line."

She left and buzzed back in less than a minute. "Mr. Dunnum is not available just now. I left a message for him to call you."

It was just past four-thirty.

"Go on home, Rose. We don't have to do anything else today."

"Yes, sir. Thank you, sir."

I ran down to the commissary to grab a ham-and-cheese on rye. Dunnum rang me up a little before six. I was sitting in my darkening office, doing nothing more than thinking and sipping on a new bottle of bourbon, knowing Harry would not approve of such behavior from his newest picture producer.

"Hughie, you got a sixteen millimeter projector?"

"No, but reckon I can glom one. What's up?"

"Hustle a projector up to my office, will you. Got some old film here I don't want anyone else to see."

"Sound or silent?"

"Silent's fine."

Dunnum arrived in thirty minutes.

"How's Harry's hotshot new director doing?" I asked as we set up the Ampro projector.

"Ridin' hard and shootin' straight. Say, I'm leaving heavies all over that back lot and my hero's kissin' a lot of horses." Dunnum put a little edge to his voice. "And I'm not gettin' anybody hurt."

We got the sixteen-mm film going and Hughie came upright in his seat as soon as it started. The nude man on the flickering screen rated about twenty. The girl—beautiful and delicate with a round angelic face—couldn't have been more than fifteen. The poor lighting and the deep shadows caused images to appear to flicker in the wavering light, but what the two performers were doing left nothing to imagine.

After a few minutes I told Hughie to turn off the projector. We threaded the second spool and started it up again. A different man, mid-twenties, loomed out of the shaded scene, dallying with the same girl, slightly older in this flickers. The naked nymph in those flickering shadows raised my hackles. No way could anyone mistake Rachel Anne Maddon.

"I'd have to say those two youngsters were almighty active," Hughie said, grinning brightly. "You make the girl?"

I nodded, said nothing. I put the two film reels back in the box, but I had no intention of leaving them in my office. "Hughie, you need to forget you ever saw this."

Dunnum picked up the projector. "Can't say I'll ever forget I saw that. But I can remember that I didn't see it, if anybody asks."

CHAPTER 18

ang on to this and don't let anybody see what's inside." I put a new metal lockbox containing the two dark nudie flickers on the corner of Mack Sanger's desk. I had taped the key to the box to the back of the bottom right drawer of my home desk, although any determined rummy could probably break into the box with a matchstick.

Sanger didn't look at the box. "I'm bettin' that thing is empty."

I grinned. "Empty as my head."

"Who does it hurt? Assuming it gets loose."

"Nobody you care about but Harry York."

"Not you?"

"I didn't think you cared."

His turn to grin. "One of the things I do best, Brand, is keep stuff that doesn't exist away from people I don't know." He fired up a Cuban and leaned back in his chair. "Who else knows about this empty box?"

"Me and Sweeney."

"Swell."

"I might ask you to get rid of it for good, or I might want it back. Right now, I don't know how it's going to play out."

Sanger shrugged. "It'll be here when you want it. If

you're protecting Harry, I've got his back. Maybe I've even got yours."

"That's why I'm entrusting this to you."

"Must be hot stuff."

"Hot enough to burn Harry's pocketbook."

The drive from Laurel City back to York Brothers gave me plenty of time to massage the inside of my conk, but I was still perched clumsily on a shaky fence when I walked into my outer office just after one-thirty. Rose stopped her rapid typing, raised thick eyebrows and rolled her brown eyes toward my private office. She hooked a finger at me, the long, red nail waving like a matador's cape.

"There's a copper in there." Her low voice fairly hissed. I smelled cabbage on her breath. A half-eaten piece of lemon pie took up space on her desk beside a mug of coffee. "He wouldn't take no for an answer and insisted on waiting in your office."

"The way to handle coppers, Rose, is to show them a little cheesecake or maybe a little cleavage and wink a lot."

Rose was still sputtering softly when I walked in on Frank Harless, sitting behind my desk with his dogs propped up. I closed the door, shutting out the sudden clatter of Rose's typewriter.

Frank looked up from the shooting script for the first Inspector Cooper picture, titled with a great deal of imagination, *Inspector Cooper*.

"Get this on celluloid," he said, smiling like a monk at a nudist colony, "and you just might go down as the greatest filmmaker of all time."

"Save your sarcasm for when you're rousting poached eggs." I dropped my fedora on the top hook of the three-prong coat rack and sat down in a chair facing the desk. "If you want to be a picture critic, Frank, maybe Lolly

can use you. It would be a step up for both the critic business and the police force."

"Got an interview with Rachel Anne Maddon,"
Harless looked at his watch, "in eleven minutes. Thought
I'd pass a little time with you, only you were out hobnob-
bing with Clark Gable or somebody."

"Clark invited me over for drinks with Jean. Or maybe
it was Claudette. Hard to see clearly with all those stars in
my eyes."

"The picture business is treating you well, I see."

I grinned. "No beef."

"You earned a break."

"Maybe not so much."

"Break like this, maybe you won't have to meddle in
cop business any more. Like the man said, nice work if
you can get it."

"I can get you on the payroll if you want, Frank. Turns
out this picture producing business is eggs in coffee. All
you have to do is separate the geniuses from the great
unwashed."

"Sounds like a motto for a homicide dick."

"Ain't much difference in the two jobs. Easy homicide
cases turn on two things, greed and hate and love. Hate
and love being the same thing. In pictures, there's only
one plot for every movie. Virtue wins out and evil loses."

Harless grinned. "Just like in real life."

"Theo Stein is one of the best writers Harry has, and
he told me a couple years ago when I was helping him on
that cop picture that he had learned the basics of writing
for pictures in one dinner conversation with Herman
Mankiewicz."

Harless shot me a funny look and shook his head.

"He's a picture writer, one of the best. Manky told him
that the hero of a novel can lay ten girls and marry a virgin, but a picture hero has to be a virgin, and that goes

double for the heroine. The villain can lay anyone he wants, have as much fun as he wants cheating and stealing and murdering his way to riches, but he has to die at the end. When he dies with a bullet in his craven heart, a respectable scenarist will have him clutch the tapestry on the wall and pull it down over his head like a symbolic shroud. Also, if the villain is covered by the tapestry— preferably one with a religious theme—the actor doesn't have to hold his breath while he is being photographed as a dead man. Many picture critics have praised Theo for the realism of his pictures, but Theo told me he ought to write movies loaded with nothing but babies, villains and wanton women. That way he could always tell the truth."

"A cop fools the crooks. A picture producer fools the public. That about it?"

I switched the subject abruptly. "You're going to talk to Rachel at the studio?"

Harless twitched his lips in a tight grimace. The good humor fled his eyes. "In Harry York's office. York will be there, along with Miss Maddon's lawyer, who is also York's mouthpiece, her agent, and somebody from the DA's office. Best I could do."

"I'm a little surprised you got that far."

"Harry's kale and his power only go so far. Things are changing in this town. It ain't like it was even three years ago. We got the bulge on this homicide and I've been turning the screws. DA finally had to give a little."

"Think you'll get anything?"

Frank shook his head slightly "Nope, but I am going to fire some hard questions and even if they don't let her answer, and they probably won't, I'm going to get to look her in that lovely pan of hers and see how good an actress she really is."

"You think she shot VanderSaant?"

"I do not, but I could be wrong. I've got a strong suspicion she knows who did and if I can push her hard enough she might give something away."

"No rubber hose?"

"No rubber hose. No veiled threats. Just a tired homicide dick in a well-mannered but fraudulent and somewhat iniquitous world covered by a thin golden sheen. And I am not necessarily talking about Hollywood."

"Just remember, Frank. Rachel Anne Maddon is an accomplished actress even at such a young age."

"I don't expect anybody to blow a wig, Neil. I have been around the block a time or two and I think I'll know a line when I hear it. I always expect an icy mitt, even when the party is on the up and up."

"And, Frank, pay attention to her posture. She's one tomato who really knows how to use her body when she acts."

CHAPTER 19

The Kentucky brown in my desk drawer came out as soon as Frank left. I poured two fingers into a paper cup and sipped slowly, my mind idling like a six-cylinder hitting on only four. The clatter of Rose's typewriter faded in and out of my conk.

The blower stayed mum and no one dropped in with urgent problems. I sipped the straight bourbon and burned gray matter and let the whole world turn hazy until it suddenly hit me between the eyes like a Jack Dempsey power jab.

Maybe I had been off the force too long. Maybe the part of me once a button with a shiny buzzer had at last vanished into whatever I was now becoming. Didn't matter. I was behind the grind on a dig I should have glommed the second homicide detective Frank Harless walked out my office door.

I buzzed Rose and told her to get me Mack Sanger right now. The horn sounded in a little more than a minute.

"What's up?" Sanger asked.

"I need that item I gave you."

"So soon?"

"Yeah, my brain's getting a little stuffed up in my old age. I'll be out to pick it up as soon as I can get there."

"I'm on my way out just now. I'll leave the item with Mike and Tank. You know where to find them. S'long."

Leaving that lockbox with Mack Sanger's two best trouble boys was safer than putting it in Fort Knox.

I grabbed my coat, told Rose to go home, and raced up to Harry's office. Betsy Hammerlin shook her lovely head and did not smile.

"Again? I have got better things to do than usher you in and out of his office. He's busy and he won't want to see you."

"Yes, he will. He alone?"

"He is. The mob just left."

"I need thirty seconds, Betsy. Maybe not even that much. It's not about my picture. It's about Rachel Anne Maddon."

"Important?"

"Bulls are about to put the screws to her."

Betsy shook her head morosely. "Okay. Hold on."

She opened the massive door to Harry's office and held it slightly ajar with her right hand to keep it from closing.

"Mr. Brand needs to see you about Miss Maddon. He says it is an urgent matter and he requests thirty seconds."

She pulled the door open and nodded to me. I took a step inside the office, blocking Betsy from closing the door. As his confidential secretary, she was privy to everything, a combination sawbones and mouthpiece in a deliciously sexy cover.

"Miss Maddon go home?" I asked.

York's face bore a wicked snarl. "What's it to you?"

"Lieutenant Frank Harless is going to get a search warrant to go through her home. Patricia Metcalf's too. You need to head that off if you can. It might be too late."

"Impossible. They both live in Beverly Hills. No

LAPD cop, I don't care who he is, is going to get a search warrant for any place up there."

"I'm betting Harless will. He's pals with Judge Willis Anderson."

Harry blanched. The hawk-faced Judge Anderson had consistently ruled against the Beverly Hills council in a series of high-profile property rights cases that had gone to the California high court, and both sides had grown to loathe each other. Besides, the moralistic Anderson was a high-minded opponent of all that was Hollywood, taking every opportunity to publically chastise Harry York and other Hollywood high-hats over the perceived wicked-ness and moral turpitude of the motion picture industry.

"What's that copper suspect to find?"

"A gun."

Harry's eyes opened wide. "A gun?"

"I'm on my way to Rachel Maddon's place. You should maybe try to get Jimmy Gallen over to Metcalf's house."

"Why? What's so important about a gun?"

"A certain gun, if found in her possession, could put her in jail for a very long time."

A stricken look creased Harry's pallid face, a face that had always been in complete control. He looked sharply at Betsy.

"Get me the DA," he thundered. "And Gallen."

I hustled my old soon-to-be-forgotten Chevy out to Laurel City and found Mike and Tank just where I knew they'd be, sitting on the back steps of the swanky Sanger-owner Laurel Hotel, the clubhouse for the man who owned practically everything legal and illegal in Laurel City.

Mike and Tank stood as I rolled up. They looked like twin Empire State Buildings. Tank held the lockbox in his meaty right hand. Either one of those boys could have squeezed that box open barehanded, but Tank held it like it was a Ming vase.

"You still drivin' that same bucket?" Mike asked.

"We heard you was the bird with the shiny feathers now," Tank said.

I didn't get out of the car. "No time to beat gums boys. Sorry."

Tank handed me the box.

"Need any help?" Mike asked stonily.

"Boss said to go with you if you wanted," Tank put in.

I shook my head. "It's all silk."

I gunned the Chevy as much as it could be gunned. I turned onto Bay Avenue and glanced sideways just as Mike and Tank disappeared inside the hotel.

Rachel Anne Maddon lived with her mother and step-father in a tidy mansion in a quiet neighborhood deep into Beverly Hills, where all the mansions were tidy and all the neighborhoods were quiet

The big white stone, two-story Colonial held down a corner lot—a covered portico on the east side fronting a four-car garage, a line of gleaming white pillars in front—befitting a nineteen-year-old budding motion pic-ture star pulling down thirty-five hundred a week, soon to turn into twice that much.

That is, if the law didn't send her over.

The butler—a couple of inches taller than my six-one, lean and silver-haired—answered my first ring. I shoul-dered past him, paying no attention to his sputtering pro-test.

"I'm from Harry York," I said. "Where is Miss Mad-don?"

"Sir." Iron gray eyes censured me. "You will have to wait to be announced. I will see if Miss Maddon will en-tertain you."

"Forget it. The police are on their way. Where is she?"

"The police? The patio, sir." He pointed down a hall-way. "That way, sir."

Rachel Anne and the face stretcher I guessed was her mother were having tea at a little marble table with straight-back marble chairs on the stone patio fronting the swimming pool. They cooled in the shade, dressed casu-ally but elegantly, while an elderly man in a white robe snored gently on a chaise flooded in sunshine.

The older woman looked up and her mouth formed a perfect O when she saw me.

"Who let you in here? Who are you?" Her husky voice bore the practiced haughtiness of the newly rich but for-ever self-important.

Rachel Anne turned to see me and put an assuring hand on the woman's arm. Her gorgeous pan lacked any hint of warmth.

"Mother, he's one of Harry York's minions."

I plopped down in one of the chairs and placed the lockbox on the table.

"You don't mind if this minion rests his dogs, do you?" I looked only at Rachel Anne and ignored her mother's simpering objection. "I'm sorry to say that your somewhat indiscreet past is about to catch up with you."

Rachel Anne charily eyed the lockbox. "What do you mean?"

I tapped the box. "It's in there, kitten."

"Young man." Her mother's voice had grown intense. I felt the tall butler coming up behind me. "What is the meaning of this?"

"What's in the box?" Rachel Anne asked, her voice as cautious as a can house pro about to roll a john.

"Two roles of sixteen millimeter film, sweetheart. I found them in a box stashed in the props department at the studio. The box belonged to Cleland VanderSaant. You know, your late dear family friend."

Mother and daughter looked at the box, and then at me. The mother's light green eyes had turned to dark stone.

"Thank you for returning them," her mother said smoothly. "Cleland had intended to do that just before his tragic death. Would you care for refreshment?"

"No thank you. The buttons are on their way, armed with a search warrant. They are going to be quite disrespectful. You might even find them impertinent."

"And what would they be looking for? Surely not what is in this box."

"A gun."

She shot a quick glance at Rachel, reset her burning eyes on me with no change of expression. "What sort of gun?"

"I don't know, but the buttons do. They'll know it when they see it."

"And what will they do if they find a gun?"

"They'll take it with them. They'll use the serial number to track down the registration. They will look for fingerprints, although, frankly, it's generally difficult to pull legible prints off a handgun. They'll run a ballistic test."

Rachel's mother took a sip of her noodle juice. Rachel did not. "What is a ballistic test?" the mother asked.

"It tells you if a certain bullet was fired from a certain gun."

"And why would they do that?"

"That you will have to ask the buttons."

"And if they do not find such a gun?"

"That's an entirely different matter. Is there a gun on the premises?"

"What makes you think there would be?"

"I get sappy ideas sometimes," I said.

"The same ideas the police have, I suppose."

"Something like that. Have you decided yet if there is

a gun on the premises? You need to pick an answer. I don't know how much time you have."

"What is your name, young man, and what is your connection with Mr. Harry York and with my daughter?"

"Neil Brand. I'm an ex-cop who used to run security for York Brothers Studio. I have recently been demoted to producing motion pictures."

"A producer, you say." Her pan warmed. "Mr. Brand, my name is Blanche Matheny Bible. I do not mean to appear rude, but you will please excuse my daughter and myself. It appears we have a family issue to discuss. If there is nothing else, Charles will show you out."

I shook my head. Blanche slid the lockbox to her side of the table.

"After you show this gentlemen to his car, Charles, please get my lawyer on the telephone. Good day, Mr. Brand, and thank you."

Rachel Anne murmured something as she stood, keeping her face turned away. Her mother picked up the lockbox. I dug the key from my pocket and dropped it on the table.

"Best be careful with those contents," I said. "They burn easily."

Blanche took the key into a manicured hand. She caught Rachel Anne by the arm and they went through a glass door behind them. The old man in the chair snored blissfully. Charles held out his arm and motioned to the door.

CHAPTER 20

Whe were just short of the front door when loud banging rattled the windows. Charles opened the door like Sir Joseph approaching the mummy's tomb.

Frank Harless nodded stoically to Charles and glared balefully at me.

Behind the lieutenant stood a knot of hard-faced buttons, along with a tall, rotund matron who looked like she could hold up the back end of a flivver by herself if you needed to change a flat tire.

"Get your mistress and be quick about it," Harless ordered Charles, flashing his LAPD buzzer. "This is police business."

"That, sir," Charles said, stiffening, "is a Los Angeles badge. I am compelled to remind you we are not in your jurisdiction."

A soft-faced man beside Harless, about half a head shorter, with sad eyes that offered an apology, stepped forward. He held out a Beverly Hills shield.

"I'm sorry. You will have to cooperate with these officers. Please step aside and inform the head of the household we are here."

Charles said nothing. He turned and plodded stiffly in search of Blanche and her daughter. I had a strong feeling it would be a while before he returned. Harless eyed me sternly, and pulled me aside.

"Brand, what are you doing here just now?" His strident whisper carried a tinge of annoyance.

"I had just come up here to see Mr. Leviticus Bible." My voice was just as low, but much friendlier. "How's that for a name? His real one too."

"What about?"

"I was going to offer him a role in that picture abandoned to my care. He'd be perfect for the part of the aging, drunken thespian."

"Half the actors in town would fit that role."

"Fact is, Frank, him being Rachel Anne Maddon's stepfather makes him a little more attractive to us. Harry's idea. I'm sure you understand."

"What did Bible say?"

"He is asleep. I said I'd come back another time."

"Uh, huh." Frank pushed his fedora back, eyed me stonily before asking, "Did you happen to say anything about VanderSaant being shot?"

"No."

"Did you mention anything about a gun?"

"Why would I?"

"It might be in your interest."

"Frank, we have a deal," I reminded him.

"You haven't forgotten it?"

"I haven't forgotten it."

"Okay then, see that you don't. Now, you want to talk with Leviticus Bible, come back some other time. You know where the door is."

I pulled my Chevy around the corner, raked it up against the curb and hunkered down to wait. I couldn't sit there long in my old heap before some nosy neighbor would grow hinky and call the bulls. It would take Harless and his crew a long time to search that big house, depending on when or if they found the gun, even with all the help he brought along. I got just over an hour before a Beverly Hills patrol cruiser pulled up beside me. A short baby grand with a florid face unfolded his chunky frame from the shotgun seat.

I already had my window down and my York Brothers identification card in hand.

"Good day, officer," I said cheerfully.

"What are you up to, buddy?" the uniformed bull asked, his voice an unfriendly growl. "Show me some ID."

His partner had left the driver's side and stood in back of the Chevy, writing down my license plate number.

"I came here to see one of our actresses. A Miss Maddon, who lives just around the corner. Just now, as I am sure you know, she is entertaining a mix of LA and BH buttons. Those boys requested I wait here."

He looked at my ID, then distastefully at the Chevy. I saw Harry's point. His people needed to drive more impressive cars.

"Who asked you to wait?"

"Lieutenant Frank Harless, homicide division, LAPD."

"You know Lieutenant Wilcox? Homicide, with us."

"Yeah, I saw him with Harless."

"All right," the cop said, handing the ID card back to me. "Get this bucket out of here as soon as you can."

Just short of two hours later, Harless and his crew spun around the corner, heading for downtown LA. A black, unmarked Ford coupe skidded to a stop just in front of me.

Harless piled out. He held up a little Colt .25 semi-automatic with ivory grip panels—the perfect size for a woman's handbag.

"I see you're not concerned about fingerprints," I said.

"No prints. Found it in a water tank in a back upstairs bathroom."

"Guess our deal's off then."

"It's off. Tell anybody you want."

"In that case, where'd VanderSaant buy it?"

"Coroner pulled a twenty-five slug from Vander-Saant's upper right chest," Harless said.

"That's why there was so little blood upstairs."

"That's why."

"Pretty much follows my hunch. Fatal?"

Harless shrugged. "Not necessarily. Doc says a man of even VanderSaant's size and health could live a long time with that little bit of lead in him. Long enough to get help if he hadn't done that swan dive over the railing."

"When did he cash out?"

"Coroner puts it between midnight and two."

"How's that?"

"Body temp, rigor, other factors."

"You turn up any witnesses?"

Harless nodded. "Two. Neighbor says he heard what he thought was a car backfiring just after midnight. Said he looked out his window but didn't see anything at first. It was a warm night and he had his window open."

"What window?"

"Front, facing VanderSaant's door."

"What do you mean, at first?"

"Neighbor says he drew the blinds after looking the first time, and then several seconds later he said he heard footsteps running down the sidewalk toward the street. He said he peeked out the blinds."

"He make the figure?"

"He was pretty sure it was a man the way he was running, but it was too dark to see anything but a vague form."

"See where he ran to?"

Harless nodded. "Car at the curb."

"Make the car?"

"Too dark."

"No body style? No color? No guess about the age?"

"Too dark."

"The other witness?"

"His bedroom window looks out over the back alley-way, with a good view of VanderSaant's back door. He said he saw two cloaked figures run out the back way a few seconds after he heard what he wired as a backfire in the alley."

"Two men?"

Frank shook his head. "Neighbor says he saw enough to know one was a woman."

"See their faces?"

"He did not."

"What did those two do?"

"Got in a car and drove away. Neighbor couldn't make the car, either. Says it was a dark sedan and looked expensive. Blanche Bible owns a sedan that fits that general description."

"A lot of sedans fit that description, Frank."

"So they do."

"Any idea who ran out the front way?"

"No idea."

"Maybe it was David Lemmert?"

"Maybe."

"You're still looking for Lemmert?"

Harless nodded. "We'll find him."

"You make the woman in that picture you found in VanderSaant's place? Or the baby she was holding."

"Charlotte Donegan. She married VanderSaant in New York City back in oh ten. They were both in the theater."

"Lemmert their only child?"

"He is. She and VanderSaant split just after the war."

"He got to be pretty big on Broadway about then," I said.

"His career washed out in the early twenties. He came out here about ten years ago with Leviticus Bible, the man you came here to see."

"They come alone?"

"I expected you knew all this."

I shook my head. "Not really. I'm just now learning the onions in my new job. I came up here just to see Bible."

"Uh-huh, so you said. And you'd give your old partner nothing but straight goods." Harless stared hard. I smiled. "When Bible came out here he brought along his wife, Blanche, a sometimes actress herself, and Blanche's little girl, Rachel Anne. You remember her. I just talked to her in Harry York's office."

"It comes back to me."

"It will keep coming back awhile. Going to be all over the papers."

"Know where VanderSaant's ex is? Charlotte."

"Might be, we find David Lemmert, we find her."

"Or the other way around," I said. "You figure VanderSaant fell over that railing on his own? Pill in the chest, went after the shooter, stumbled."

"Not on your life. Somebody helped him take that tumble."

"The shooter?"

"Not likely. I peg the trigger man as either Rachel Anne Maddon or her mother, Blanche. I peg one of them as the twist the neighbor saw fleeing the scene. Neither one is likely to have thrown him over that high railing. Not by herself, anyway."

"The man with her?"

"Something to consider."

"See anyone who looks like they might confess?"

"We'll run ballistics, trace the ownership of this gun, and go from there. If it's this piece that put the slug in VanderSaant, we'll know it's one of the two of 'em. They'll come clean when we separate them and get down to business."

"DA might not let you. He and Harry are pretty tight."

Harless grinned mirthlessly. "Somehow, I have a feeling—a strong hunch, let's say—that this is going to be leaked. When the newsboys get ahold of it, the DA will feel too much heat to run along with Harry this time."

"Who says you are a fat-headed flatfoot?"

Harless grinned again, this time with humor. "Lots of people." He leaned forward. "That a line from that picture you're making?"

"I have the writer's ear. Or he has mine."

"Speaking of ears, the Maddon dame's mouthpiece has hers. He was still there when we left. I think he's waiting for you."

"Waiting for me?"

"I told him you'd likely be hiding around the corner, waiting for us to leave, and you'd be back when we did."

I grinned. "Very thoughtful of you."

"You know me. I try to be helpful."

"When did the mouthpiece get there?"

"About a half-hour after we started. All bluster and legal mumbo-jumbo. Read the warrant and warned us we couldn't seize anything we found in the house except that gun. Anything else would be illegal."

"Was there anything else?"

Frank shook his head. "Nothing that matters, although I wonder why someone would have a little fire going in a fireplace on a day like this."

"I think you might have brought a little chill into the house, Frank. Did you go through the ashes? You know, looking for a gun."

"Matter of fact. Looks like somebody was burning film up in a back bedroom where it would take us a while to find it."

"What was on it?"

"Wouldn't know."

"You didn't heist a piece?"

"Not in the warrant. Besides, not enough of it left to tell us anything. How about you, Neil? Got any idea what that film was?"

"Might have been an old picture Rachel Anne Maddon was in. I understand some of her early stuff didn't show her to best advantage."

"You didn't bring that old picture with you when you came up here?"

"I told you it might have been. It could have been a hundred different things, and none of them having anything to do with this. You could have asked them."

Harless pursed his lips and shook his head. "If they were burning that film to keep me from finding it, and I think they were, they weren't going to spill it."

"I didn't see them burn it, Frank."

"So you say. And how old can a picture of Rachel Anne Madden be? The girl is only nineteen, I'm told."

"I told you why I came up here, Frank."

Harless leaned back from the window and straightened his shoulders. "Uh, huh. I hope you're playing level with me, Neil. I'd hate to think you're trying to street me."

CHAPTER 21

Which one of you bumped VanderSaant?"

Rachel Anne Maddon glanced at her mother. Neither said anything. Rachel Anne found entertainment in the carpet. Her mother stared at me thornily. The two had sought refuge in a large room filled with pricey furniture, a grand piano, thick carpeting, paneled walls loaded down with leather-bound books and a big Gobelin tapestry, and a wet bar big enough to hold a submarine. Most of the framed paintings decorating the walls looked expensive.

Mother and daughter sat side-by-side on an oxblood divan. The man I figured to be Leviticus Bible, still wrapped in a white robe, sat forlornly at the bar, a tall drink in his shaking right hand. A bottle of Cutty Sark took up space beside his left hand. Their lawyer, a dapper little fellow introduced to me as Montagu Whitesell, hovered over the room like a hyperactive ghost, twitchy and excited and volatile.

Jimmy Gallen, nattily dressed in a dark blue double-breasted gabardine suit, sat off to the side, almost behind the divan, wiggling impatiently. A decidedly unhappy look creased his handsome pan.

"Which one of you bumped VanderSaant?" I asked again.

"Don't answer that question. Don't answer that question." Whitesell pointed a buffed finger at me. "You have no right to ask that."

"Bulls pulled a twenty-five slug out of VanderSaant. If that slug matches the gat they found here, they'll be back with another warrant."

"Yes, thank you for that, but I am their attorney and I will take up that issue when the time arises. If you have advice to offer, based on your knowledge of this case and your position with York Brothers Studio, we will listen appreciatively, and we will respond accordingly. You will not, however, harass my clients with untoward questions. I assume that you perfectly understand our position and that you will respect it."

"Anybody call Harry York?" I asked.

Gallen nodded. His blue eyes briefly met mine before he dipped his head toward Whitesell, who regarded Jimmy in the same way he'd glare at a cockroach crawling across his dish of sturgeon caviar.

"Yes." The lawyer gave me the same look. "I called Mr. York on Miss Maddon's behalf immediately after the authorities departed. Miss Maddon and I will be in Mr. York's office first thing in the morning. I think, Mr. Brand, we have nothing left to discuss."

"Bosh." The cry was part sneer, part moan. Leviticus Bible stirred from his seat at the bar, waving his glass-filled hand in tight circles around his white-maned head, amber fluid spilling onto the bar top. Every eye in the place went straight to him.

"When I was a mere lad, a young sprite just starting out on his life's mysterious journey, learning his trade of trodding the boards, his overpowering interest in life being the pursuit of the imperial female form in all its unsheathed purity, I found myself in the lovely and enchanting city of Constantinople, where I chanced upon the

Babylon of brothels, a magnificent palace of lavender and white, gleaming floors littered with luxuriant, cloud-like pillows that cuddled the buttocks and soothed the scrotum, splendid food and grand beverages unending, glorious young ladies with resplendent thighs and come-hither smiles and superlative bosoms descending directly from the heavens. I found my poor, undeserving person in that fabulous mecca of debauchery for an entire month, my every need..."

He paused, holding his booze-ravaged but somehow still handsome head in profile. "But I am afraid I digress."

The great actor took another long swig from the glass and his head collapsed into arms folded across the bar top. The tall glass, about half-full, somehow remained upright, still clutched in a now-still hand.

"I must apologize," Blanche said in a calm voice not at all apologetic. "My beautiful Leviticus does go on as if an enthralled audience clamors for his every word. Ah, well, what can I do? He is every inch the magnificent performer and I love him so."

I wondered how anyone so besotted could manage to speak so dramatically. I cast a sideways glance at Whitesell, but the learned counsellor couldn't take his unamused eyes off the suddenly snoring Leviticus. Gallen stirred in his empire chair and I thought he might leap to his feet in wild applause.

I looked at Blanche. "You've been married for some time?"

"Almost twelve years now, although I have known Mr. Bible for twenty years and more. He was so charming in those days. Charming and the most handsome man I have ever known, considered by many to have been the finest Hamlet the theater has ever seen. When we first met I was married to Rachel's father, Leonard Matheny, an exceptional man and wonderful artist with finely-honed talents whose fate, sadly, was to die during the Great War when Rachel was merely a toddler. I desperately needed Leviticus then. He and I had become lovers while Rachel's father was serving his country. I was a Florodoro girl at the time, and very beautiful, everyone said. When Leonard died I yearned desperately for Leviticus but he was in London, engaged in a long run as Hamlet. I remarried in haste. That was a dreadful mistake I rectified immediately when Leviticus returned from his triumph on the London stage. Shortly after his return from that engagement, we were married."

"Rachel would have been about seven when you married Bible."

Blanche nodded. "She was five months shy of her eighth birthday. A most beautiful girl with the most exquisite golden tresses."

"Bible know about that film?"

"Film?" Whitesell came out of his trance and swung curious eyes at Blanche. "What film is that, may I ask?"

"Do not concern yourself about that, Monty. In fact, I believe our business is done for the day. Rachel will see you at Mr. York's in the morning. Mr. Brand, will you kindly stay for supper? I fear we have much to discuss."

"Blanche." Whitesell sprung to his feet. "I advise you strongly against any discussions with this man, Harry York or no Harry York. He does not have your best interests at heart. I urge you in all sincerity—"

"Enough." A hand shot in the air, the palm facing Whitesell. "Rachel will see you in the morning. Charles will show you out." Charles suddenly materialized, Whitesell's hat in hand. "Good night, Monty," Blanche said sternly.

Whitesell stammered his protestations, but he was soon out the door.

Blanche looked at Gallen and then at me.

"Jimmy stays," I said. "We are going to need him."

Blanche motioned to an overstuffed chair closer to the divan. Rachel sat unmoving, her beguiling eyes now fixated on the wall tapestry. Gallen slumped deeper into the empire chair. I could almost hear the spinning wheels churning inside his conk. Leviticus Bible continued his gentle snoring.

"When I married Leviticus," Blanche said softly, "I thought he would always be the brightest light on the Great White Way, but he soon mistakenly allowed the temptress called motion pictures to seduce him. He saw the promise of fame and riches, and for a while it all came deliciously true, and the entire world was finally seeing his greatness. He was an actor like no other, Mr. Brand. He painted grand words in the air with his voice and with his gestures. If you have seen the Hagia Sophia or the Taj Mahal. If you have seen the Sistine Chapel or the Great Pyramid at Giza, then you have seen my husband perform. On stage he is one of the wonders of the world. He has enthralled thousands. You might not see that in him now. The pictures stole that greatness from him as surely as a thief in the night steals your jewels. The roles became less and less important, the parts merely caricatures. His career began to unwind as age encroached and the solace of the bottle lured him. He had always been a heavy drinker, but as his drinking intensified his health declined and the roles dried up. Now, regrettably, you see only the dregs of the greatness that once was Leviticus Bible."

The woman missed her call. She should have been an agent.

"He know about that film?"

She looked uneasily at Gallen.

"Forget he's here," I told her. "He's the one who will

control the media, and he will have to know everything. I'll wire him about the film later. He's completely trustworthy when it comes to you, your daughter, and the studio. His job depends on his loyalty."

"Mrs. Bible," Gallen said, "Mr. York sent me here for the express purpose that Mr. Brand has outlined. Consider me to be your doctor or your lawyer, inasmuch as anything that is said within these walls is strictly confidential. You are going to have to put your full faith in Mr. York, Mr. Brand, and myself."

"Does Leviticus know about that film?" I asked again.

She nodded. "Certainly. I tried to keep its existence from him, but he could see something was obviously wrong. Cleland was always around, and as my dislike for the man became more and more palpable, I had no choice but to inform Leviticus. He raged to the gods and threatened Cleland with the vilest of plagues, but as we did not know where that awful film was, what could we do about it?"

"What did VanderSaant want? I think it was more than money."

"He wanted money, of course, but not much. He pursued other matters. He weaseled Leviticus, who was then still a major star, into giving him his start as a director, then a producer. Cleland had been a legitimate stage actor and had gained some fame, but audiences found his florid style too old-fashioned by the end of the war, and he faded quickly. Leviticus, an old friend from their stage days, helped Cleland get a toe-hold out here, and then Cleland's career started to die again, after some very poor reception of his productions. So he repaid our kindness, our beneficence, with pure treachery, and resurrected his career through Rachel, who was growing into the lovely and vibrant creature motion picture audiences will soon clamor to see. We all saw her promise when she was so very young, but Cleland—as wretched an ingrate as the world has ever known—took advantage of her youth and her beauty and her trusting adolescence and filmed her in those abominable flickers. Then he blackmailed us, money at first, and then he used Rachel's growing prominence to worm his way back into the pictures."

"Who was the man in those flickers with Rachel?"

"One is unknown. The other is VanderSaant's son, David."

"Do you know where David is?"

"I do not."

"Rachel know?"

Rachel shook her head. Tears welled in her eyes. I wondered if she was a good enough actress to cry on cue.

"I am sure he is staying with his mother, Charlotte," Blanche said. "I believe they are in Los Angeles somewhere, but I do not know where."

"If there are copies of that film and David has them, you'll hear from him. If you do, agree to whatever he wants and then call me at the studio. Can you do that?"

Rachel shuddered. Blanche stoically nodded her head. "Yes, of course."

"What about VanderSaant's wife? Patricia Metcalf."

"What about her?"

"Did she wire the blackmail angle?"

Blanche shook her head. The wall tapestry consumed Rachel's interest. "I don't believe so."

"Why do you think that?"

"I'm sure Cleland would not have told her. It was a business arrangement between me and my family and him. We all wanted to keep it strictly personal. The arrangement was based on the fact that no one else would know."

"How did you pay him?"

"Monthly, in cash."

"He come to you to pick it up?"

"No," Rachel said softly, not looking at me. "I delivered it to him."

"At his home?"

"Sometimes at his home. Sometimes at the studio."

"He blackmail you into his bed?"

"Yes." Rachel did not look up. She whispered the word but the sound of it bounced off the walls in that quiet room.

I looked at Blanche. "And you let it happen?"

"Rachel had a career to safeguard."

"And you were the doting mother who knew just how to do that."

"We all did what was necessary."

"Was it worth it?" I asked Rachel.

There was no expression on her face. "He was gentle and kind."

"And he helped you with your career?"

"Very much."

"The more kale you bring in, the bigger cut he could take."

"It was a small price for her to pay," Blanche said. "My child is going to be a major motion picture star."

"We all have our crosses."

"Mr. Brand, sarcasm is not appreciated."

"Which one of you shot VanderSaant?" I asked again.

Nothing registered on either face. "We did not, either of us, shoot Cleland," Blanche said.

"But you knew he had been shot."

Their eyes flashed at each other but neither said anything.

"Who pushed him over the railing?"

Both of them raised their heads, their eyes shining with surprise.

"The newspapers say he accidentally toppled over the

railing," Blanche said, "and the fall killed him by bashing in his head."

"Somebody shot him. It wouldn't have been fatal, but the fall over that railing did the trick. Maybe the shooter pushed him, maybe not."

"Neither of us shot him." Rachel looked at me. "Neither of us pushed him."

"We were both here in this house the entire night that Cleland died." Blanche's eyes locked on mine. "Here with Leviticus. We had dinner and enjoyed a relaxed evening at home."

"Will the servants back you up?"

"Certainly," Rachel said.

"The servants were allowed the rest of the evening off, after dinner was served about seven," Blanche said.

"That's convenient."

"That's the truth. Besides, if the bullet was not the fatal blow and he was, as you say, pushed over the railing, it could not have been us. We are two slight and not very strong women who are physically unable to do such a thing."

"One of you alone, maybe. The two of you together could do such a thing. Or it could have been somebody with you."

Blanche clucked. "Nonsense."

"The buttons might not think that. I'm told they talked to a next-door neighbor of VanderSaant's who can identify you."

"The neighbor is mistaken," Blanche said coldly.

"The slug pulled from VanderSaant will match the gun they found here. If that gun belongs to anyone in this house the bulls will find out. If neither of you shot him, how'd the gun get here? Who tossed it into a bathroom water tank upstairs?"

They were both as still as the bride and groom perched atop a wedding cake.

"There will be lots of questions," I said. "Harry can't step in for you because the buttons got the bulge on us, and if you two get indicted and this thing goes to trial it will burn up the papers and the radio from here to the China wall. If that happens, good luck trying to hang onto a movie career. The pictures have fed the public too much nightly pap for too long for anyone to survive this mess."

Rachel buried her face into hands. Gentle sobs shivered her silken body. Her mother put a reassuring arm across Rachel's shoulders.

"Mother, what are we going to do?"

"We will be strong," Blanche said, looking at Leviticus. His snoring had stopped, but he had not moved.

"You might have safeguarded her career right onto the cutting room floor," Gallen said. "I don't think there's much Harry can do to salvage it."

"Rachel's picture is nearly finished and I am promised it will be a large success. The public will see my precious child as I see her. They will adore her."

"Let's hope Harry can get it released before the papers start smearing you," Gallen said. "We can rush the final print."

"Smearing us?"

"That gun comes back to you and the ballistics match, the bulls will haul you in," I said. "You will both be charged. They'll think one of you shot him and both of you tossed him over that railing, or one of you had help doing it. They'll work you two inside out, playing one against the other until someone spills."

"I told you, we were not there."

"The buttons will crawl all over your servants and at least one of them won't stand the gaff. If you're lying about anything, it'll come out. The buttons will also need a motive. A shakedown will give them a pip."

"They couldn't possibly find out."

"Don't underestimate them. Don't expect these boys to be anything like picture cops. They're smart and they dig with a purpose. And they'll gashouse the two of you until you fall apart."

"We certainly won't talk, I can promise you that," Blanche said indignantly.

"You just think you won't. Buttons have grilled plenty who had that same idea, and they know ways to make them spill." I pointed toward the rummy at the bar. Bible had somehow drained his glass and was snoring again. "And what about your precious Leviticus? He knows all your dark secrets."

"My Leviticus loves me. He will remain quiet."

"Your Leviticus also loves his hooch. Give the buttons a fried barfly with the shakes and they know how to gas him. When they tighten the screws he'll fall apart like a cheap coat."

"Montagu can prevent that."

"Montagu is worthless in this. You're going to need a smart, hard-nosed mouthpiece who knows the ropes. Harry will help you there."

"Mr. York will see that nothing happens to us," Rachel said.

"I told you, there's little he can do this late. Harry's lawyers will stall all they can and drag this out and throw up as much smoke as a five-alarm, but they can't keep this mess out of the papers forever."

"Surely he can do something," Blanche said. "He has a very lucrative property in my daughter and he will protect it."

"You have to understand," I said grimly. "Guilty or innocent won't matter in the public eye. Remember Fatty

Arbuckle? Guilty or not, your daughter's precious career won't survive this trouble any better than his did."

"Surely, there must be something we can do."

"Don't talk to the buttons. Don't talk to the newsboys. Don't read the rags and glom ideas. Stay off the radio. Refer all comment to your lawyers. Put it all in their mitts."

"And meanwhile, we will be captives in our own home. We will be at the mercy of every reprehensible gossip with a platform."

"Rachel," Gallen snapped.

She had been staring vacantly at the wall again. Her head jerked toward Jimmy but her eyes remained empty except for the tears.

"Finish that Crusades picture," Gallen told her. "I will impress on Harry that you need a long vacation. He'll see the advantage of a cruise around the world or a tour of Europe. He can send a studio escort with you and book everything under the escort's name. That way, the three of you can travel as secretively as possible."

"You think that will work?" Blanche asked.

"No," I said "At the best it will drag things out a while and maybe somebody will come up with something to keep some of the mud off you."

CHAPTER 22

I nursed the Chevy out to Marathon Street and found the place I wanted only a few blocks from the Paramount Picture's lot. The bungalow VanderSaant had paid rent on—a white Spanish style in the middle of a nondescript block—bore a dark red tile roof, dark red shutters, a small front stoop badly cracked on the front left, and a split driveway with no garage and no car. The scant yard needed to see a lawnmower. I parked on the street and knocked firmly on the front door. I knocked three times, stirred up nothing.

The tiny window on the door allowed no view inside and curtains covered the window just to the left. It wouldn't do to peer in or walk around to the back. A nosy neighbor probably already had me in the crosshairs.

I drove back to the studio, relieved when Rose told me I had no messages and no calls. I rang up Betsy and asked if she had heard anything of any interest.

"You have a bizarre sense of humor," she said, and filled me in.

Jimmy Gallen had been buried in Harry's office a little more than an hour, laying it all on the line for moviedom's currently most distressed mogul.

The alabaster curlicues on Harry's ceiling had probably turned every color in the spectrum while Harry cursed, screamed and denounced the unscrupulous gods who had callously interfered with his well-structured plans. York had summoned Betsy five different times, she said, and had briskly ordered her to unearth a dozen different underlings—off and on the lot—and get them to his office without delay.

Fortunately, I escaped that list.

I asked Betsy to have Gallen drop by my office as soon as he got out of Harry's clutches, no matter how late it was.

"Jimmy might not be able to walk by then," Betsy said, and I had a hunch she could be right. "But I will pass along your message."

I called Alice and told her not to wait dinner on me. I said Harry was calling out the militia to deal with some vexing issues at the studio.

"You don't have a casting couch, do you?" she asked sweetly.

"They just moved one in. It's big enough for three people."

"Is that so? You and Harry York and who else?"

"Jimmy Gallen." I said I loved her and hung up.

Nearly an hour crawled by before I heard Gallen talking to Rose. I opened my private door and ushered him in. He draped his suit coat over a chair and plopped into the other chair in front of my desk. His floral print tie was loosened at his neck and his face bore the desperate look of a bruno who had just wrestled an alligator to a standstill. I dug out the bourbon and two crystal tumblers and set them on my desk.

"Pour a little for yourself," he said. "I'll take the bottle."

"That bad?"

"And how."

I spilled three fingers into each glass and pushed the bottle closer to Jimmy. The bottle was a little more than half full. I hoped that would be enough.

"What's Harry going to do?"

"I don't know, Neil. He's rounding up a half-dozen lawyers and all his top execs. Right now he's talking to Leo Collier. It is going to be next to impossible, we think, to get that picture out before the fire engulfs the frying pan." He smiled lamely. "Harry's phrase."

"Got a hunch?"

"My hunch is he'll cut down Rachel Anne Maddon's part, reshoot most of her scenes with another actress—yet to be named—and edit in a few more action scenes than were called for. I hear Hugh Dunnum has a lot of action in the can. I hear we have you to thank for that. I think the original hundred and thirty minutes will be cut a reel, and he'll get the picture out there with as little delay as possible."

"What about Rachel's contract?"

Gallen arched an eyebrow. "You mean the morals clause? Sure there's that, but just because VanderSaant's dead doesn't mean she's in violation."

"Don't be too sure."

"If Harry has standing to invoke the morals clause and ditch her, then he'll no longer try to protect her."

"No, he'll go the other way to show cause. He could just cut her out of the Crusades picture, send her off on a long vacation, keep her deal and wait for this to blow over. She might still be valuable property."

Gallen emptied his glass, reached for the bottle. "That's an option, but at thirty-five a week, it's an expensive proposition. And it's seven grand a week by the time her deal runs out."

"Fish or cut bait."

"Listen, Harry's still got a shot for a successful release, but if he tries to get it out with Miss Maddon intact it's almost a sure bet he'll take a bath."

"Guilt by association?"

Gallen nodded. "In the public eye, you bet. It's a fight for every scrap out there these days and the country's full of do-gooders."

"And there's Joe Breen to think about."

Gallen took a long pull at the bourbon. "There's going to be a firestorm, no matter which way we twist."

"Even Harry might get burned."

"We'll know more tomorrow after he finishes with his people and meets with Miss Maddon and his lawyers."

"That puts her in a tight spot, Jimmy."

"Neil, play this thing as tight to your vest as you want, but there are things I need wired into. I can't deal when the deck's stacked."

I filled him in on everything. I told him about the film and VanderSaant's gouge. His eyes glazed when I told him about the gun, the slug in VanderSaant's chest, the witnesses, police theories and my hunches. I took mercy on him and left out the little white bungalow on Marathon Street.

"If that gun turns out to be what I think it is and the newspaper boys find out they'll throw a front page orgy," I said.

Gallen drained his glass again, and sunk into his own personal gloom. He glumly shook his head and pursed his lips.

"If that happens, Harry's gonna have to drop her. That's his only option He might even like her, personally, and he's poured a lot of scratch into building her up, but he'll have to let her go. Breen's brought in a circus, you know, and everybody's on a high wire. If the morals clause in her contract gives Harry an out, he might have to use it."

"That picture was going to make her a star. If Harry cuts her out, only a few will notice."

"That's too bad." Gallen reached for the bottle. "I like Rachel. I like her a lot. She's basically a sweet girl who goofed up big time, but she's got a pushy monster for a mother and a wasted derelict for a stepfather. She's never had a chance. I'm certain she saw VanderSaant as a way out, wrong-headed as that was, and it would be easy to forgive her for her youthful indiscretions. I'd say VanderSaant got what he deserved, but she's getting the short straw."

"She looked pretty willing in what I saw."

"God, let's hope there aren't any copies of that out there."

"That might not matter, Jimmy."

We both fell silent. Gallen refilled his glass.

"I did a lot of dumb stuff when I was nineteen," I said after a while. "I joined the Army with my brother and went off to fight a war."

"If only she had kept her clothes on."

"World is filled with ifs, Jimmy."

"There are a lot of actors—men and women—around this town who couldn't keep their clothes on, and they're doing just fine."

"They didn't get caught. Not yet, anyway." I lifted my glass. "Here's to secrets."

He nodded. "And to beautiful naked nymphs in dark flickers who know not what unholy mischief they create."

CHAPTER 23

Lights in the curtained front window of the little bungalow on Marathon Street threw weak but eerie shadows across the small yard. Two cars filled the short, split driveway—a medium green Ford Model A coupe in front, a dark yellow Alfa Romeo 6C behind it. I pulled my bucket to a stop at the end of the driveway, blocking the two vehicles. I looked at the license plates on both jalopies—1934 California issue, black numbers against an orange background. I jotted down the numbers and moved to the cottage's front door.

I knocked loudly, keeping my eyes on the curtained window. After a few seconds I pounded the door again, harder. A shadow moved across the window and the curtains fluttered slightly. I felt eyes staring at me. I stepped back and kicked the door hard, rattling the peep window cut about head high. The knob turned and the door creaked open about four inches. Cold eyes exactly like Cleland VanderSaant's studied me, and thin, colorless lips parted in a practiced sneer.

"You tryin' to knock the door down?" a tough-guy voice asked.

"That's the idea."

"Whatever you're peddling, pal, we don't want any. Screw."

"Sorry to crash your party." I leaned my one-ninety against the door, and pushed my way inside against the thin man's feeble struggles. His face set in a hard line and I made him as the same gink I had seen in the second stag flickers, coarsely cavorting with Rachel Anne Maddon. Three or four inches shorter than me, sallow skin covered his spaghetti thin frame. A shock of light brown hair almost stood straight up.

I glanced around the small front room, saw no one else. Fairly expensive furniture filled the parlor, and a dark red throw rug with beige curlicues covered most of the brightly polished hardwood floor. An antique brass screen hid some of a large, dark wood fireplace. I could see into the dining room and a portion of the kitchen. A hallway led past two closed doors, ending at a third door slightly ajar. I could feel eyes poking at me from behind the door.

"All right, pal." The mug squared his shoulder and glared at me. "You got your slant of the place. Now drift or I call the cops."

I handed him one of VanderSaant's rent receipts.

He looked at the receipt while he chewed his lower lip. The paper shook slightly in unsteady hands. "Okay, who are you?" I caught a tone of worry in that tough-guy voice.

"I'm the fella you need to talk to, David. If you're the gink who threw your father over the railing tell me now."

He tore the receipt in half and let it drop to the floor. "You're not the cops, and I told you to screw."

He stepped around me to the still open door.

"I've got plenty of those receipts, David. Close the door and get your mother."

"I said beat it. Mustard plasters give me the jeebies."

I turned to the door, slammed it shut and pushed David backward. His foot hooked against one of the throw rugs and he collapsed onto a brocaded sofa.

"I want to talk to you and to your mother. She here?"

"None of your beeswax. Screw while you still can."

"Okay, tough guy, here's the lowdown. My name's Brand. I'm from York Studio. Your father left a box at York full of a lot of stuff. Chief among them receipts like the one you glommed and two reels of a nudie flickers. I'm pretty sure the images on that film wouldn't surprise you."

He jerked like a marlin that had just taken the hook. Frightened eyes flicked down the hallway and his tongue traced the line of his bottom lip. He straightened up on the sofa, his bluster gone.

"This a shakedown?"

"Get your mother. I need to talk to someone with ears."

"She's not here."

"Cut the static, David, and wise up. She'll want to hear this."

The door down the hallway swung open and a handsome woman in her late forties stepped out, carefully closing the door behind her. She paused, raising her hand to adjust tightly curled auburn hair that came well short of her shoulders. She was an older version of the lovely young lady in the photos at VanderSaant's townhouse. Her expensive pink silk robe bore the initials CV in script over her heart.

She came easily into the room, in complete command of herself. She smiled and motioned graciously to a chair.

"David, you are being very rude to our guest."

"Mother, he's just a cheap grafter looking for a chizz."

"No, David. We need to extend our courtesy to the gentleman. Please sit down, Mr…"

"Brand. Up until a few days ago I ran security for York Brothers."

"And now?"

"I took over your ex-husband's job. The production part."

"You are somewhat atypical from most picture producers I have known." She relaxed onto the end cushion of the sofa.

"I'm sure."

"And what is it you want?" She smiled like a schoolgirl showing her father an all-A's report card. "Excuse me, where are my manners? I am Charlotte VanderSaant. May I offer you refreshment. Scotch, perhaps. You look like a man who needs to relax."

I shook my head. "You can feed your whelp the plaid. He's gonna need it. What you can offer me is the straight goods to a few questions Who knows? Maybe I can help you with the buttons."

She shrugged, seemingly unconcerned about the law. A sudden smile that showed perfect, white teeth engulfed me in its warmth. She crossed her legs and flashed a slice of nice gams she quickly covered with the robe. She twisted her head at a slight angle and raised her chin. Dark brown eyes regarded me openly.

"What do you wish to know, Mr. Brand? My son and I have committed no crimes. Unless your questions are of a deeply personal nature, I see no reason not to answer. We really have nothing to hide."

"Did you shoot Cleland?"

"What do you mean? Cleland was shot?"

I nodded.

"But the papers—"

"Forget the papers. The news boys are chasing moonbeams. Cleland was shot. Was it you, David?"

Charlotte jerked upright. "Heavens no. Whatever would give you such an astonishing idea, Mr. Brand? Neither David nor I would in any way injure poor Cleland. He was very good at providing for my son and I, even after our divorce."

"Somebody shot him. Buttons want to talk to the two of you about that."

"We have nothing to hide, I assure you."

She reached for a deck of Turkish cigarettes. I shook my head at her offer. She struck a match and eyed me through the gasper's curling smoke.

"David worked for his father, you see. Now, David and I have no income and our future is a little doubtful."

"Hard times come a'knockin'."

"Indeed."

"David kill him?"

"I guess you are a picture producer. Your head is thick enough. David did not kill his father, and for the same reason I did not."

"Any more of those nudie flickers lying around?"

"That was an unfortunate decision on David's part, but he was young and unwise." Charlotte watched the smoke curl upward from the cigarette. "He was simply innocent clay in the hands of a master sculptor."

"Nobody's that innocent."

"Perhaps a better choice of words would have been naïve."

"Perhaps. Any more of those flickers hanging around?"

"We have no knowledge of that. We do know, of course, that Cleland had the originals in his possession, but if he made copies I am unaware. We have been living separate lives from him for a number of years."

"Not too separate. VanderSaant was paying your rent. Your son was working for him, doing a lot of odd little things."

"All menial and for an insignificant remuneration, I assure you. As for the rent, that was mostly a boon to David. Cleland's pathetic way of attempting to be a good father."

"David had a room in VanderSaant's townhouse."

"His duties to his father oft times kept him there overnight. He divided his time between his father and me."

"Did you see VanderSaant often?"

She blew smoke out of the corner of her mouth. "Seldom."

"Do you know where he kept those films?"

"We did not. He, of course, would not say. They were, obviously, not at his residence. We expected he kept them in a safety box at a bank or at his studio. Out of our reach at either place."

"They were at the studio."

David snorted. "So you said."

Charlotte glanced at her son. "David, hush."

"You do realize VanderSaant used those films to bleed Rachel Anne Maddon and her family," I said. "One of the reasons he could keep you so comfortable."

"Of course, but don't make me laugh. Cleland was making a very obscene amount of money and we were seeing very little of it. As you can see, we are not living an opulent lifestyle, and David was, I remind you, forced to work for his father."

"There could be an inheritance."

"No, Mr. Brand. We got our first look at Cleland's will just today at his attorney's office. David and I are left a mere pittance. Not enough to live on for even a month. We could contest the will, of course, but our attorney was not too enthusiastic about the outcome."

"The buttons have been searching for your son."

"David has been right here, living under his real name, and making no attempt to hide from the police."

"Why Lemmert?" I asked. "Not VanderSaant."

"Lemmert is my maiden name. Cleland did not want

David using the name VanderSaant. My husband was very vain and did not wish it to be common knowledge the young man working for him was his flesh and blood."

"David could have gone to the police. Most flesh and blood turn a little gloomy over the sudden death of a loved one."

"Indeed."

"They'll throw some hard questions at David." I glanced at him. He looked like a lost puppy. "Him laying dormy like this makes the buttons a little hinky."

"They can be as suspicious as they like. David has done nothing wrong and has broken no laws. When the police come to our door, we will invite them in. We will answer their questions and we will hold nothing back."

"Hold back all you want, but don't lie to them. The buttons can get a little self-righteous when they get lied to."

She offered a tight smile. "I do understand such things."

"They'll be around before long, with bright, shiny buzzers, long scowls and hard questions. David's a suspect in his father's death. So are you. Now that I know where you live I'll have to tell them."

"I expect no less. One must do his civic duty." She ground out the stub of her cigarette. "Am I missing something here? I was told Cleland's unfortunate death was an accident. Yet, you tell me he was shot."

"He was, but the slug he caught didn't do the job. Not quick enough for whoever pushed him over that railing."

Her eyes blinked rapidly and she shot a quick glance at David, who looked at her and shook his head slightly.

"It wasn't David," she said.

"You trying to assure yourself or me?"

"I am assured. As for the police, you may do as you wish and as your conscience dictates. We will be living here until the end of May, and then we will be forced by circumstance to make other living arrangements."

"You never remarried after VanderSaant left you?"

"I did. A terrible mistake."

"Worse than VanderSaant?"

Her face crinkled around her eyes. "Do you question a woman's heart?"

"A woman's heart is a deep mystery to me. But you're still using VanderSaant."

"I decided to go back to that name rather than to my maiden name, for perfectly legitimate reasons that are mine alone. If the police wish an explanation as to that, I will be mostly happy to oblige them."

Charlotte VanderSaant was starting to sound a lot like Blanche Matheny Bible. The two came from similar backgrounds, were about the same age and had likely spent a lot of time in each other's company.

"How well do you know Rachel's mother, Blanche."

"We practically grew up together. We remain dear friends, although I am afraid this ugly episode with Cleland has put some strain on our relationship."

"No doubt."

"I hope that in the near future that can be rectified."

"My sense is that won't be simple."

She nodded. "I dare say."

"If money's the object, you're trying to drill a dry hole," I told her.

"I don't understand."

"If there are more of those nudie flickers, or copies of them, blackmail has gone out the window. You can't bleed a stone."

"Whatever do you mean?"

"The bulls know about those films. They might even be considered evidence. They will at the very least provide a motive."

She gave David a quick glance. "For whom?"

"For anyone going to that well again."

"I am sorry for them, but it is a wicked, unsure world."

"So there are no more films or copies, to your knowledge?"

"There are no more nudies of sweet little Rachel Anne," David smirked, "doing nasty things that would horrify her adoring fans."

Charlotte shot her son a quick, warning glance and took a long draw on another gasper. "I told you, Mr. Brand. Not to my knowledge."

"You two alone just now?"

I asked the question with my eyes firmly fixed on David. His mother was not going to give anything away. David blinked rapidly and his eyes again flicked briefly down the hallway, quickly turned back to me.

"None of your beeswax."

"Of course," his mother said smoothly. She did not look at her son.

"There are two cars in the drive."

Charlotte smiled condescendingly. "There are two of us."

"That sedan out front Cleland's?"

"No, it is mine."

"David was driving Cleland's car? Where is it?"

"If the police ask me, I shall gladly tell them," David said.

"All right, you should know one more thing."

"And that would be?"

"Rachel Anne Maddon was fifteen in those films. The young man performing so fervently with her could possibly be charged with statutory rape."

David jerked his head toward his mother. Charlotte remained placid. She gently spread out a fold in her robe.

"Really, Mr. Brand, you are becoming quite tedious."

I looked at David. His jaw clenched and empty eyes stared at the fireplace. He had clammed for the night.

"Someone would have to prove that was my son. The image on that grainy celluloid and in that flickering light is rather unclear."

"You've seen the films?"

"Certainly. Cleland wanted me to see them. He had a strange, even indelicate, sense of humor. I think you were acquainted with him, so you understand exactly what I mean."

"Even so, if you have copies of those films, burn them. They're worthless now. They'll only be an embarrassment."

"For whom?"

I smiled. "Maybe only for the bulls."

CHAPTER 24

My Chevy puttered nervously as I circled the block and stopped down the street in the darkest spot I could find in the middle of the block. Streetlights illuminated the street corners, giving me a good view of the two cars in the driveway. I didn't know how long I would have to wait, so I hunkered down. I might have been off the force a while, but it didn't require honed instincts to figure someone else in the house had been eavesdropping. Possibly someone who wasn't going to spend the night. It would only take a little time to find out.

Thoughts of my twin brother came out of the darkness. Two standard fare California kids, growing up playing baseball and football, frolicking on the silky beaches and swimming in the clear blue ocean, and chasing girls. We joined the Army in 1917, and went overseas together in 'eighteen, serving together in the same AEF unit. Nelson took a lungful of mustard gas in our first fight, and was soon in a field hospital, then in a hospital far to the rear. They sent Nels home and sent me to hit the Huns again and again in a bunch of places forever marked on the blood-stained maps of world history.

When the war ended I got back home just in time to be Nels' best man at his wedding. A few years later, he returned the favor. Nels joined the police force, pleasing our Old Man, then a desk sergeant downtown. Three years later, I joined. Mom contracted cancer and died in '23. Nels' wife split when the mustard gas and the cancer wasted him. My pregnant wife took a bullet meant for me from a gunsel turned loose by a crooked bull named Elmo Jones, my one-time partner. I took my revenge, got myself suspended, and kicked off the force. Nels' fading health soon forced him to retire.

Nels died in early '32. A bitter shell replaced our Old Man. Each day he drew closer to a dead son. Each day he pushed his other son farther away.

Memories sank in and I wanted to scream. I shook my head and rolled down the window, even though a strengthening fog chilled the air. I thought of Alice. Nearly two years into our marriage, she wanted to start a family. At eight years younger than me, she thought it time. Maybe so. I wondered what kind of father I would be.

More pleasant thoughts had begun working their way into my head when I saw a tall dark-clad figure leave the bungalow and head for the dark yellow Alfa Romeo. It wasn't David Lemmert. I could see him clearly in the lit doorway. David watched the gink settle into the Alfa's front seat and then he closed the bungalow door.

The 6C backed out and headed away from me, toward downtown. I fired up my bucket and pulled out, a full block away. Lack of traffic made the shadow job both good and bad. I could hang farther back and keep an eye on the Alfa, lessening the risk of being seen. In the darkness, however, the driver ahead could see my headlights and it wouldn't take long for anyone paying the slightest attention to grow suspicious.

He stopped for one of the new electric traffic lights the city had begun installing. His arm went out the window and he gave the signal for a right turn. A block behind him, I turned right, went one block and turned left. I was halfway down that block when the Alfa Romeo passed in front of me, gathering speed. I turned right and dropped behind nearly two blocks.

Traffic began picking up and I closed the distance. He made a left. I got behind a Ford sedan and followed along, far enough back to know if the 6C turned either left or right. The driver went straight a couple of miles, and then hung another left. I turned behind him and saw the distinctive 6C taillights a block and a half ahead, just past another electric traffic signal. I started to speed up but the signal turned bright red and I had to stop for other cars crossing the intersection. Ahead, I saw the 6C turn right.

I ran the red light as soon as traffic allowed, hung a right at the corner, and gunned the Chevy. I dodged a streetcar and tried to get around several boilers in front of me, but I was shut off on both lanes. I drove straight, checking the side streets as I passed them, and got around slower cars as quickly as I could.

I couldn't see any dark yellow vehicles on the street.

I checked more side streets and crisscrossed a couple, but the dark yellow Alfa Romeo had disappeared. We were close to downtown now, with traffic getting thicker, and I had to admit to losing my quarry.

The Chevy admitted it, too. The radiator suddenly sprang to life, spewing boiling water high over the hood.

"Okay, sweetheart," I said. "That makes the both of us."

CHAPTER 25

My involvement in anything to do with the VanderSaant case was finished, I told myself. I gave the VanderSaant rent receipts to Harless and told him how I had come across them. I wired him on the Alfa Romeo and gave him the tag numbers. I did not mention the dark flickers. Somebody else might, and likely would. Somebody might connect them to me, and tell Harless, but I wasn't concerned. Frank might get a little peeved I had kept them to myself, but he would get over it.

I got down to the business of producing my first-ever motion picture. Harry had decreed each entry in the *Inspector Cooper* series would run no less than sixty-four minutes and no more than seventy-two minutes. Our working budget topped out a little higher than Harry's lunch bill, but Southworth and his cameraman, Chick Wheeler, hid the shabby sets demanded by the budget behind dark shadows and harsh lighting. Anyone on the set with an idea helped fix drowned dialogue. When stage directions didn't work out, Eddie and Chick came quickly to the rescue. Southworth often shot a scene with three cameras rolling, cutting down valuable time by speeding up shooting.

"We can meld the different camera angles in the cutting room," he said. He became a pro at using as little film footage as possible, leaving little extra for the cutting, but saving more money in the long run.

One brief scene required a ritzy set and I found one on Stage 18 that would be deserted Thursday morning. The set designer nodded less than vigorously as he listened to my plea but he allowed us two hours on the set with the proviso we were done by eleven. Two people were needed for that scene: our intrepid inspector and a washed-up ham actor, but it was a pivotal point in the tale. The ham actor was about to give Inspector Cooper the key clue to solving the murder of the much-despised chemistry professor.

I needed an actor for that part, which took up less than two minutes of screen time, and the name came to me in a murky cloud of inspiration. I remembered the reason I gave Harless for being at the Bible mansion.

"You're nuts," Southworth said.

"You have a death wish?" Eban asked

"It's your ass," Harry told me after I assured him I could land Leviticus Bible for a song. Harry understood that Bible's name on the billing—no matter the part lasted only a couple of film minutes—would put a few more butts in the seats.

Bible no longer had an agent so I took the script directly to him. I found him alone in the big house, accompanied only by Charles. Early morning light streaming through opened windows helped Bible clear out last night's hangover. He had a short start on his buzz for the day. He agreed to do the part, no matter the brevity of the role.

"There are no small parts," he uttered, showering me with his magnificent profile. "There are only small actors. Or is it small actors have small parts. I disremember."

A lot of time had passed since he had last worked and

I could sense his anxiousness about getting back into harness. I think he would have taken any part offered. I told him the terms of his pay and that he had to show up sober, that the scene had to be done in the early morning and if it wasn't finished by eleven he was out of the picture for good. He agreed without hesitation. His demands were small: a chauffeured car—a Rolls Royce Phaeton—to and from the studio, he would keep his wardrobe, he would have a dressing room with a bath and fully stocked bar—for after the scene, of course—and he would be served lunch in the dressing room no later than thirty minutes after the scene wrapped. He would, naturally, bring Charles as his dresser and Charles would be paid by the studio for that service.

I left a few pages of script for him to memorize and he promised not to disappoint.

Regal and sober, Bible arrived on time Thursday morning, a stoic Charles in tow. The crew lined up to scrape and bow when the great actor appeared. Southworth shook Bible's hand and told him how proud he was to direct such a legend.

I sat in while Charles helped Leviticus dress. I asked Bible as diplomatically as possible if he had the part memorized.

"I can recite it backward, if you prefer."

"I'll settle for straight-through from the start. Just be the artist you are."

"Artist? Bosh. Acting is not an art, you understand." He stared into the brightly lit makeup mirror. I wondered if the eyes staring back were as sad to him as they were to me. "Acting is a junk pile of all the arts."

"I remember Ben Hecht once saying an actor is the only man in the world who can do anything because he uses emotions rather than be used by them."

"Bosh. It is a scavenger profession, but I make this

boast. An actor is much better off than a human being. He isn't stuck with the paltry fellow he is. He can always act his better self, the nonexistent self."

"I have heard people say you were the greatest Hamlet of them all."

"What a scurvy drip of a man, that Hamlet. A ranting, pious pervert if ever there was one." Bible raised a finger and his eyes danced. "But clever, mind you, as are all homicidal maniacs. I love to play Hamlet. He and I were made for each other."

His dressing finished, I ushered in the makeup lady, a middle-aged, married woman grown slightly plump in her duties. Her name was Martha. She gushed about the honor and leaned over to begin on Bible's face. He reached a hand up her dress, and she jumped away.

"Mr. Bible, please."

"My love, your objections are noted. Please continue without apprehension. I assure you I will be the essence of a gentleman."

Martha hesitated briefly, but got back to her work. In her business, a hand up the dress—by man or woman—was only slightly juvenile and never totally unexpected.

I said something about Bible's famed London performances in *Hamlet*. I had been briefed by Jimmy Gallen.

"You mentioned the honored Mr. Hecht," he began. "If memory serves, he is the only man I have ever told this to, although there may have been others present at the moment. I do not recall. Those London notices are the only criticism I have ever hoarded. I've kept them to read on the day I might become vain and fancy myself a man of artistic qualities.

"You see, shortly after I arrived in London, I fell madly in love. I have caddishly forgotten her historic name, although I seem to recall she was a duchess. Or was it a Dame? No matter. I fell madly in love and I spent every

hour of my idleness trying to seduce the lady, one of the
worst examples of that strange blight known as female
chastity. I sang for her. I danced. I recited the poets. I fell
to her feet. I plied her with wines. I wept and pawed her
body hour after hour. Her clothing was glued to her body.
I could get my hand no further up her dress than her
kneecap, one of the least interesting of all the female outposts. I had despaired of mounting the lady when a mes-
senger came for me the morning I was to open as Hamlet,
inviting me to her castle for lunch, where the lady await-
ed me alone.

"A memorable afternoon, sir, with opening night to
follow. I weighed the matter carefully and decided I
could arrange both. The lady lowered the drawbridge and
I entered with gonfalon high. At seven, I was lying ex-
hausted in her bed, trying to revive myself with bottle on
bottle of her finest wine. The more I drank the sleepier I
became, but being a man of resource I switched to scotch
and with the help of two servants I was dressed and on
my way.

"I arrived at the theater a half-hour before opening and
passed out cold in my dressing room. My man Charles
whacked me with wet towels, shoved lumps of ice into
my costume as he dressed me, poured pots of coffee
down my gullet. I was the first American to play Hamlet
on the London stage, and the first drunk to play the role
anywhere. I reeled out of the wings barely able to stand.
The heat of the footlights made me dizzy. I had to lean on
Claudius to keep from falling on my face. I made several
unrehearsed exits in order to vomit in the wings. Unable
to stand, I sprawled in a chair and recited my soliloquy
while trying not to black out. I was drunk as a fiddler's
bitch through all five acts, but I missed no cue. I missed
none of Will Shakespeare's magnificent words.

"The marvelous reviews the next day praised me as

the greatest Hamlet of the ages. Every one of my drunken staggers to the wings to vomit, my reeling into a chair to recite 'To be or not to be' was hailed as brilliant artistic interpretations. I have kept those notices to remind me of the foolishness of fame. It is why I have accepted this wretched little part I am to play for you today. You have required me to be sober. I am, but I am a much better actor when I am not."

Martha, who had started smiling at Bible's rambling and could barely contain her laughter at the end, finished her work and fled. Bible watched her leave with a mischievous eye.

"She reminds me of the ethereal lady I reminisce about. Now, I require a slice of pie, if you will be so kind."

"Pie?"

"Yes. I cannot perform without pie. It replaces the substance you have requested I abandon until my scene is completed."

"What kind of pie."

"It does not matter. Any slice of that delicate pastry will do handsomely."

I hunted up Southworth, who dispatched his gopher to the commissary to commandeer the demanded goods. He returned in two minutes with the despondent news the commissary had as yet not baked the morning pies.

"No pie? Bosh." Bible glared at me. "Call the props department."

"There's a drugstore two blocks down Sunset that has a lunch counter," I told the gopher, handing him a fin. "They probably serve pie."

"I know the place, and they do." He was gone, only to be back in twenty minutes with a slice of fresh apple pie and one of peach, and no change for me. "Got two, just in case."

Leviticus ate part of the apple and turned his attention to the peach. The set was ready, the crew prepared, everything in place. All we had to do was twiddle our thumbs while the great Hamlet of the stage consumed a piece of pie.

"Do you know why motion pictures are so exquisite?" he asked between bites. "They are so because they allow me to sit in the audience and watch myself perform. Oh, the marvelous magic of the age."

The first part of the scene went flawlessly. Bible played his small role as if he, indeed, were on the stage as Hamlet. A sober Hamlet. Between camera set-ups, he performed a little soft shoe and sang, displaying a lovely voice. He finished the rest of it and retired to his dressing room surrounded by applause.

Southworth let out a long sigh. "Okay, Neil, you were right. The man was brilliant in a dull, commonplace part. A knockoff part for any other actor."

"Let's go tell him."

Bible pulled a bottle of scotch from his lips as we entered the dressing room. He accepted our congratulations without affectation and inquired about his lunch. The steak—rare—and all the trimmings were soon brought in, and Southworth slipped out. By then Leviticus Bible had gotten himself plastered. He ate sparingly, drank copiously.

Southworth slinked back in and whispered to me. "I need him."

"What?"

"I need him."

"For what?"

"I've got a cutaway closeup," he whispered. "He needs to look into the camera and say go."

"That's all?"

"That's all. Go."

"If he can play Hamlet fried, he can say go."

Fortunately, Bible's contract allowed him to keep his wardrobe and he was still in it, minus the coat jacket. Charles got him into the jacket and we helped him stagger onto the stage, explaining what was needed.

Bible nodded his head, stood on his mark, looked around and inquired, "Where is my cue card? I must have my cue card."

"Mr. Bible," Southworth said soothingly, "all you need to do is look at the camera and say the word go, forcefully."

"Where is my cue card?"

"You don't need a cue card. Just look in the camera and say go."

"Forcefully," I said.

Southworth gave me a look of quiet desperation.

"Fine," Bible said. "I need my cue card."

"You don't need a cue card," Southworth said firmly. "Just say go. What could possibly go wrong?"

Bible held his head in the manner he had practiced his entire professional life, and looked condescendingly at the director. "Well, I could say stay."

Southworth turned to a script girl chewing her lip to keep from laughing. "Get a big piece of white cardboard and write the word go on it in big, black letters."

She quickly produced the cue card and held it up beside the camera. Bible nodded, looked dead at the camera and without a glance at the cue card, intoned, "Go."

The A picture set designer immediately stepped out of the darkness and looked at his watch. It was a couple minutes after eleven. Southworth and his crew set about getting their equipment off the set. I hustled the wobbly Leviticus Bible back to the dressing room.

Over his fervent objection, I removed Charles from the dressing room. I poured more scotch into the glass for

Bible, some into a glass for me that I had no intention of drinking, and lied to him about how I had followed his career and admired his talent.

"You, sir, are a fool."

I thought the VanderSaant case and I were history, but I was wrong. Enough cop hung around inside me to not allow me to miss this opportunity. I started Leviticus talking. Half-seas under, he stood ready to regale me with wild tales of his days of glamor touring the world, giving one brilliant stage performance after another. I listened to him a long time, laughing and consoling and slowly turning the conversation to Mrs. Bible. He rambled on about her, saying nothing of any consequence.

"You must love her very much," I said at length.

"Ah, she is the light of my life. She understands my weaknesses, my foibles, and yet she remains staunchly by my side."

"And Rachel."

"Rachel is a precious, sweet girl, although a bit impetuous. The unspeakable sin of youth, I fear. I love her as if she were my own daughter, you know."

"You'd go to any length to protect her."

"That, sir, goes without saying."

"I know her mother would."

Bloodshot eyes raked me. "Certainly."

"Tries to shield her from the misfortunes that can accompany such a lovely young lady in Rachel's position."

"Yes, those misfortunes are varied and unending it seems."

"I'm sure Mrs. Bible has her hands full. There must be a lot of young men clamoring for Rachel's attention. Mrs. Bible has to constantly be on the lookout for her daughter's well-being and pursuit of happiness."

I was starting to sound ridiculous, but Leviticus earnestly nodded his head. He finished the brown plaid and I poured another three fingers for him. His hand shook so violently he could hardly get the glass to his mouth. His lamps were slowly being taken hostage by a vacant glare. He yawned prodigiously and burped loudly. The long fingers of his bony right hand fluttered around his right ear.

"Yes, she is untiring in her maternal exertions," he said, the words slightly slurred.

"I'm sure she frets, as all mother's do, when her charming, precious daughter is out in the company of other men?"

"As any mother would, naturally." His eyelids drooped, barely open. "And as I do as her doting stepfather."

"Is that why she was with the two of you the night Cleland died? A beautiful, wealthy young kitten of nineteen, content to sit around demurely on a Saturday night with just her mother and her stepfather."

"Bosh. I remember that night. Who says Rachel was sitting around forlornly, only her mother and wasted would-be father for companionship?"

"You mean she wasn't?"

"She was out enjoying life as it was meant to be enjoyed."

"Where was she?"

Bible drained the glass, set it on the dressing table. I made no move to refill it. His head leaned against the chair back. His eyes closed. "I do not know."

"Surely, Mrs. Bible knew."

"Mrs. Bible was as perplexed as I by Rachel's absence. She pestered me for an hour about where Rachel had gone. She made several frantic phone calls. She called Cleland. No answer as I recall. She rang Rachel's agent, and a confidant of Rachel's—a young lady whose name escapes me, although I remember fondly the rest of her—and there were other calls."

"But no one knew where Rachel was?"

"Mrs. Bible could ascertain no definite answer." His eyes opened briefly. "That is why she went out."

"She went out? What time?"

His eyes squinted as he raked his muddled memory. "About eleven, I judge."

"Did she say anything?"

"She seemed confident her Rachel was with Cleland at his townhouse. The thought rather set her on edge."

"Did she take a gun with her when she went out?"

He sighed. "I could not say. I am afraid I did not fulfill my obligation as husband and father. I regret to say I did not accompany her on her noble mission."

"But Rachel had gone out before. She didn't sit at home every evening."

"Assuredly not, sir. Sweet Rachel is no…what is the expression?…chunk of lead. She is a beautiful, well-rounded young lady."

"So what made that night different?"

"Different? I am not entirely certain I derive your meaning."

Bible's chin lolled onto his chest and he began that same gentle snoring I had heard before. I would get nothing else out of him. I rustled up Charles and we got Bible into the Rolls. Charles threw an annoyed look at me. I ignored him. The Rolls rolled off and I went back to work. Several actors had told me a motion picture producer was the lowest form on earth, and I was beginning to believe them.

CHAPTER 26

The first *Inspector Cooper* rolled merrily before the cameras when another slight problem cropped up. We needed a nightclub scene in which a canary warbled sixty seconds while the inspector entered the club, crossed the floor, and slid into a booth occupied by our prime suspect. I wanted an original song for that brief spot, but the budget allowed for no songwriters.

One day on the set—filming wrapped for the day and the stage clearing out—Bob Gibbon sat down at a piano and began singing:

"I'd rather be lucky than good.

"You know I need luck, that's understood.

"I'm lacking skill, 'cause I'm over the hill.

"I'd rather be lucky than good."

Bob played piano in a style that might have brought forth thoughts of Hoagy Carmichael—if there had been a little more style—but his voice put nobody in mind of Bing Crosby.

"That's the chorus," he told us. "First verse:

"When I'm playing golf and my timing is off,

"I feel like I'm swinging a pole.

"I'm needing some luck 'cause my game is a cluck,

"And I can't get the ball in the hole.

"Chorus and then second verse:

"I know it is true when I'm pitching woo,

"And my baby sees Gable walk by,

"I'm needing some help 'cause I'm just a whelp,

"And I know I can't compare to that guy."

Gibbon repeated the chorus and regarded us expectantly. "Sixty seconds," he said.

"You can't use Gable," Southworth said stiffly. "He don't work for this studio." He walked off without another word.

"We just need to change the canary to a man," Gibbon told me.

"Do we really need sixty seconds of music?" I asked Southworth later.

"Not that sixty seconds."

We decided to open the scene with the inspector sliding into the booth and kept pushing toward the wrap. The daily rushes showed promise and I started to feel better about the whole thing. Then, two-thirds through the shooting, Browner dropped in with a chunk of bad news. "Billy Lyons busted his leg in a couple places yesterday sliding into second. We won't be able to use him for several weeks."

Lyons had the second male lead in our little drama.

"Why was he sliding into second?" I asked.

"He was trying to stretch a hit."

"Baseball?"

"Mushball."

"His contract says he can't break his leg while he's working on a picture."

"Why don't you write that on his cast?"

I snorted. "I don't think he can read. Can't his agent read?"

"Let's just say he was improvising."

I called in Bob Gibbon. He lay unmoving on my

couch, hands clasped behind his head, staring at my office ceiling, his mouth working a wad of chewing gum as I told him about Lyons' misadventures on a softball field.

"We cannot reshoot Billy's scenes," I told him. "It will cost too much and will put us too far behind schedule."

"No problem. I'll add a line or two about his character's mother dying or that he ran off to China with some dizzy blonde. Whatever. Won't matter. We bring in another actor, make him the same character but with a different name, and keep going."

I told Eban Browner of Bob's solution and Eban gift-wrapped a replacement courtesy of Harry York—an enormously unhappy and agitated Russell Cave.

"I thought Cave was strictly A list," I told Browner. "Isn't Harry trying to make him the next Cooper or Montgomery or whoever?"

"Not anymore. When VanderSaant bought it, Cave took up again with Patricia Metcalf. They tried to keep it from Harry, but you can't get away with that hooey. Harry intends to teach him a lesson and you're the instructor."

Cave heartily cursed Harry soundly and at length, but most people who worked at York Studio had that routine down pat. His career on a shaky high wire with no net beneath, Cave went to work and we wrapped our little masterpiece a day earlier than scheduled and a few clams under our measly budget.

In the meantime, Rachel Anne Maddon and her mother and stepfather romped around inside my conk like circus acrobats. The buttons would have matched the .25 gun they took from the Bible house to the slug in VanderSaant by now. Harless would have tracked down David VanderSaant and his mother, but I heard nothing on any of that. Plenty of time had passed for the buttons to determine ownership of that gun. The newspapers and radio were mum on the subject—Harry York doubtless had a hand in that. Harless was holding his cards close to his chest, and Harry had to be working the district attorney—and nothing cheap about that.

The loop closed without me in it. Trapped in the fantasy world of dauntless *Inspector Cooper*, where everybody wanted me, proved darb with me.

Blanche Bible called me one day to thank me for allowing her husband one more chance to pursue his craft. She told me they had just taken Leviticus to the hospital again in dire condition. Her soft sobs sounded genuine. She said the police had come around once to ask a lot of silly questions, but otherwise were leaving the Bible family alone.

"Go about your daily business," I told her. "My best to your husband."

The *Inspector Cooper* editing process passed quickly and simply. Southworth left little extra film footage to work with. He had shot the story with his eye on cutting and he did that work in jig time, using just his assistant cutter, with me sometimes watching and learning. We had the thing ready in two weeks for Harry to screen, sixty-nine minutes of fast B picture action. Cops and heavies, the right amount of sex to please the audience while appeasing the censor, good triumphing, evil defeated, movie-goers feeling good as the music swelled for the main feature.

Harry York never screened the lowly B pictures, but he ran this one in his private projection room, sitting just behind Eban, Southworth, Gibbon, Wheeler and the three main players. I sat beside a nervous Virginia Lodge, who dug her nails hard into my arm each time she appeared on the screen.

Russell Cave was noticeable by his absence. I didn't

know if he skipped the screening on his own or under York's orders. It didn't matter to me.

Harry said nothing when it was over and the lights came up. His stogie had burned to a stump and Eban held a match while Harry lit another. He looked at me and I could tell—or at least thought I could—by a glimmer in his eye that he was at least not unhappy.

"Chief, what do you think?" Eban asked.

Harry turned for the door, without looking at anybody.

"Sixty-nine minutes is exactly what I wanted." He started out the door but stopped and looked at Eban. "Who was that blonde dame? I don't remember having any broads who look like her working at this studio."

Eban pointed to Virginia. "She did that part on a one-picture deal. Her name is Virginia Lodge and I think she might have a future."

Harry nodded while eyeing Virginia. His peepers raked her head to toe, and then up again. She reached for my arm and her nails began digging some more.

"Use her in the next one. Same deal. I think they'll like her."

Harry was gone then, cigar smoke trailing behind him, and the entire room started breathing again. Everybody but Eban, who had tranquilly absorbed what had been an ordeal for the rest of us. It didn't mean a thing to him.

CHAPTER 27

Erle Stanley Gardner rang me up four days after the *Inspector Cooper* screening. The ink had barely dried on his deal with Warners and Warren William—an A-list Warner star—had signed on to play Perry Mason. Gardner wanted to know if I was still in the market for his Mercedes. I met him downtown at the state motor vehicle bureau, where my wife had worked until we got married.

Alice turned in her two weeks' notice the day after we got back from our honeymoon and spent three days training her replacement before the boss showed her the front door.

She went out laughing and never looked back.

Gardner and I completed our transaction without fuss, although he seemed a little bit preoccupied. Maybe second thoughts about turning his prize cow over to the Warners meat plant gnawed at him.

"Things don't work out with Warners, give me a call," I told him. Maybe I could induce Harry into adding a *Perry Mason* series to my workload. Gardner's first five books had hit the best-seller list and it occurred to me Perry Mason had better legs than Inspector Cooper.

"I'll keep that in mind," Gardner said. He jumped into the passenger seat of a new stake-bed pickup driven by a handsome bruno wearing a white Stetson. The gink could have been the model for Perry Mason.

I was quickly on my way home to Alice, finding out quickly how much I liked the roadster's smooth power and easy grace. I had to admit it was a long way up from the dilapidated boiler I had been driving.

Alice, excited and pleased, hugged me, admired the deep shine on the Mercedes, jumped into the passenger seat, caressed the plush leather and ran a hand over the polished woodwork. She nodded in approval.

"Now this is proper for the man I married."

"I would have gladly taken it back without your endorsement."

"Endorsement?" She laughed lightly. "Now that you're not hanging around so much with homicide dicks your language is improving."

"I rise to the level."

"Uh-huh."

"You should hear how some of those actors I have to deal with talk. Especially the ones trained in the theater."

She grinned impudently. "Take me for a ride, big boy. Thrill me with the power of your big engine. Have you had lunch, yet?"

We drove. I headed no place in particular but we soon found ourselves along the coast, the early afternoon sun warming us, the wind in our hair cooling us. We headed north, stopping for a late lunch at the pricey Laurel Beach House. A booth on the west side of the large dining room offered a remarkable view of the Pacific Ocean through a long glass window.

"I remember this place," Alice said after we ordered. "You brought me here on one of our first dates."

"I did indeed."

"That Sanger character isn't here, I hope. What I have heard about him since our first meeting has not been very flattering. I assume he still owns this place." She grinned. "If he isn't in jail. Or out there in the ocean with cement for shoes."

"Now look who's been hanging around too many homicide dicks."

"I'm picking up picture patter."

"Next thing I know you'll want to be in them."

The soft light in her eyes caressed my face. I felt a shoeless foot working its way up my pants' leg. "I am very content, Mr. Brand."

I tried to match the soft light in her eyes. "Me, too."

"That makes me even more content."

"To answer your question, Sanger does own this joint and he is in fine fettle, far as I know. And I thought he was a perfect gentleman the night you met him."

Alice wrinkled her face. She was twenty-eight, with smooth, unblemished skin and large sparkling brown eyes. Her pert nose accentuated full red lips and her slightly rosy high cheeks added to the waterproof pan.

"He was a pip," she said, "but something about him made me a little suspicious. Smooth and debonair, but the edges were still a little rough."

"Sanger's edges will always be a little rough."

"I can, however, thank Mr. Sanger for getting you to marry me."

"Mack Sanger had nothing to do with that."

"Oh? You must adjust my somewhat faltering memory, my dear Mr. Neil Brand."

The waiter appeared with our drinks. I raised my glass. "A toast to Mr. Mack Sanger and to all he has done for us."

Alice sipped her Manhattan. "As I said, it was a nice evening."

"Yes, it was. All of it."

"I'm thinking we could have another nice evening."

Alice smoothed her napkin across her lap and gazed steadily at me. "Neil, you know we have talked about starting a family. With your new job, I think we should get serious about that."

I grinned. "We could work on that this evening."

"It would be the ideal time."

We ate and discussed the future. Alice had her mind set on expanding our family, and she wanted a new neighborhood for the expansion. Our place was old and small, too far from the York lot and offered no comfort for entertaining.

She made it clear she wanted bigger and newer, with a nice yard for an expanding family.

"In your new position, you're going to have to entertain. I know how much you like that, but it will be necessary."

I agreed, although I knew only a few people at York I wanted to entertain. And other than Frank Harless and his wife, no one outside York came to mind.

"It won't have to be lavish, but we need a little upgrade. Something we can now easily afford without going overboard."

"I told you Harry liked what he saw my first time at bat. He said to drop in on him in a couple of days to discuss my future. I expect he'll offer me a seven-year deal, that's pretty standard. Something along the lines of fifteen a week the first three or four years, then a weekly increase for the rest of it. Say five hundred. Either that or he'll give me the air."

"Don't be foolish, darling. Harry owes you plenty for Johnny Cutter. You know that and he knows that. And Harry is sold on your first picture. Don't look down on yourself."

"You have a lot of faith."

"And well placed, darling. A seven-year deal works

out to be a nauseating amount of money, but we'll take it."

"Go ahead and start house-hunting," I told her. "Keep in mind we should look for something we can pay off before any deal I get expires. There might not be another."

"You get a long-term contract we could buy San Simeon from Hearst."

"That would be a long drive to work."

"If you insist, I'll find something a little closer and a little less ostentatious. But I don't want to think about it anymore today." Her eyes twinkled. "I have other things in mind for the rest of this evening, my lovely Mr. Brand."

"I'm right with you, my lovely Mrs. Brand."

CHAPTER 28

Having *Inspector Cooper* in the can made me a man of leisure for a few days before we started on our next six-reel adventure, tentatively called *Inspector Cooper Returns*. That would be followed by exciting adventures with titles like *Calling Inspector Cooper, Inspector Cooper Catches a Killer*, and *Inspector Cooper Catches Moby Dick with a Safety Pin*. I figured by then the public would have demoted the inspector far down the B list and I would be on to something different, assuming I still had Harry York's best regards.

I washed down a late breakfast—a stack of wheats—with a cup of hot, black joe. Alice kissed me and retired to the bathroom to put on the finishing touches, leaving me to take care of the dishes. She and her mother were going house-hunting this morning—two places in Brentwood and another up in the hills. I had been invited along, but I shuddered at the thought and turned to the newspaper.

I read a little—mostly the sports pages and the funnies—and had just set the paper aside when Alice came in to kiss me before leaving. She was dolled up in a conservative gray number that still managed to show off the curves, her pan mostly free of makeup.

She was no flour lover, anyway, and she certainly

didn't need the munitions. An automobile horn blew out-side.

"That's mother. I'll be home in time to make dinner." She kissed me. "You have a good day. Don't work too hard."

I watched her leave and my eye fell on a book I had pulled off the shelf a couple of days before. Three years ago, Theo Stein had given me a copy of Jack Pershing's memoir, *My Experience in the World War*. I wasn't ready to read it then. The Great War was still too vivid in my mind. Now I felt ready. I took a little more coffee, read an hour, and had finally turned to the dishes, wondering if I was even going to the studio today, when Frank Harless called.

"Hoped to catch you at home this morning," he drawled when I answered the blower. A strange noise on his end of the line caught my attention.

"Where are you?"

"I'm down at the port. Imagine you being a playboy. You're not even keeping banker's hours these days."

"I'm just kicking back and raking in the mazuma, Frank. You ought to try it yourself."

"One day, maybe. Just now, my days seem to be get-ting more and more interesting. Want to see the latest?"

"Down at the port?" I asked.

"Big ship called the *California*."

"I'm told that ship plies the seven seas in the swell lap of luxury, all orchids and silk."

"So I hear. But that doesn't go for everybody."

"Meaning?"

"Come on down and see. Art Stiles will be looking for you."

"On my way soon as I wash the breakfast dishes and get dressed," I promised.

"Maid's day off?"

"No, baby's going house-hunting."

"And you're not?"

"She's going with her mother."

"Gotcha. Look up Stiles when you get here. The *California*."

I didn't have any trouble finding the massive luxury liner—its two red-white-and-blue funnels loomed high above the docks, poking holes in a cloud-ridden sky that threatened rain. Art Stiles, hemmed in by a mob of noisy reporters and hard-faced uniformed bulls, his brown fedora pushed back on his balding head, stood with his feet spread on the gangplank like Douglas Fairbanks Sr. fending off the hordes in *Thief of Baghdad*. He motioned at me and the hordes parted like the Red Sea, but kept shouting out questions.

More uniforms and several homicide dicks in plain clothes hung outside an open door on the first deck of air-conditioned luxury cabins. I stopped at the doorway, where a figure covered by a black sheet hugged the floor in macabre silence. An LAPD photographer snapped shots with a Speed Graphic and a flash from another camera went off inside the cabin. Frank Harless and a couple of other homicide boys rousted about the cabin.

Harless saw me and stepped to the doorway. He pointed at the black sheet. "I think that's somebody you know. David Lemmert."

"VanderSaant's kid?"

"The same. I believe you've met."

I shrugged. "Briefly."

"Keep your hands in your pockets and come on in."

Another figure wrapped in a black sheet slumped on the bed, head over the edge, arm dangling. It was a woman's arm.

"Charlotte Lemmert?"

Harless nodded. "You know her, too, I believe."

"I met her once."

"Looks like the two of them were planning to go on a cruise."

"To Davy Jones' Locker?"

"Probably not what they had in mind?"

"You know what happened?" I asked.

"No gunshot wounds on either body. No marks of any sort that indicate something of a violent nature. Cabin undisturbed."

"No one to hear. No one to see."

"That's right," he said. "Looks like David Lemmert managed to get the cabin door open before he dropped dead. We found a snub-nosed Smith and Wesson .38 Special with a full chamber on the floor beside him."

"Hadn't been fired?"

"Safety's still on."

"Ship ready to sail?"

"If Lemmert hadn't gotten the cabin door open, it could have been a few days before anyone found the bodies."

I frowned. "One cabin?"

"Adjoining cabins. Figures out to around two grand for the trip."

"That's a lot of kale. I had the hunch these two were on their uppers."

"We got a look at Cleland VanderSaant's will," he said. "It's still in probate, but it leaves only a century each to his wife and son."

"Two hundred clams is a spit in the ocean to him."

"Rest goes to his wife, Patricia Metcalf. I hear they'd split."

"Mental cruelty. Irreconcilable differences. Wouldn't cut his toenails. Too much drama over her lovers and his mistresses."

"And these two practically get cut out of his will."

"Cut out for good, it seems. They know about the will?"

Harless nodded. "So says VanderSaant's lawyer. I thought maybe you knew that."

"You've found out a lot in a hurry."

"We've been digging into these two ever since VanderSaant bought it. Any idea where they might have got their scratch?"

I ignored the question. "Cut out of the will and with no prospects, so they decided to take a powder. Where were they headed?"

"Tickets say they were bound for Havana."

"Not a place to go without funds."

"They had two other tickets. Havana to Rio."

"That would take a lot more than two grand." I indicated the finely furnished room. "This is a first-class cabin."

"Two large would only get them as far as Havana, forgetting Rio for the moment."

"I take it you found no more dough."

"Nothing." Harless tapped four fingers in succession. "No cash, no checks, no bank books, no jewelry. Nothing. Between the two of them we counted out a little under seventy bucks. The purser says they didn't give him anything to keep in the ship's safe."

"Any idea how they bought it?"

"Figures to be poison. We'll know more when the coroner gets them."

"Hunch?"

"Same one you got. It ain't hard to figure." He eyed me stonily, went on. "What we don't have are any witnesses. We can pin it down pretty solid. Looks like they bought it late last night. Ship was to sail this morning and it was a pretty busy place last night. You could probably have slipped a marimba band on board without it being seen."

"You've got people to see, Frank. Why bring me down here?"

"Might be the people we want to see belong to your pal Harry York in one way or another. Thought I'd give you a heads up."

"Hand me another line, Frank. You wanted to see my pan when I glommed this."

He grinned. "That too."

"And see if I wanted to tell you anything before you talked to the people you need to see. The ones you think belong to Harry."

"The very ones."

"I'll tell you this, Frank. Harry no longer cares about any of them. There'll be no interference. No stall. No more payoffs."

He nodded. "I figured that since we got access to Metcalf and to the Maddon doll without strings, it was shaking out that way."

"I figure I'll be seeing some of those people in the course of business."

"Go ahead, Neil. At least one of them already knows we're on our way."

CHAPTER 29

I drove up to the Bible mansion. The late morning sky had turned sparkling blue, leaving only a few wispy clouds to prowl the distant mountain tops. A couple of palookas in stained dungarees pushed two-wheeled mowers across the manicured lawn while an older man similarly dressed fooled with the hedges bordering the portico. Another man, dressed in white linen with a black tie tucked under the third button of his shirt, walked around with a clipboard, studying the house and making notes.

I parked on the street and crept up the long walk.

Leviticus Bible had fooled them again, returning home from the grave the day before. Five times in the last two years he had been taken to the hospital to die and five times he had cheated the Grim Reaper and returned to his home. With each triumphant return, the odds grew heavier on the Reaper's side.

A sad-faced Charles answered the door, seemed to brighten a little when he saw me. Behind him, several pieces of furniture had disappeared and portentous white sheets covered a number of other pieces. Several paintings had been taken from the now-deserted walls and were leaning against the corner like children being punished.

"Mr. Brand, good to see you. I believe Mr. Bible will be quite happy." Charles bent forward. "It is he you have come to visit, I trust."

"I wanted to see the entire household."

"My apologies, sir, but the mistress and her daughter are at the moment unavailable. They are out on…shall we say, business."

"Say anything you want, Charles."

"Yes, sir. An unhappy business it is."

"In that case, I'll settle for a few words with Bible."

"Only a few if you don't mind."

"How is he?"

Charles shook his head sadly. "He is confined to his bed. The doctors have, once more, forbidden his drinking. Mrs. Bible has had all the alcohol in the house taken away."

"And how is he?"

"He is drunk, sir?"

"And how does he manage that?"

"I am ignorant. Mr. Bible is a cunning man with a great deal of resourcefulness. He is apparently stealing his sustenance from somewhere beyond our means to detect."

"What does Mrs. Bible say?"

"Sadly, Mrs. Bible has accepted the inevitable."

I looked around. The place seemed haunted. "What's going on here?"

"The house, I am sorry to say, is being placed on the market. The mistress has determined that under the circumstances this splendid dwelling is no longer necessary for the needs of herself, her daughter or her husband."

"What about you and the servants?"

Charles let moist eyes sweep the morgue-like room. "The new owner may very well want to retain the servants. I shall stay with Mr. Bible as long as he requires."

"That go for Mrs. Bible?"

"I am afraid not, sir. Neither the mistress nor her daughter shall require my services after the house is sold. At least, not until Miss Rachel secures a lucrative contract with another motion picture company. They remain hopeful. I, on the other hand, am of the opinion that such security may not be forthcoming."

"You're hitting on all sixes there, Charles." I abruptly changed the subject again. "How long have you been with Bible?"

"Nearly forty years, sir. I began as an actor myself, but my talents were dreadfully lacking. Mr. Bible despaired of my abilities and asked me to be his dresser, and I have stayed on in that capacity and in others."

"You were with him in London?"

"Yes, sir. Finest Hamlet of the ages."

"Drunk or sober?"

Charles allowed a smile to play at the corners of his mouth. "Yes, sir."

"How well did you know Cleland VanderSaant."

"Quite well, indeed. Mr. VanderSaant became Mr. Bible's protégé and a rather well-known performer in his own right."

"How did his talent stack up?"

"Mr. VanderSaant was a quite talented actor, although not of the stature of Mr. Bible. Very few through the years have been so privileged."

"What happened?" I asked.

"Mr. VanderSaant, unfortunately, had a very nasty proclivity towards acts of cruelty. He was most difficult to work with and many of his peers refused to appear with him. His roles became less and less important."

"Then you knew Charlotte Lemmert?"

"Of course."

"And David."

"Certainly."

"Charlotte seems to still love VanderSaant," I said.

"That is also my opinion. It is remarkable to me that a lady of her charms and sweet character should be so enamored."

"How so?"

"Mr. VanderSaant was incapable of loving anyone but himself, and I sometimes wondered about that. He returned love with callousness."

"They divorced before he came to Hollywood?"

"Yes, sir, but she tagged along after a discreet period of time." Another shake of his head, sadder than before. "It was quite sad to see, although I suppose she thought her son needed his father."

"How'd VanderSaant take that?"

"I could not say, sir."

"Leviticus and his family?"

"Mr. Bible followed when the motion picture divinities beckoned him. I believe you know the rest of that tragic story."

"All right, Charles. May I see Mr. Bible now?"

"Certainly, sir. However, I am not certain he will be lucid and I beg you to stay only a few minutes. He is not at all well."

A grandfather clock echoed somewhere in the quiet house. The sound bounced off the walls and crawled up my spine. Dust particles danced in the bright sunlight filtering through the tall windows.

Early morning shadows writhed ghost-like through the deepening stillness. Following Charles up the winding staircase reminded me of David Manners creeping up the steps behind Dracula in that old, decrepit Universal Studios castle.

Leviticus, his white-maned head propped against numerous pillows, resolutely clasped the King James Version of the Good Book to his chest when Charles ushered me into the immense, cheerfully lit bedroom. A long, quivering finger marked a place on a page and his crumpled mug turned toward me. Sunken eyes blinked and tried to focus through wire rim cheaters. Leviticus Bible looked closer to ninety than to sixty-five.

"Bosh. What is this interruption?" His sonorous voice belied the emaciation of his body.

"Mr. Bible," Charles said softly, "Mr. Brand is here to see you. He modestly requests a few moments of your time."

"Bosh. Show that rascally drip to my despoiled bedside. Despoiled by my own shameless actions, I admit. I should have words with him. He is the one true friend who has not found it within him to abandon me. You may leave us, Charles."

Charles bowed slightly. "Sir, I shall be just outside the door if my assistance is required." He looked at me openly, his meaning clear. "Please, Mr. Brand, I ask that you do not linger for more than a few minutes."

I dragged an armless chair, a little round thing with a padded seat and wired back, to his bedside. His mammoth bed, a four-poster with an impossibly large headboard, could have doubled for Noah's Ark. Shelves cut into the headboard held a lamp just above Bible's head. A number of leather-bound books—all Shakespeare and the classics, along with what appeared to be playbills—filled the shelves.

Bible's haggard face glowed like fresh milk on a vanilla cake, his withered hands as dull white as the sheet underneath him.

I nodded at the heavy, leather-bound Holy Bible opened across his chest. "I thought you were an avowed atheist," I said.

"Yes, indeed." He tapped the Good Book. "I am looking for a loophole. It has come to me that I might very well soon be in need of one."

"A little doubt creeping in?"

"A man in my precarious position must consider the other side of the critical question. On occasion in my wasted years, I have been wrong-headed, and it now occurs to me I might be erroneous again. A little bird—or perhaps it is the devil himself—sits treacherously upon my shoulder and constantly whispers to me in sinister tones that I will not be making many more ruinous mistakes."

"Charles tells me you're still drinking despite the insistence of your doctors and the pleas of your wife."

"Bosh." His eyes lit up like Shylock spying money. "How is it that those scurrilous miscreants think they can change in a wink the habits of a half century of living? A pox on them."

"Charles says Mrs. Bible has removed all the booze."

"I love her with all my heart and I labored under the impression that she loved me. Tell me, valued friend, how can a woman of just senses connive so unabashedly against the man who adores her and to whom she professes her complete and undying love?"

I chuckled lightly. "I think that might be why."

"Bosh. What is love but a fleeting sentiment that cannot be vindicated against the flood of emotions that rise up to overwhelm a defenseless man? What is a man to do against such forces as that?"

"Mrs. Bible and Charles are a little bit curious. They can't figure out where the booze is coming from."

"Mrs. Bible and that slinking Charles are not the only ones in this house who profess to love me." He closed his eyes and smiled. His eyes jerked open, glinting madly. "There is another, and her love rings true."

"Rachel?"

"A dear child, but no." He wiggled a finger for me to lean closer. "It is a fetching maid who has from time to time allowed me to explore the innermost of her feminine outposts. I implore you not to turn on her."

"I came up here to tell you I can set up a private showing of your latest motion picture, if you'd like to watch it."

"That is quite kind of you." He worked at a smile. Sandhogs took less effort to dig tunnels. "Quite kind, indeed. I shan't think, however, that such a gesture will be necessary. I am looking ahead to the future. To the next great role I am to play. Audiences of a far different complexion will be entranced." His head fell back on the pillow and his eyes closed. "I beg you, sir, to forgive my insufferable rudeness. I am suddenly very weak. I must rest for my next performance."

His chest rose heavily against the weight of the book. He began to mutter, lowly at first in words I could not understand, but the voice grew stronger and his eyes suddenly opened, staring at the ceiling, unblinking.

He was Hamlet again, lost in a soliloquy, magnificent in his drunken majesty, his mind treading the London stage, enthralling audiences of a time long past. He was again in full command of his junk pile.

I quietly slipped from his bedroom, gently closing the door. Charles, erect and stoic as ever, stood near the head of the stairs.

"He is asleep?" he asked.

"He is reciting Hamlet."

"I see. Sir, Mr. Bible has asked me to show you a few items that might be of passing interest. If you would follow me?"

"Asked you when?"

"During his latest stay in the hospital, sir."

Charles escorted me down the hallway and into a large

Egyptian-themed room decorated in a style that had been the rave a decade ago. Workers moving out furniture from the house had not touched this room. He unlocked the bottom drawer of an enormous cupboard decorated with various carvings of Egyptian symbols and extracted a gold-inlayed, cherry wood case about a yard long, half as deep and about six inches high. Charles set the case on a polished table and produced another key from the side pocket of his jacket. He unlocked the case, revealing all manner of interesting objects. Many of them looked valuable.

"During the course of his long and venerated career, Mr. Bible has amassed an immense amount of keepsakes. A few of his most prized are contained herein." Charles extracted a large manila envelope conveniently left atop several others. "He thought you would find these of particular interest."

"What is it?"

"Photographs, sir."

"Photographs?"

Charles nodded. "Mr. Bible has a number of photographs covering the fifty years or so of his professional life. This envelope contains his most treasured. He says you may take anything that pleases you as a memento, with his deep gratitude."

Most of the photos—some no larger than my hand, some barely able to fit into the envelope—were of Bible on stage, performing, alone and with others in the cast. One of the photos was a close-up of Bible's legendary profile. I recognized Blanche in one photo, clutching Bible to her breast, apparently in the role of Juliet. Cleland VanderSaant appeared in several of the photos, in a number of roles. Each photo bore a signature.

"You might particularly enjoy this photograph," Charles said, sliding out the bottom photo and handing it to me. Bible, with Blanche clutching his left arm and VanderSaant on his right, glared at the camera with his head held high in a familiar pose. VanderSaant—holding a clock in the crook of his right arm, the green-and-yellow atrocity I had seen in his townhouse—seemed slightly uncomfortable.

Charles tapped the photo. "Mr. Bible was under the impression that this photograph would interest you in particular."

"I've seen that clock before."

"Yes, sir, who could forget it. It was a gift from Lady Dorchester, presented to Mr. Bible the night of his opening performance as Hamlet on the London stage."

"He told me in some detail about that night."

"Yes, sir. When the company returned to America, Mr. Bible presented that clock to Mr. VanderSaant as a measure of his esteem. Between you and me, sir, I believe Mr. Bible no longer wanted to look at it."

I nodded "Who would want to look at it?"

"Not only that, sir, but the gift reminded Mr. Bible of a lady he had lost complete interest in shortly afterward."

"And VanderSaant kept it this long?"

"At least thirty years, sir. I do not quite understand why, other than it was a gift from Mr. Bible. Quite unsightly in any setting, sir, even as a doorstop."

"Do you mind if I keep this picture."

"Not at all, sir." Charles managed a thin smile. "I had rather imagined you would find that particular photograph of prevailing interest."

"You imagine right." I looked the man straight in the eyes and he returned my stare. "Charles, showing me these photographs was not Bible's idea, it was yours."

"You are correct, sir. I thought you should know."

"Who else knows?"

"Only the mistress, sir. She was present."

"Not the daughter?"

"No, sir." His eyes bored into mine.

"You've told me so you must have thought this out."

"I have indeed, sir. In order to save the mistress and her daughter further embarrassment and shame, I have decided upon a course of action."

"Why are you telling me?"

"You have been most kind to Mr. Bible. You have tried to help the mistress and her daughter, to no avail, but due to no fault on your part. You were instrumental in terminating this long ordeal, and although my personal feelings are not in the least relevant I thought to repay your efforts in the only way I knew."

"Terminated." I said the word quietly, staring at the big cupboard. The carvings seemed to drill holes through me. My eyes went back to Charles. "You're talking about that flicker of Rachel Anne."

"Correct, sir."

"And now?"

"I will call upon the authorities and confess to my sin. That is a promise, sir, and I implore you to accede to my request."

"When?"

"The very moment that Mr. Bible no longer requires my services. I fear that moment is very rapidly approaching." Charles held out his hand. "I am not accustomed to this, sir, but I would consider it an honor."

"And if I told you not to do it"

"I am afraid it would make no difference, sir. My mind is resolute and cannot be changed. I implore you not to make any attempt to do so."

I clasped his hand and nodded.

I went quickly and silently down the long staircase, passed through the dancing dust in the fading shafts of sunlight in the east windows, hurried through the great, quiet rooms with their staring bare walls, and out the heavy front door and into the resurrecting sunlight. The mowers and the man with the clipboard were gone. I soon followed, leaving the burdened Bible mansion to its solitary and sorrowful memories.

CHAPTER 30

Alice—vibrant, perky, lovely and sexy as Anita Page and Marlene Dietrich put together—ran out of the house and met me at the car. After my grummy morning on *California* and at the Bible mansion, I wanted nothing more than to take her to bed—an idea Alice did not discount—but she had found the perfect house in Brentwood, anxiously determined I should see it this afternoon. Somehow, she had talked the realtor into giving her a key to the place.

I had to admit the place was ideal: A large, white New England two-story with black shutters and dozens of big windows, a three-car garage, plenty of shade trees, a tidy front lawn and a big back yard, fenced-in, with an oblong swimming pool and a rear patio that ran the length of the house. A tidy light green guesthouse in the back, partly hidden behind pines, promised to be ideal for Alice's fifty-two-year-old widowed mother. A tall eucalyptus dug its sturdy roots into the ground behind the guesthouse.

Alice gushed over every room in the main house and I found nothing to dislike, except its sheer size—and the price tag. Alice had always longed for a big, white house on a street corner and this seemed to be it.

A large room in the back right corner, off the master suite, offered a built-in bookcase along the inside wall and lots of dark, solid wood. Large windows on two walls let in plenty of light and presented fine views of the yard. The hardwood floor gleamed in perfection. Alice saw it as a perfect library/study for a fledgling motion picture producer with a brand new seven-year deal in his hip pocket. The room sealed the deal for me. The feeling gnawed at me that I had little choice in the matter.

A bar in the corner of the room came well-stocked with a single bottle of bourbon I could lay on Alice's doorstep. She poured me a stiff drink, smiled sweetly, and told me the house's asking price. After I gulped down the potion, Alice bent her head in that way she had and asked me what I thought.

The York Brothers contract—seven years with regular raises—I had signed added up to more money in its course than a gink like me should make in ten lifetimes. In one of those lifetimes, I had been a frightened dough-boy with no thought in his mind other than killing Huns and making it through another day, somehow lasting to the end of the war and coming home. I had basically those same thoughts as an LAPD flatfoot. Another life-time found me married and most likely soon to be a fa-ther. I shrugged and called the idea nifty and poured an-other drink while Alice danced around the room. She had taken ballet lessons in her youth and it was kind of comi-cal watching her try to remember them.

Alice stopped dancing.

"Say, you, the guesthouse in the back comes com-pletely furnished. All the rooms." A light flamed in her eyes and beckoned me. She struck a provocative pose. "Care to check it out with me, sailor boy?"

I did indeed.

CHAPTER 31

Harry York decreed three new *Inspector Cooper* pictures in the next year, a fresh programmer every four months. From the time Bob Gibbon hit the first keystroke until the edited version shipped to theaters, the first in the series took two months, and that included putting the unit together. Gibbon worked with a relentless discipline and had the inspector deep into his second mystery before cutting finished on the first installment. He had outlines for the third and fourth scripts, and an idea for a fifth. We determined we could easily complete the other three in six to seven weeks, start to finish, which left me with a lot of time on my hands.

I went to Harry. I don't know how many picture producers ask for more work, but Harry glared at me in that way of his—York's razor-sharp scowls were of themselves meaningless. Harry would scowl at a nude Barbara Stanwyck—and finally asked if I was trying to gouge him for more mazuma.

"I can sit around and drink bourbon on your dollar, or I can work. I'd prefer to work but I can go home and do the other if you'd rather." I grinned at him. "My wife and I are trying to make a baby. I don't think she'd mind me being home."

Harry immediately assigned me to three other pictures,

all B productions, all at one time planned for Vander-Saant.

One, an overly cute family romance, came with a dollop of humor and a hackneyed storyline replete with phony platitudes. The other, a fantasy tale of murder and revenge, turned the police into mere signposts in the yard. The third starred the two wacky Vincent brothers—Mackie and Mickey—who had honed their comic craft through a dozen years in vaudeville and four years of motion pictures. The Vincent formula was down pat and I was as necessary to that picture as a giant wart on Myrna Loy's lovely fanny.

And so it went. I put in my expensive time on those three pictures, got the ball rolling on *Inspector Cooper Returns*, signed the multitude of papers for the big house in Brentwood, helped Alice and her mother pick out furnishings—I had as much to do with that as on the Vincent picture, except for the library/study, which was all mine—bought Alice a new car, nodded politely to the middle-aged woman Alice hired to help clean and cook now and then, and regarded with wonder my fat monthly paycheck.

Slightly less than two weeks after I had last visited him, ambulance attendants rushed Leviticus Bible to the hospital for the sixth time. It turned out to be the famed actor's final curtain. At a scarcely-attended private memorial service three days later his ashes, ensconced in an engraved silver goblet that had been a prop for every drunk or sober performance Leviticus Bible had ever given as Hamlet, passed to his grieving, black-clad widow, her face hidden behind weeds. When the brief service ended, Bible's stepdaughter—undistinguishable from her mother in her matching black weeds—escorted Blanche Matheny Bible to their rented Rolls Royce limousine. I stood beside Charles Goriot as the Rolls disappeared into a murky sunset behind a row of king palms. No cameras clicked, a message we both understood.

"A fitting farewell," he said softly. "A major star who never achieved stardom. I don't expect Rachel Anne's adoring public will ever see her again." I nodded in silent agreement.

Early next morning, Goriot—tall, lean, stoic and giving his age as sixty-two and his nationality as British—walked into the downtown police clubhouse, asked for Lt. Frank Harless, and solemnly confessed to the murder of Cleland VanderSaant. It made all the papers. Lolly Parsons devoted fifteen minutes to the story on a special afternoon broadcast with a hook-up across the nation.

The over-the-moon district attorney preened and smiled for the daily rags, modestly consented to be interviewed by anyone who asked, and even once briefly mentioned the police. An editorial writer for one of the daily papers unflinchingly promoted the DA as the next mayor, telling his beloved readers it was time honest voters culled out the undesirable element from city politics. I couldn't positively say—my invitation apparently lost in the mail—but I suspect the moralistic writer and the honorable district attorney were having dinner together—on the DA's pad—when the mayoral idea magically struck.

Alice and I moved into our new cave, got settled without fanfare, and decided to throw a little housewarming party. She invited a few close friends. I invited Frank Harless and his wife, the *Inspector Cooper* crew, along with Betsy Hammerlin, and Hugh Dunnum and his wife. Harry York politely declined, as I had hoped he would, but he sent over a lovely and very expensive painting as a housewarming gift, along with two bottles of Krug 1928.

Russell Cave didn't bother to reply, and sent no gifts. Neither did my old man. I had hoped both of them would be there, although for two completely different reasons.

Toward the end of the evening, I asked Frank if he could hang around. He grinned and said he intended to do just that. When the last guest had left, Alice and Miriam retired to the living room for girl talk. Alice's mother pleaded exhaustion and disappeared into the guest house. Frank and I wrapped ourselves inside the wood and leather of my new library. I had started calling it my get-lost room. We sat in plush chairs facing each other, a bottle of top bourbon on a table in front of us. Every light in the room burned cheerily.

Frank shook his head as he looked around. No smile creased his lips but his lamps betrayed no hint of the hardness of a homicide dick on the prowl. He removed his suit coat and dark blue tie with the white sea gulls painted all over it, and sank into the chair. His broad shoulders accentuated a slender frame. Wavy, dark brown hair cut to a deep widow's peak centered over wide-set, dark brown eyes and a straight nose over a slightly rounded chin. His arms, long and well-muscled, ended in big hands. One of them held three fingers of bourbon in a tall crystal glass Alice's mother had picked out. Pushing fifty, Harless barely looked older than me.

"Neil, I gotta hand it to you. I never saw this coming."

"Yeah, covered in slop and smelling like a garden of roses. I only wish Nels was here to share it with us."

"What about your father? Miriam told me on the way over how much she hoped he would be here tonight."

I shook my head. Silence has a way of booming off closed-in walls. After a while I said, "Wire me about Charles Goriot."

"Figured you had him in mind. You already know most of it."

I nodded. "I just want to hear it from you."

"Correct me if I'm wrong?"

"Don't know if I can. I don't expect you're wrong

about much of it, if any. You certain Charles threw VanderSaant over that railing?"

"He confessed."

"I don't think Charles plugged him," I said.

"You think he's shielding someone?"

"I think that's a good hunch, Frank."

"Why would he go to jail for those two? Especially since he surely knew we'd never be able to pin that shooting on either of them."

"A sense of loyalty or an obligation, maybe."

"Maybe he's got a conscience." Harless shrugged, took a short pull of the bourbon. His eyes roamed the room before landing on me. "I don't think he intends to tell anybody the why of it."

"Maybe he hopes to clean the slate for both of them," I said. "Give Rachel Anne another shot at keeping her career alive. Charles was completely devoted to Leviticus Bible and by extension Bible's family."

"That's a hell of a thing to do for anybody."

"I think he is thoroughly lost after Bible's death and figures this is the last service he can perform for the family."

"Sounds like applesauce to me. But then I'm just a dumb flatfoot."

I took a sip of the brown. "Maybe you should ask an alienist, Frank."

"I don't think I'll ask anybody."

"Pull up a rug in VanderSaant's place and suspects might come scurrying out like ants at a picnic. Didn't anybody look deep into that guy?"

Harless shook his head. "I don't need any more suspects. Charles Goriot confessed and that's good enough."

"You could make a case for Rachel except for that door being propped open. She could just walk in and turn on the lights. Blanche would want to sneak in."

"Goriot says he pulled the trigger. Says he tossed VanderSaant over the railing. Says he propped the door open. Says the gink got what he deserved. That suits everybody but you, Neil."

"Charles showed me an old picture of VanderSaant holding that clock. Took pains to tell me the clock was ugly even as a doorstop."

"Proving he knew the door had been propped open with that clock. Only someone who was there would know that."

"I said he took pains, Frank."

"I get you."

"Who grilled him?"

Harless shrugged. "Forrester, along with a couple of his boys. But it was no gashouse, Neil. Charles Goriot wired the tale straight down the line, with all the trimmings."

"Those baby grands could have helped smooth out any rough spots."

"I told you, Neil, Goriot sang for free. It's all according to Hoyle."

"And the DA wants to buy that. It gives him a clear-cut case."

"And a clear run for mayor."

I grinned. "Dragging in the women complicates things."

"Makes it very muddy. He can't get a conviction on either one of them unless he drags out a confession. At the best he could only get attempted murder. The last time we tried to talk to those two, they clammed and yelled for that shyster mouthpiece of theirs."

"Whitesell?"

"That's the one."

If Whitesell stayed on the job, it meant Harry York had washed his hands of Rachel Anne and her mother.

That left Charles to try to pick up the broken pieces.

"So Charles is made to order."

Harless shrugged, poured more bourbon. "He tossed VanderSaant over the railing and that's what killed him. Everything he told us fits to a tee."

"I read the papers."

"Goriot's story is that Rachel was out the night VanderSaant dried up and her mother grew more and more concerned. It didn't make sense at first, the way he told it. Rachel is nineteen, a knockout, and she's no ostrich. Twist like her is not going to sit at home on Saturday nights playing hob with the old folks. No reason for her mother to be more worried than usual."

"Any fingerprints on that clock?"

Harless shook his head. "Not a one. Maid was in Friday and dusted everything."

"If Goriot propped open the door using that clock he would have left prints."

"Not if he was wearing gloves."

"Frank, Goriot told you Blanche was fretting Saturday night about Rachel. She insisted he drive her to VanderSaant's. Why would he bother about gloves?"

Frank sipped the bourbon, eyed me over the rim. "So? When he moved the clock, he remembered not to leave prints."

"VanderSaant was blackmailing them."

"You know what he had on them?"

"Didn't Charles tell you?"

Harless nodded. "He told us."

"Blanche told me part of the gouge was Rachel playing house with VanderSaant." I drained my glass, reached for the bottle. "I think sweet little Rachel didn't mind that too much. He was a big shot and being with him gave her career a welcome boost, as long as her adoring public stayed in the dark."

"Her mother seemed not to mind at all."

"I'm not sure how Blanche really felt about it."

"Goriot said she was going along with it all right, but that ended when the film turned up." Harless looked hard at me.

"The film?"

"Seems VanderSaant had a motion picture—I think those of you in the picture business call it a flicker—that showed Blanche in what Goriot described as a compromising situation. Goriot says Blanche got her mitts on that film. That's what we found the remains of in the fireplace when we searched the Bible house."

"He said Blanche?"

Harless nodded, flashed a crooked grin. "He said Blanche, okay. You asked that like you had another twist in mind."

"He say how she got the film?"

"He says he doesn't know. He didn't ask her and she didn't say." Harless spread his hands, careful not to tilt the glass. "After all, he's simply the hired help. It's all hinky and I'm inclined to think it was Rachel in that flicker and not the mother. That makes more sense. I thought perhaps one of them wired you about it."

"Any one of them getting their hooks on that film would take care of the hold VanderSaant had on them."

"It would. I think Blanche made up her mind right then to kill her blackmailer. When her frantic phone calls couldn't turn up her daughter that night, she figured Rachel to be back with her sugar daddy. That would have set Blanche off, all right. She grabbed her gun and got Charles to drive her to VanderSaant's place. She has no license to drive and Charles said she didn't know how, anyway. Blanche had a key to the back door."

"Rachel's," I said.

Frank nodded. "Goriot said Blanche had slipped it

away from Rachel and made a copy. Goriot said he took the gun from Blanche, skated into the house, propped the kitchen door open with that clock so he could see his way up the stairs without turning on lights, and shot Vander-Saant. He says VanderSaant came at him and got thrown over the railing. Goriot said he had just gotten to the bottom of the stairs when Blanche came in after hearing the shot. Goriot claims she never saw VanderSaant on the floor and had nothing to do with his death. They went out the back, got in Blanche's car and drove off."

I nodded. "Neatly explains the witness seeing a woman out back. That'll play well in court."

"Easy conviction."

"Isn't that what you want?"

"It's what the DA wants, Neil, but what I think is they both went inside, snuck up the steps and Blanche shot him. VanderSaant staggered at her and she panicked. Goriot tossed him over to protect Blanche and the rest happened just like he told us."

"Find Goriot's prints anywhere in the place?"

"No. Blanche's neither. He could have bumped VanderSaant without touching anything."

"He says he touched the clock. Anybody think to ask about that?"

Harless shrugged. "Maybe I'll get around to it."

"And where was Rachel all this time?"

"She might have been watching. She might have been somewhere else. She might have been the one who pulled the trigger. Goriot's the only one who's talking."

"What about the other neighbor?"

"The one who saw the figure in the front?" Frank nudged his head sideways. "All right, he saw someone who might have been a man running down the walk. He didn't see the figure come out of VanderSaant's. We can't tie that figure to the crime scene."

"That loose trail won't please the DA, Frank, although Whitesell isn't the gink to worry him. The DA's got a confession in hand and the two broads are nothing to him, unless there's still a bite left in that cheap squeeze."

"You think?"

I shook my head. "They're washed up, Frank. Nobody in the business is going to touch either one of them."

"Leaves one other question."

"The Lemmerts. Anything on that?"

"Dry well so far."

"But there's a rattle in your head."

Frank grinned. He set down the empty glass but ignored the bottle. "VanderSaant gets bumped, couple of days later his kid and his ex-wife get the same treatment. You're right. That coincidence rattles around in my head."

"How'd they buy it?"

"Poison. I know you figured that when you saw the scene. Same as me. Probably cyanide. That stuff's deadly but you can't smell it and most people can't taste it, especially when it's hidden in something like champagne."

"LA Port, vintage 1934?" I asked.

"Stomach contents included champagne. You can put poison in the stuff with a hypo and not break the seal. You pop the cork, pour the bubbly, drink to a happy voyage, only you just pretend to drink, then you put the cork back in the bottle, gather all the glasses, put everything in a big bag and walk leisurely off the crowded boat. At your first chance, you pour the champagne down a drain and toss everything else in some deep, dark place."

"And the boat goes to sea with two bodies in a cabin the killer thinks won't be found for a while. No trail left behind."

Frank shrugged. "That's the size of it."

"So the Lemmerts would be expecting somebody."

"My hunch is somebody with money to fund their voyage. Otherwise, those two would have been stone broke long before they hit Havana."

I nodded. "Somebody who wanted to keep the money."

"And silence the Lemmerts."

"Wonder why."

"You know as well as I do, Neil."

"Suspects?"

"Not a one. We know most of the answers except that one."

"That's the big one, Frank. Whoever killed Vander-Saant likely bumped off mother and son. Goriot didn't kill any of them."

"Not a stretch to think he did."

"If he confessed to one, why not to both?"

"His confession to one is all the DA needs to put the VanderSaant case to rest, Neil. As for the Lemmerts, we'll keep digging. You got a shovel?"

"Frank, I'm just a lousy movie producer. The stuff I'm shoveling these days won't help you solve any murders."

CHAPTER 32

Alice and I fell into bed shortly after Frank and Miriam left, putting off the clean-up until the morning. We wrapped ourselves around each other, not ready for sleep. The warm smoothness of her skin overwhelmed me. She nestled her head on my shoulder. We talked of nothing. We talked of everything. We entertained the pillow for nearly an hour.

Afterward, I lay in the darkness, listening to her rhythmic breathing. I lost myself in thought, but the thoughts that settled in my head did not settle well. A big, beautiful, snazzy bow wrapped the VanderSaant killing in glistening righteousness. The district attorney had caught his man, a conviction assured in a high-profile case that could be the kick the gimp needed to grab a higher office. The DA could send Charles Goriot over for a long stretch, and the man who had watched over Leviticus Bible for half his lifetime didn't seem to mind the beef. The buttons could pull the case from the blotter and stick it in a soon-to-be-forgotten file down in the basement, just the way they had done with Rachel Anne Maddon and her mother. The forgotten Lemmerts would go the same way. The sweet smell of rose oil caressed everybody's senses but mine.

One thought troubled me above all others. For the

moment, that simple fact shut the others out. Charles Goriot had lied to the bulls and I knew it. The men with long shovels had planted Cleland VanderSaant in the deep, cold ground days before I had found that nudie flicker and given it to Blanche Bible.

I should have wired Frank Harless the night before while he sat smug and comfortable sipping my bourbon, but I had something I wanted to do first.

Instead of driving to the studio the next morning, I headed for the city jail before breakfast. A light fog perfectly fit the mood that enveloped me. Nobody at the jail wanted to let me talk to Charles Goriot, and I bounced Harry York's name all over the place without a sniff of success. Finally, with the immediate offer of a spanking new Ben Franklin and a promised nod to the request of a snippet of Catherine Holmes' pubic hair—along with an autographed photo of Harry's top star—I convinced one of the jailers to give me a few minutes alone with Goriot. The jailer—a tall, gaunt gink with a wall eye—escorted me up the back stairs to a detention cell on the second floor, tucked close to the stairs. The cell's steel door snapped shut behind us. The jailer stood to one side as Goriot shuffled in handcuffed, another jailer firmly holding his prisoner's right elbow.

The striped, formless jail outfit didn't become the usually dapper and perfectly groomed former man Friday, but Charles didn't seem to mind. A fine grayish stubble marred his chin but his eyes allowed no emotion. He sat across the table from me, erect and stoic as ever. I only had a few minutes and no time to chew gum.

"You lied to the police, Charles."

"Yes, sir."

"Want to tell me why?'

"No, sir."

"VanderSaant was dead before you got that flicker.

You didn't kill him. Neither did Blanche. Neither did Rachel. And certainly not Leviticus. None of you would have done that for fear that dark flickers would get out to the public."

Charles didn't twitch a muscle. "If you say so, sir."

"But even so you still think one of them did it and you're taking the fall. Leviticus didn't and you wire that. That leaves two people."

"Yes, sir."

"Who do you think it was?"

"I am sorry sir."

"That's it? Spill, Charles. Tell the truth and stay out of jail. That's no house for a gentleman like you."

"That is of no consequence."

"Your life matters, Charles."

"Pardon me, sir. If I might say, the only possible way the authorities will know is if you tell them. I think the police might construe that as obstructing justice. I am told that is considered quite a serious offense."

"And you're willing to spend the next decade or so in prison?"

"Quite so, sir. My usefulness to this world is ended. I cannot even imagine at this stage of my life taking on a new station. The only service I can perform now for anyone is the service I am implementing. I cannot say anything else."

I stared at him. "I can."

"Please do not do that, sir. I beg you. It would serve no good purpose in the long run. I am not at all certain anyone will believe you and I will insist I had possession of the film in question the day Mr. VanderSaant died, and that is why I killed him. It occurs to me and surely to you that you could not prove differently."

"I might get somebody to believe me."

"I am afraid it will sound like you are inventing a way

to keep me out of prison. The man was a vile human being and got what he deserved before he could wreck any
more lives. That is the fact that is most relevant. There is
nothing you can do."

"I can tell the truth, Charles, and keep you out of jail."

"No, sir, the die is cast."

"You're runnin' out of time," the jailer said dully.

"We have all strutted our little bit on the stage and
now it is time to bid that hour a pleasant farewell,"
Charles said. "You are indeed a sweet prince, sir, but I do
what I do with my eyes wide open and with no regrets for
my actions."

"You should have tossed the gat, Charles."

His eyes betrayed no emotion. "If you say so, sir."

"Bulls didn't find your fingerprints anywhere in
VanderSaant's place."

"I took precautions."

"How so?"

"I thought it might rain that night. I put on my raincoat
when the mistress and I departed. There were gloves in
the pockets from the last time I wore the coat. When we
arrived at Mr. VanderSaant's I thought it would be wise
to put them on."

"Blanche's prints were not found anywhere in the
place."

He blinked. "She was in there only a very brief time
and did not touch anything."

"Not even the door?"

"The door was open sir. I might add, sir, that being a
proper lady, Mrs. Bible was wearing gloves that night."

I heaved a long sigh. The man had it covered.

The gaunt bull I had bribed loomed behind me and
clutched at my arm. "Gotta go. Now. They see you here,
it's my ass."

"Good day, Mr. Brand." Charles stood and bowed. His

gray eyes burned my face, begging. "Please do not call again and I beseech you to not do anything rash. Please believe me when I say this is all for the best."

The second bull led Charles away and the jailer who had me by the arm tried to jerk it off. "When do I get that…you know?" he grated.

"I don't have it on me," I said, trying to think of a willing young extra with the same hair coloring as Catherine Holmes who might help me out for another yard of green with Ben Franklin's puss on the front. To sweeten the pot, I could toss in a speaking bit in my next *Inspector Cooper* masterpiece.

"Stop by the studio in a couple of days and I'll have it for you. Maybe I can get her to give it to you personally."

CHAPTER 33

I left the Mercedes in the jail lot and walked over to the LAPD clubhouse. The early fog had lifted and the cool air warmed quickly as the cloud cover broke up. It set up to be another warm, sunny day. It didn't matter. I could feel a deep chill lashing at my insides and it shaped up to cling to me a long time.

Frank Harless sat alone in his office, looking over the morning reports while he sipped coffee—black, no sugar—from a large, dark brown cup. A boxing trophy Frank had won as a light heavy before my time propped the door open and I strolled in. LAPD citations adorned the walls of the little office. Harless looked up from behind an age-beaten desk, frowned slightly, and put down the reports. "Is the early bird looking for a worm?"

I got right to the point. Beating gums gave me no bulge. "Frank, Charles Goriot did not kill Cleland VanderSaant."

Harless nodded at the coffee pot on a little table underneath a window. The Venetian blinds were still drawn snugly against the strong morning light. A thin layer of dust clung to them like chimney smoke on a cold morning.

An open cardboard box on the corner of his desk held two glazed doughnuts. "Have a cup of joe and a sinker."

"You heard me."

"We've plowed this ground before, Neil."

"The Bible family did not get their hands on those nudie flickers of Rachel Anne Maddon until after VanderSaant died."

"How do you know?"

"I gave them to Blanche Bible the day you showed up to search the house. I was there for that, not to see Leviticus Bible."

Frank's eyes turned to dark marbles. The ticking of the white-faced clock on the wall filled his office, growing louder with each pulse of the second hand. Standing appeared to be an expenditure of great effort.

Harless pushed the boxing trophy aside with his foot, allowing the door to close gently. He slowly opened the dusty blinds. Sunlight exploded into the room.

I expected another explosion, but Frank sat down behind his desk and stared into the brightness of the window.

"Suppressing evidence, Brand, is a felony."

"What evidence? Nobody in the Bible family was going to bump off VanderSaant until they got their hands on that film."

"That would be the smart play, but when you get caught up in this sort of a mess you don't always make the smart play." He turned to look at me. His eyes hadn't softened. "You are exhibit one in that regard."

"First off, the DA would have to prove VanderSaant had possession of that flickers. You'd need witnesses who saw him with it."

"My hunch is you found that film in VanderSaant's office before I came in to search the joint. You remembered to wire me about the rent receipts for that place on Marathon but then you conveniently forgot the film.

Somebody other than me might draw a hunch that you had some nasty intentions for it."

I shook my head. "I didn't find that flickers until after you searched the office."

"All right. Where was it?"

"Stored in a box down in the props department. A fella who works there brought it to me after you left."

"You should have wired me right then."

"I had no reason to think that flickers was evidence of anything other than VanderSaant's depraved habits."

"You should have wired me."

I decided to move on. "Second, you'd have to prove VanderSaant was blackmailing the Bibles. Blanche won't admit to it, and you've got no bulge to get her to talk. The last thing she wants is the knowledge of that flickers to be made public. What else do you have? Rachel? Same with her."

"We're digging. Quietly."

"Third, the DA would need a way to get that film introduced in court as evidence if he could prove the first two points."

"The DA would start with you. What the hell were you thinking?"

"The girl was fifteen at the time, Frank. That's underage in anybody's district."

"I'm guessing VanderSaant shot that film. That alone would have sent that rat to the pen for a long stretch."

"The only thing that would come out of that grift going public would be the ruin of her career. Rachel was young and foolish, but she didn't have to pay for that mistake the rest of her life. Maybe that film was in VanderSaant's possession. Maybe he was using it to bleed that family dry. The DA won't find any evidence of any of that. Where's the proof that flickers didn't belong to the family?"

"Dammit, Neil, I don't like being played for a sap, especially by you. I think about that a little I could get miffed as hell."

"I admit I should have told—"

"Admit? Damn you, Neil."

"Frank, that film is not evidence, but it muddies the water. It would have ruined that entire family, not just Rachel Anne. Whoever killed VanderSaant either did not know about that film or didn't care. It doesn't figure in his death."

"Doesn't mitigate the facts. You held out on me. You kept information from me that would have pointed me in another direction."

"I get you. If I had known what was coming—"

His hard eyes raked me. "You knew what was already here."

"Puts another slant on the Lemmert killings."

"It certainly does, dammit, and I would have liked to have known that at the time we found them. You were there, Neil, and you still didn't kick in, damn you."

"We can beat that bangtail some other time, Frank. Let's get back to Goriot. That's why I'm here. What are you going to do?"

"What do you think?"

"Take me to the DA."

The grating sound that came from Frank's throat might have been a laugh.

"Not a chance," he grunted.

"I'll tell him I held out. He's got an innocent man locked up."

"No, Neil, he's got a man locked up who confessed."

"Wise up, Frank. Charles Goriot is taking the rap for someone else. Someone he desperately wants to protect."

"You decided who? Is it the mother or the daughter?"

"I don't know, Frank, but he obviously thinks one of

them killed VanderSaant, despite their not knowing where that film was hidden."

"Unless he rescinds his confession and starts yelling his head off the DA is not going to cut him loose."

"Let me talk to Goriot, with the DA and whoever else he wants present. I can convince Charles that neither Blanche nor Rachel killed VanderSaant. If Goriot believes that, he'll wire us the straight goods."

Harless shook his head. "DA won't go for it, Brand. You know what kind of sap that makes him look like? Got his pan spread all over the papers, he was all over the radio, his ears ring with praise, his back is sore from all those hand slaps, and a bunch of high-hats are pushing him to run for mayor. Cutting Goriot loose will mean the DA admits he goofed. They'll have a field day and the DA will be lucky to find a job cleaning fish up at Arrowhead." Harless let out a long, slow blow. "Now get out of here."

"I still want to see the DA."

"Why? You want to offer him a job as an assistant ass for you?" Frank nodded at the door. "I told you to get out of here. Dangle before I go ahead and decide to pinch you for obstructing justice. You think Harry York will pull you out of that beef?"

"If you won't go to the DA, Frank, I will."

"That'll get you a big laugh."

"I've been laughed at before."

"Not a chance in hell you'll get in to see him," Frank said, "and if you do, he won't believe a word you pipe. He'll write you off as a crackpot or think you're just trying to drum up hoopla for a movie, or that you're a pal of Goriot's desperately clutching at straws to get him out of jail. He'll think you're trying to street him, just like you did me."

"Frank, I owe it to Goriot."

"You owe him nothing. It seems to me you might owe me a little besides a stab in the back. I told you to dangle."

"If nothing else, Frank, help me figure out who killed VanderSaant."

"I'll figure that out. And who killed the Lemmerts. You go back to those ivory towers you've moved into and go to work on your precious motion pictures. Make some flickers of your own. Do whatever the hell you want. Keep on selling your soul to Harry York and to the rest of that damned bunch."

Harless stood slowly and rounded the desk. He held the door open without looking at me, standing ramrod straight. His face froze in a rigid mask, and all emotion drained from his eyes. A bunch of curious homicide dicks outside his office silently stared at us.

"Don't call me," he said. "Don't call the district attorney. And don't try to call any more angles for me. Now dangle."

The door slammed hard behind me.

CHAPTER 34

I drove back to the studio, knowing I wasn't going to get any work done, but not wanting to be at home alone with Alice the way I felt. I fooled around with a sandwich at the commissary, alone at a corner table, but ate little of it. A mid-morning quiet settled over the place, but my head roared too much to wonder why. I strolled up to my office.

Rose, stiff-backed at her typewriter, stopped her furious typing when I opened the door.

"Who is Mr. Joseph Breen?" she asked guardedly.

"Why?"

"I saw him this morning on my way up here. I stopped for a Danish and coffee and ran into Mr. Breen just outside the commissary. He was with several men I hadn't seen before. Mr. York was with him. Alfred Marks' secretary told me his name, but she was in too much of a hurry to say anything else. Who is he?"

"Production code," I told her. "Don't worry about it."

"He seemed very officious."

"I'm sure he is."

"You don't know him?"

"Never met the man."

She seemed not to be convinced. "He and Mr. York and several of Mr. York's top executives were going into the commissary. I think they were meeting in Mr. York's private dining room."

"It has nothing to do with you, Rose. This place is not doing to shut down, and you don't have to type so fast."

"It was just so mysterious, that's all. I have never seen Mr. York act so unassuming before. He was…" She tilted her head. "Obedient. Quite strange."

I closed the door to my inner sanctum and Rose began firing away again at her mill, finishing the final script for one of my pictures—I had no idea which one—so it could be mimeographed for the cast and others who needed it. You would have thought she was typing the Declaration of Independence for Thomas Jefferson.

I sat glumly at my desk, listening to the faint drumming of Rose's Remington, turning a rush of ideas over in my head, and throwing them into my brain's wastebasket. I thought about the bourbon, ignored the idea. I didn't want anything to drink. I just wanted to be alone to think. I needed a smart idea.

Rose went out about noon and, shortly afterward, Hughie Dunnum walked in unannounced, wanting to know if I'd go to lunch with him. He had a couple of hours before he had to get back to the latest oater he was filming. He told me he planned to spend the afternoon shooting a gunfight he and his stunters had worked out that morning.

I said I thought maybe I'd come down and check it out.

Dunnum stretched out on the couch. "I hear Joe Breen and his cronies are in the house this morning, kicking up a fuss."

I propped my feet on the desk top. "Rose wired me."

"More rules I reckon," Hughie said to the ceiling. "I hear he's in deep parlay with Harry and a bunch of the boys who'd probably like to get drunk about now. You not being a part of that tells me you don't rate as high on the executive scale as you might think."

"Lucky for me. Breen is cracking down on the rules we've been skirting for years, Hughie. Nobody's paid much mind to that production code since they thought it up, but that's changing in a hurry. I don't know why we have Technicolor when everything to those moralists comes out black and white."

Hughie rolled his neck to look at me. "Moralists on a soapbox, Neil."

"Everybody devoted to the same creed."

"Yeah, I know." Dunnum put his head back and admired my ceiling. "Let's see. From now on, the rules for making pictures say no sex, no liquor, no crime, no fun. That about it?"

"Pretty well nails it down. A board of review will have to stamp their approval on all pictures before they get released. The censors have taken over the asylum."

"Gotcha. A Jewish owned business foisting Roman Catholic values on a protestant America. That's what I call a democratic society."

I grinned. "And a picture maker's paradise."

"Whaddya think? Maybe I should switch out all the six-shooters for pillows when I do my big shootout this afternoon."

"Instead of a fight scene, Hughie, how about a cowpoke knitting party?"

We went to lunch. I had a light salad, which drew Dunnum's confused stare, but he didn't say anything. Hughie had a steak with all the trimmings and we passed the time beating our gums until he had to go back to the set. I could tell Hughie knew something bothered me. We had known each other long enough for him not to read me clearly, but he didn't ask. I walked to his set with him, remembering my days as a stuntman while watching him kill off a dozen or so black hats, but my mind kept wandering and before long I was doing the same.

The York Brothers Studio sprawled over several hundred acres of prime California real estate, most of it picked up for pennies back in the dust cloud days when Harry got off the train and immediately saw the boundless possibilities of sunny Hollywood. While his brother Louis greased the money boys back east, Harry started their picture studio with one building and one camera and an unending flood of big ideas.

Eighteen years later, thirty-two sound stages and three times that many buildings for one use or another worked their way around streets that could stand in for European cities, the Old West, modern America, and anything in between. Come up with that rare but different picture idea and a street with phony facades could be built in a few weeks. The York lot came with ponds and parks, woods and glades. A railroad track wound its way around the lot for almost a mile and several locomotives that could serve any era of transportation waited to haul armies or cattle or whatever the script called for.

Brawny action pieces could be staged in the far back lot and if you needed something better Harry had a ranch up in Lone Pine that could double for almost anything. Whatever the needs of any picture, York Brothers had the answer.

And the York Brothers had done it all on their own. They worked unceasingly—disregarding everything else in their lives—paid back the moneylenders, bought back the shares they had sold for financing, and now had nobody to answer to but each other.

I roamed the massive lot, wandering through a few of the sound stages in use, stopping at a couple of outdoor shoots to watch directors at work—one of them being Leo Collier filming a traffic accident for a big budget comedy with a top cast—and lost myself in troubled thought through a long afternoon.

The orange sun began losing itself over the far mountains, sinking just like me. Between us, only the sun was sure to come up in the morning.

I turned the corner of one of the stages and glimpsed a dark yellow Alfa Romeo 6C rolling past one of the props buildings. I raced to the end of the long building just in time to see the 6C hang a right toward the side gate. I couldn't make the driver but I glommed the wary beaver on the tag. The car had vanished by the time I got to the gate. A wide-body studio cop named Karl Behm, a former World War I German army infantryman who had come on board four years ago, had the gate.

"Who was driving that dark yellow crate that just left?"

"I wouldn't call that a crate." Karl's mastery of the English language had greatly improved since I had hired him.

"Call it what you want, Karl. Do you know the driver?"

"I have seen him a few times. He is a new actor, I believe. One whose stiff nose is always sniffing the air."

"Remember his name?"

Behm pressed his lips into a fine line and rapidly tapped his palms against each other. His eyes searched the heavens.

"Yes, sir. It is something that sounds like bushel."

"Bushel?" I could think of no one on the lot.

"His last name is the same as those big holes in the ground you can walk into. What do you call them? Caves?"

"Russell Cave?" I asked.

"If you know his name, why do you ask me?"

CHAPTER 35

Wallpaper samples and paint colors had Alice's lovely head wrapped in decadent dreams when I phoned just before six. I told her I was on my way and to dress up and we'd go out to eat, anywhere that pleased her. I hadn't eaten anything all day except the commissary salad that had wrinkled Hugh Dunnum's nose and I was suddenly very hungry. I agreed to take her to a picture show after dinner. She wanted to see the latest Clark Gable programmer, a slick MGM cops-and-robbers tale called *Manhattan Melodrama*.

It was darb with me. It would give me a chance to sit in the darkness, hold Alice's hand and think. I was beginning to hatch another idea.

Rose had a mimeographed copy of the shooting script on my desk when I got there the next morning. I took a quick look, told her it passed muster, and she called a runner to take the copies where they needed to go.

I got police headquarters on the blower and asked for Detective Sergeant Calvin Forrester. The sergeant served as one of the department's top goons, a beefy baby grand with a thick head, thicker neck and hands the size of a catcher's mitt.

He wasn't in the office. I left my number and said I had a hot tip for him. Forrester called back about two hours later. He listened quietly and said he'd be at my office at 5 p.m. sharp. He bored me with the standard warning about playing around with the cops. I told him his line intimidated me enough that I could guarantee it would be worth his time.

At lunch time, I hunted up Russell Cave. I found him on Stage One, the oldest and smallest on the lot. Harry had ordered Cave to be cast as another bland juvenile in another bland B picture.

It was the kind of role certain to go completely unnoticed, further sinking Cave's career. Russell sat alone in a dressing room he shared with another minor player, dressed in wardrobe's idea of a South Seas beach bum, with a stubble of beard darkening his chin. He rapidly closed in on the bottom of a bottle of expensive brown plaid. He did not bother to use a glass, and he tried hard to ignore me.

A wooden, cathedral-style Philco radio danced across a small table in the corner while a cat with a golden horn cut a mighty rug on *Potato Head Blues*. It could only have been Louis Armstrong. I listened a few seconds before switching off the radio.

"Hey, who do you think—"

"I need to hear."

"Why? I got nothing to say to you, Brand."

"Doing anything at six?"

"Not with you."

"Why don't you come up to projection room C about six?"

Cave cocked his head sideways. "For what?"

"I might have a way to get you out of B pictures."

His eyes widened. "Is this on the level?"

"Room C, about six."

"Okay, then. As long as you're on the up-and-up."

That gave me about six hours, more than enough time

to set up what I needed. I asked Hughie Dunnum to be there with me.

"You might have as much fun as you do playing polo."

Hughie grinned. "I'm in."

The projection room lights glowed brightly when Russell Cave walked in. He had on a brown tweed sport coat and no tie. He made no offer to shake hands and ignored Dunnum.

"What is this about?" he asked, taking a seat beside me in the third row down. The brown plaid was strong on his breath.

Hughie found an empty seat behind Cave and to his right.

Cave sneered at him. "If you think I'm doing one of his lousy oaters, you can go climb up your thumb."

"What were you doing at the Lemmerts the other night?" I asked.

"What? What is this? I thought I came up here to talk to you about pictures, not about where I spend my evenings."

"Oh, we're going to talk about pictures. Just now, I'd like to know what you were doing at the Lemmerts the other night when I called on them."

He hesitated and I thought he was going to deny being there. He plucked a deck of Old Golds from his pocket. "Do you mind?"

"Go ahead." I said.

He stuck a gasper in his mouth and struck a match on the bottom of his Aurlands. He blew a puff of smoke and looked at the blank projection screen.

"Maybe I need to repeat the question?" I said.

"Not necessary. The answer is that it is none of your affair."

"You kill 'em?"

Cave's dark brown eyes jerked wide open. The Old Gold dangled and he had to grab it to keep it from falling into his lap. He crushed it against his jacket lapel. He brushed off tobacco ashes and threw the wasted cigarette to the floor. He reached inside his pocket for another smoke. I sat calmly as he lit it, waiting for him to think up an answer.

"You're full of static," he finally said. He looked at me calmly and blew a smoke ring.

"What were you doing there? You knew the Lemmerts. Somebody killed them. Buttons would like to talk to you."

"The police have already asked me a number of questions about David and Charlotte. I wondered how the cops caught on I knew them. Now I know. What I don't know is how you wired it was me."

"That Alfa you were driving has license plates," I said.

"Damn, you are a smart ex-cop, after all. That sort of thing really takes brains."

"Now that we got that settled, tell me why you were there."

"I told the coppers exactly why I was there. It was purely a social call. I had been invited over for dinner. I don't have to talk to you, Brand, but the story's the same."

"You could have come out and said hello to me instead of hiding in the bedroom."

"I did not wish to engage in any conversation with the likes of you. You had already interrupted what was going to be a pleasant evening with two friends."

I nodded. "A pleasant evening just visiting."

"Just visiting."

"A little going away party?"

"Listen, I've had it with you, Brand. You want to talk about your lousy movies, swell, but you and me ain't gonna talk about my private life. Pipe that?"

He tried to stand. I grabbed the tail of his jacket and jerked him back into the seat. Dunnum reached out and patted the top of Russell's shoulder.

"No reason to play rough," Cave grunted. "I told you why I was there. There was nothing sinister about my visit, no matter what you think."

"They were sailing to Havana."

"So?"

"Where'd they get the kale?"

He jerked at my question. "How would I know?"

"First class cabins. Barely enough scratch on 'em to last till Havana, never mind about what they live on when they get there. Bulls haven't been able to find anything more than the few plasters they had on 'em."

He took a long pull on the gasper. "I heard the cops think they were murdered but you ain't the cops anymore. So what makes you think I'll talk to you?"

"Your façade is slipping a little, Russell. Juvenile leads need to have a little more culture in their voices."

"I'm thinking of giving up the acting profession." He smiled coldly and blew another smoke ring. "I'm considering a career change."

"Don't care for the life of a beach bum?"

"Miss Metcalf has asked me to be her personal manager."

"She's already got one." I reminded him.

Cave grinned tightly. "He has resigned. Her agent, also."

"You taking that job, too?"

"As I said, I'm considering a career change. Is there anything else? Did you just lure me up here to ask a bunch of insipid questions?"

"You plan to marry Patricia?"

"That, Brand, is not your affair."

I shook my head slightly. "Harry wouldn't like it."

"Harry York can go to hell, and you can tell him I said so. He's set about ruining my career, so we'll just see how he feels when I'm Miss Metcalf's personal manager."

"And her agent?"

"Laugh if you want. That's very likely."

"Last I heard Miss Metcalf had kicked you out." I said.

"Maybe you heard wrong."

"I heard it straight from her."

He raised his chin. "I love Miss Metcalf and she has told me she loves me. That, Brand, is all you have to know. You can save your questions for your fairy godmother."

"She tell you she loved you before or after?"

"Before or after what?"

I grinned and leaned in closer. "Before or after you found those nudie flickers of her that VanderSaant shot."

That hard jab was pure hunch and I had nothing to back it up, but it hit Russell Cave flush in the belly. He covered it quickly with a phony cough, but the flash in his eyes told me what I needed to know. He stared at the blank projection screen. He took another drag on the Old Gold, and dropped the spent gasper into the tin container on the back of the seat in front of him.

"Goofy, that's what you are," he said.

In the corner of my eye I saw Dunnum lean forward.

"VanderSaant had nudie flickers of other actresses," I said. "You know that, so don't try to gas me. It occurs to me that among those flickers would be some of Patricia Metcalf. He married her just as she was trying to get a start in the business, so why not make some flickers of her. It will occur to other people, too."

Cave's tongue traced his lower lip. "Like who?"

"Bulls. Gives you a helluva motive for murder."

He sneered. "More static."

"And for gouging her."

"Like I said."

"David Lemmert was VanderSaant's son," I said. "He was in some of that rot VanderSaant filmed, maybe with Patricia Metcalf a time or two."

"Beat your gums somewhere else. Miss Metcalf is a serious actress and you're having nothing but a fantasy."

"David's old man was bleeding her, but not necessarily for the sugar. His gouge came in another form. David wanted to blow but he was on the nut. He had another grift in mind, a one-time bite for the case dough he needed to set him up down in Rio. Being Patricia's personal manager, was it you who closed the deal on David and his mother that night?"

"I will not answer any more of your insulting questions," Cave said and looked furtively at the closed door at the top of the stairs. Dunnum rose from his seat and loomed menacingly. I wondered vaguely how much time had passed since Hughie had clipped somebody.

"You go with Patricia to the *California* to pay them off that night, only not the payoff they were expecting? Or did you go alone?"

Cave stood unsteadily and started up the steps. Hughie blocked him.

Cave turned to look at me, all the while pointing a quivering finger at Dunnum. "Tell him to get out of my way."

"You tell him."

"I'm leaving here whether you like it or not. You can't stop me."

"You gave them money, they gave you the film," I said. "You fed them poison, and they politely returned the scratch to you."

"I am going to sue you for libel."

"This would be slander, Russell."

"Call it what you want, Brand, but you're all wet. Even if you wired that chisel and such a film did exist, don't you think it would have been destroyed by now?"

"I would think."

"And this little flight of fancy of yours would have no substance. The cops would do nothing more than laugh in your face."

"I would think that, too."

Cave squared his shoulders. "So get out of my way. We are done here."

"Except for one thing."

Cave let out an exasperated breath. "And that would be?"

"VanderSaant had copies of those other flickers he shot. Don't you think he might have copies of all of them, just in case?"

Another hunch, another swift jab that caught him flush. A little twitch bit the corner of his kisser and his dark eyes again flashed briefly. He leaned against one of the seats, his posture that of a man reeling under the hard body blows.

"You're just guessing," he said weakly.

"And if he had made copies and somebody found them, just maybe it was the bulls. They searched Vander-Saant's place after he died. They searched his office here. I'm told he had a box of stuff down in props and the bulls went through that."

Cave tried to gather himself. "What's that to me but grease? I didn't kill anyone. Neither did Patricia Metcalf."

"Doesn't matter."

"Why do you say that?"

"She's painted herself into a tight corner, but there's a

couple of ways for her to get out from under this mess."

"And what's that?" Cave asked.

"Confess her sins to Harry. Promise him she'll be a good girl. Of course, that means she'll have to toss rats like you off her sinking ship. But you'll be too busy with deeper worries to pull a lousy shakedown on her."

"She has no reason to do that."

"You mean she can't do that," I said. "Not as long as you've got the bulge and can put the bite on her. But that bulge goes away if Harry York decides she's too much trouble. Where do you stand if she doesn't have a career to look after?"

"She's got a contract with Harry York. She's one of his studio's biggest stars. If I know one thing about that bastard, it's that he'll protect his investment."

"As long as there's a payoff at the end to make it worth his time and money." I shook my head. "The law of no return catches up sooner or later."

"Listen, Brand. If you have nudie flickers of Patricia, you need to produce them. Put them up there on that screen. Prove they exist. Isn't that why you brought me up here? Or is your angle just a rotten bluff?"

"There's a second way out for her. She can tell York what you're up to, and he'll personally put you under glass for keeps."

"Go to the cops, you bastard. Peddle your blackmail and murder hooey all you want. You can't do that because those pictures don't exist, and you're damned insulting by suggesting otherwise. Now get out of my way."

"They exist, Cave, and you know it."

He clenched both fists. "Are you going to let me leave?"

"Why don't you ask Patricia if she thinks VanderSaant made any copies?"

"I won't insult her by suggesting any such thing."

"The buttons will, and strongly," I told him. "What do you think she'll do when the bulls stick their long horns in her? How much gaff will she stand when she can finger you for the fall and sweetly skip away? Better for you to get ahead of her."

"Don't try to pull that old dodge on me."

"All right, wise head, how about this angle? How many times did you meet Rachel Anne Maddon at the Braebern? You two were seen there together at least twice. The help there said she had a habit of slipping out before daylight."

Cave let out a long breath. "You go too far, Brand. There is no reason to drag her into this."

"She's already in it, Cave. You two find time to whisper sweet nothings about VanderSaant and the nudie flickers he shot of Rachel five or six years ago? You try to crab a way to get your mitts on that film, too?"

"You son of a bitch, let me out of here."

"Walls have ears, Cave, especially at the Braebern."

I told Hughie to step aside. Cave started for the door.

"And by the way," I said, "if you're trying to bleed Patricia you'd really need to know if there are any copies."

Cave ignored me and jerked open the door. Detective Sergeant Calvin Forrester glowered at him. The sergeant put a meaty hand on Cave's chest and held up his police buzzer. Another baby grand stepped out of the shadows behind the sergeant.

"Not so fast, buddy," Forrester growled.

I grinned at Cave. "Russell, this gentleman has been watching you up in the booth and he's wise to everything you've spilled. He has some questions for you, I believe. The sergeant would very much like to be the fella who solves the Lemmert murders."

"I got nothing to say."

"Buddy," Forrester sneered, leaning in on Cave, "I think you got plenty to say. We're gonna shake your tree till something falls out and busts wide open."

"Russell," I said flatly, "these boys are going to take you downtown. Doesn't matter if you don't want to go. They are going to take you downtown and show you a little room in the basement that has a small table, a few hard-backed chairs and a bright light. You won't like the place. They are going to tighten the screws and sooner or later you're going to spill like a busted box of rice."

"I demand to see a lawyer."

"The sergeant will be happy to oblige."

"Sure, buddy, sure." Forrester grinned broadly. "We'll hunt one up for you in two or three days." He leaned in closer, his mean eyes black spears. Standing behind Cave, I could feel the heat of Forrester's breath. "Maybe sooner than that," the sergeant said. "Paperwork sometimes gets misplaced, sometimes shows up in the damnedest places. Me and you and some of the boys are gonna kick a few things around before that happens."

Forrester eyed me. The mean look was gone but he didn't smile. "Thanks, Brand. Maybe I owe you one."

"Maybe you'd like some pubic hair."

The hard look returned to Forrester's pan.

"Sorry, bad joke," I said.

"That was some crack," Dunnum said when they were gone.

I wired him about the bull down at the city jail. "I slipped a lovely bit player a yard to cut me a snip," I told him.

"Hundred bucks is an expensive snatch. And now she thinks you're a satyr."

I grinned. "Of course, she does. I'm a motion picture producer."

"You watch her cut it? I mean just to be certain it was authentic."

"She offered to let me. Poor thing couldn't understand why I wanted the swag but refused to watch her perform the deed."

"It's a strange world." Dunnum got us back on track. "How long you think that gink will hold out? I doubt he makes it through the night."

"Cave won't make it an hour, Hughie. They'll take him downtown and smack him around a little and after a bit somebody will drive a rubber hose into his kidneys a couple of times. He'll start lying to fend them off but the bulls will twist him up in his lies and they'll wave that hose around and smash the table with it, and he'll dirty his pants and crack open like a rotten walnut. Cave's built for speed, not distance."

"You make it sound like you've played that scene before."

I nodded. "I sat in on a few gassers in my time, Hughie. Bulls like Forrester are real pros at that game."

"Maybe that bimbo will sing before they even get him downtown."

"He might at that. You may as well go home, Hughie."

"It's been fun. Don't worry. I'm mum on your snatch story. Although I'd sure like to glom the look on Alice's face."

"You'll get a close look at my fist if you tell her."

Hughie grinned and went out the door. I got Alice on the blower and told her not to expect me home until late, maybe not until morning. I fended off some hot questions and told her to stay close to the phone.

"Mother wants to go to a movie. I was hoping you'd come with us."

"Nix that. I need you to stay by the phone."

"Important?"

"I'm counting on you."

"Ooooh, I feel like I'm in an Inspector Cooper picture." Her tone changed from playful to serious. "Say, you aren't in some kind of danger, are you?"

"No, sweetheart. It's just business. I'll tell you all about it when I get home."

I called Jimmy Gallen's private home number. He answered on the second ring.

"Jimmy, we need to find Patricia Metcalf and hide her out. Police will be coming after her and you don't want her found."

"What the—"

"No time to talk. Beat it to her house and if she's there, take her somewhere the bulls can't find her. Send some of your boys out to scour the town, anywhere they can think to look. Tell them to hide her out if they find her. I'm going to the Braebern. If she's there I'll take a room and stash her in it and call Alice. If you can't find Metcalf, call Alice and take it from there. If you find her, hide her good and wire Alice. I'll check with her. Got it?"

"On my way."

I turned out the lights and found my way down to the Mercedes. I took a locked box out of the back, opened it and pulled out the Colt .45 automatic—the 1911 model I had used in the Great War. I had two full clips with it and a shoulder rig.

I had no ticket to wear iron anymore, but that rated only a minor beef. I hadn't used the Colt in a long time, other than target shooting in the far back lot with Dunnum and some of his boys. I didn't intend to use it this night, but I had decided the night before to put it in the Mercedes. I had a hunch I might want the bulge.

I fired up the roadster, pulled out of the studio lot and turned right onto Sunset, headed for the Braebern Hotel.

CHAPTER 36

The sallow-faced night clerk holding down the Braebern's main desk tried not to lick his pale lips as I slowly counted out five double sawbucks and arranged them invitingly on the polished wood in front of him. I covered Ben Franklin's face on one of the bills with my York Brothers identification card.

"How may I help you, sir?"

"Is Patricia Metcalf in? This is studio business and I need to see her without delay, and without turning any heads."

The gink's lamps had a hard time switching from Ben's puss to mine. He pulled it off and nodded at me. "I will ring her, sir."

"Don't bother her just yet. I need a room on the ground floor, in the back and as close to the back door as you can get me."

"Yes, sir." His noodle bobbed like a rowboat on a stormy sea. His right hand twitched as he tried not to reach for the scratch. "I can get you a standard room very close to the rear exit. Number four. Would that be acceptable?"

"That'll do," I said amiably. "I'll need it for an hour or two and nobody else needs to know. Got that?"

"Of course. You may trust our discretion, sir." He

picked up a pen beside the registry. "What name shall I record in the register?"

"Forget the register."

The clerk didn't bat a peeper. "Yes, sir, as long as you require the room only for an hour or two the register will not be necessary."

"Two hours tops, and keep it to yourself."

"Of course, sir."

"She still taking room eight-forty?"

His head bobbed. "Yes, sir, she reserves that room."

He handed me a gold key hooked on a gold ring attached to a flat gold tab with room number four stamped on one side and the name, address and phone number of the hotel on the other.

"I'm not here. You never saw me." I put my hand on the Franklins. "That goes for anybody who asks. Pipe that?"

"Yes, sir."

"Do that and there's another century for you."

"Yes, sir," he said. I never saw a brighter smile. "Am I to understand, sir, that you specifically mean Mr. McLain?" he asked.

"You're a bright chap, brother."

Number 4 was the only room off a short hallway at the back of the hotel. A few steps past the door, the hallway ended at the rear exit.

I left the lights burning in Number 4 and the door unlocked. A sleepy-eyed elevator operator rode me to the eighth floor. I slipped him a sawbuck and told him to hang an out of order sign and to keep his cage handy.

"Mister, for ten bucks I'd ignore the queen of Sheba."

I rapped lightly on the door to Patricia Metcalf's suite. A tall, robust bruno with bright blue eyes and lots of blond, wavy hair answered, fully dressed except for his tuxedo jacket and shoes. A black bow tie hung loosely around his neck. His jacket lay on the bed beside a mink stole.

Behind him, Patricia lounged comfortably on a chaise, her dark red evening gown showcasing her ample charms. The slit in the dress showed a shapely gam up to where it started. She held a gasper in a gold holder in her left hand, a champagne glass filled to the brim in her right hand. She craned her neck to see who was at the door, but didn't crack her pan when she made me.

"What is it?" the bo asked me, poker faced.

"Let him in, James. He's a producer at my studio."

James's pan lit up and he shoved a hand at me. "Yes, sir. Pleased to meet you."

"Me too," I said. "Now pin on your diapers and dust."

The showy smile left his handsome puss. Patricia set down her glass and regarded me curiously. I shouldered past James. He reached for me and started to say something but Patricia hushed him with a shake of her head. A serious look spread across her waterproof face. Her eyes warily searched my mug. "I have a feeling you didn't just show up for caviar and bubbly."

"We have to talk, sister. Alone."

She smiled softly at James. "I'm sorry, darling, but it appears our evening has been tactlessly interrupted. I must ask you to leave quietly. We can take this up another time."

I looked blandly at James. His eyes darted from Patricia to me, back to her. He nodded. "Yes, I see how it is."

"Pal," I said, "you'd outrun Man O' War if you had any clue."

"I didn't expect you to give in so soon, my love," Patricia purred.

James reached for his shoes. He and Patricia tossed me inquisitive looks as I ambled around the room, nosing behind pictures on the walls, examining the lamps, peeking behind the pricey furniture. Behind the chaise, a thin wire snaked down a leg and disappeared into a tiny hole in the floor. I found another wire in the adjoining room behind the bed's headboard.

I came back into the sitting room. James shrugged into his tuxedo jacket, and gave Patricia a brotherly kiss on the cheek and let his hand rub her leg. He snatched his top hat, gave me a friendly nod, and was gone.

"Who's the jobbie?"

"A new player at MGM." She smiled lustily. "I think he's going to be a star."

"You getting in on the ground floor?"

"I told you once before that a lady must keep her options open. But he's yesterday's wash, now that you're here."

"You might want to keep him hanging on the line a little longer."

"Oh? So why are you here?"

"Bulls picked up Russell Cave about an hour ago and took him downtown." Her eyes turned blank. "How long do you think he'll hold up under a hard grill?" I asked.

"How hard?"

"A gashouse. The works. They know he was in on the Lemmert deaths. They know about the nudie flicker you made for VanderSaant."

"How do—"

"Cave spilled to me and the bulls were listening in. The bulls have already started looking for you. Cave will spill about this place. My hunch is he already has, and the bulls won't waste any time getting here."

She studied my face. "You seem awfully certain about Russell."

"You know that egg better than I do. How tough would you say he is?"

"He might give my hairdresser a close race." She exhaled smoke, inhaled champagne, treated me to a lusty smile. "And you have come to my rescue again on your white steed. What is it you want me to do?"

I picked up the stole. "Put your shoes on. I've got a room on the first floor, in the back."

I slipped the elevator boy two fins from my nearly empty pocket and told him to keep his yap shut. He nodded, slid the two bills into his uniform pocket, and took the cage down to the first floor. We waited outside the elevator until the doors closed, then made it unseen to room four.

Patricia sat on the edge of the bed, shaking slightly. She lit another cigarette, this time not bothering with the holder. She took a long drag and pulled her mink up so that it modestly covered the long slit in her dress.

I rang up Alice. She wanted desperately to know what I was up to. Gallen had just phoned and said he would call back shortly.

"Can't talk now, sweetheart. I'll be home as soon as I can. Tell Gallen I just called. He'll know what to do."

I hung up to shut off more questions until I got home. I faced Patricia. I spread my feet and dug balled fists into my hips. "My hunch is Cave will say you killed the Lemmerts."

"No. No. Why would—"

"He's facing the gallows, sister. He'll talk his head off and say anything he thinks might help soften the beef."

"No. Russell is—"

"Break it off," I said sharply "You said it yourself. That cake-eater won't stand the gaff. His best way out is to make you the patsy."

Her face turned to me, mouth open, her perfect white teeth clenched. Hard trouble had smacked her on the jaw and her acting talents couldn't mask her fear. Real emotion or phony, tears formed in her eyes.

"I might nurse you through this mess if you come clean."

"Russell killed them. I didn't mean for him to…I just wanted to pay them off and get them away from me. I had no idea he—"

"They were gouging you over your nudie film."

"It is not what you think." She ground out the gasper in an ashtray, pulled a frilly hankie from her handbag, and dabbed gently at her eyes. She blew her nose lightly and held the mop in clenched hands folded across her lap. "I made that film for Cleland just after we married. I was sixteen and just getting started and needed the money. That was long before I—"

"Cleland bleed you over it?"

"No. Never. It made us some money, but then a far better opportunity came along."

"Yeah," I grunted. "Leviticus Bible and his stepdaughter."

"Cleland said it was a gold mine. I didn't want anything to do with it. Blanche and I had become friendly and I begged him to let it go—"

"Stop it. We don't have the time for that. I know how VanderSaant liked to pass his time."

"David said that for fifty grand he would give me the film and I would never see him or his mother again. He said they were going to Rio and that I wouldn't have to worry about them coming back for more. He said we all had plenty to be ashamed of. He just wanted out."

"So you decided to pay him off."

She nodded. "I could easily afford it."

"And you believed him?"

"Yes. Yes, certainly. After all, he was still my stepson. Cleland had treated David miserably and, frankly, I thought David deserved the money. Do you know Cleland cut him out of his will? David and his mother. Left it all to me. I felt sorry for both of them."

"So you okayed the payoff and gave Russell the scratch."

"He was to take it to the boat the night before David and his mother sailed. I was terrified to go myself for fear I'd be recognized. I knew the ship would be packed that night. What with Cleland's death and our pictures in the newspapers, well, I needed to avoid being seen."

"Giving Cave that payoff was a dumb play."

She lit another gasper. "Yes, I see that now, but I trusted Russell. And I thought he was dizzy for me."

"And when you found out how things stood with him, you ran straight to me for protection. You needed someone you knew could handle that fancy sharper for you. That was some act you put on in my office."

"It wasn't entirely an act."

"But a girl has to keep her options open."

"You mock me."

I snorted. "I might get around to apologizing if you keep feeding me the straight goods. Did David say there were no copies of those flickers?"

"He promised me. Cleland had told me before there were no copies and that he was keeping the only one he had plenty safe. He knew what it would do to my career if it came out. Believe me, he was as invested in my career as anyone."

"But David found it?"

"Yes, and after his father was killed he wanted nothing more than to sell it to me and clear out. His father's death scared him."

"Did David know who killed his father?"

She took a long pull on the gasper. "If he did, he didn't say."

"But he promised you a one-time deal?"

"Yes. If I had the film, I was safe. I have a lot at stake

and that film could ruin it all. Fifty grand was a small price to pay under the circumstances."

"Where's the scratch now?"

"Russell kept it." Her eyes dropped and she let out a loud sigh. Her hands began fumbling with the hankie. The cigarette dangled from her lips. "And he has the film."

"No, sister. I don't think so. Shapes up that someone else has it."

The shock on her face was no act. The second gasper went into the ashtray. I sat beside her on the bed and asked softly, "But Cave was shaking you down?"

"Yes."

"My guess is more than money is involved."

"Russell wants to be my personal manager. And my agent, and all for a big cut of what I make. And I have to marry him."

"That won't be what he's spilling to the buttons," I told her. "He'll have a different story for them if he can keep any sense about him."

She shuddered. "Russell doesn't think that fast."

"If he does, he'll tell them you killed the Lemmerts. He'll spill the works. If he can pin the cure on you, he can make a clean sneak."

"I did not kill them. Please believe me. I was very fond of my stepson. And Blanche. I would not have done anything to hurt them."

"Even though they were bleeding you?"

She shook her head. "I did not resent them asking for money. I thought at least half of Cleland's estate should have gone to David, anyway. And David promised I'd have the film and he would be gone for good. I gave Russell the money. He was supposed to give the money to them at the boat and bring the film to me."

"Okay, sister, sit tight. Don't leave this room and

don't phone a soul. Jimmy Gallen will be up here in a little while. Pipe that?"

She nodded. She took a deep breath and seemed about to pop open. She was twisting her hankie into a pretzel.

"Thank you. Thank you. It seems you are indeed my white knight. No line, Neil, I didn't kill David and his mother. I just wanted to pay them off and destroy that film."

"It's a cinch Cave didn't destroy it."

Her eyes widened. "You mean...that means the police..."

"That's right, sister." I stood. "Be ready to dangle the second Jimmy shows up. Tell him to call me in your room. I'll be waiting up there. Now, do one other thing. Call Beck McLain. Go through the switchboard. If he isn't in his room, have them hunt him up. Get him up to your room right away. Don't mention me. Be sexy and mysterious. Let him think he's got a chance to seduce you. Say there's money in it for him. Say anything to get him up there to your room. Give him an Academy Award performance, but leave me out of it. Got it?"

"And then?"

"Sit tight and wait for Gallen. Do anything else, sister, and you might be putting your lovely neck in a tight noose."

CHAPTER 37

I left the door to Patricia Metcalf's suite slightly ajar and dragged a chair over to a small table in the right corner of the front room, facing the door. I took the .45 from the shoulder rig and a full clip from my coat pocket, racked the slide and laid it on the table within easy reach of my right hand. I took off my fedora and placed it over the Colt, leaving the grip exposed just enough so I could easily get to it. I didn't figure to use it, but it gave me the bulge if I needed it. I turned out all the lights and settled down to wait.

A soft knock sounded within two minutes. The door crept open a few inches and the hallway lights threw harsh shadows over Beck McLain's face.

It reminded me of a scene late in *Inspector Cooper* when a shaft of light from a doorway slowly crawls across the killer's pan, exposing him to the hopefully surprised audience.

"Miss Metcalf?" His soft voice carried a hint of expectation. "This is Beck McLain. You asked me to come up."

He pushed the door a little harder. The shaft of light from the hallway fell across my feet. I switched on the lamp beside the chair.

"Come on in, Beck. Miss Metcalf had to step out."

McLain's pan drew a harsh mask. He stepped inside and pushed the door closed. He spread his feet and put his hands on his hips, leaning slightly forward. I caught the faint whiff of cheap aftershave.

"This about that security job?" he sneered. "I tried to call York back and couldn't get past the girl at the switchboard."

"You'll be lucky to ever get that far again."

"Okay, Brand. You're here for a reason. What's the beef?"

"Have a seat. Some bulls you might know are on their way."

"On their way, why?"

"Think about it, Beck. I want to talk to you before they get here."

"Why? Tryin' to peddle more phony jobs? Spread more lies about me. Maybe you got some spare kale you want to slip me, just for old times' sake."

"I want to tell you a story."

He sneered. "Funny or sad?"

"A little bit of both, Beck. But it's got an ending that'll knock 'em dead."

"You can stuff your ending. Why are the bulls coming?"

"Beck, you need to learn patience. Your lack of patience—and a little bit of temper—cost you two fights against me when we boxed back in the day."

"Maybe you were just lucky."

"No, Beck. Two hard right crosses to the jaw, not luck, cost you those two fights. You have a bad habit of dropping your left when you throw your right jab, and you were easy to beat to the punch. Now sit down. It's a long story."

"Anything from you would just be static, Brand. You and me are on the outs, permanently. Anymore trouble from any of your York pastries and I'm calling the buttons and you can deal with the publicity."

"I wouldn't worry about that too much, Beck."

"And why is that?"

"You're going to be moving on tonight. The Braebern will be looking around for a new house dick come tomorrow morning."

McLain's eyes closed to slits. "You got something to say then spit it out."

"You told me a lot of things that day at the studio when you thought a cush job was on the line. I got to wondering how you glommed all that dope. So I nosed around tonight. Found your wire behind the chaise in this room and the headboard in the other room. I bet you put wire in every room high-pillows keep on a regular basis. That alone will get you a hard bounce from the place. It'll also buy you a bit in an upstate can."

Beck's pan went blank. "It's a security measure."

"Who's squealing static now? No, Beck, it's an extortion measure. Wise head like you can crab all sorts of rumble on a wire, including nudie flickers and sugar payoffs. He can hear just about anything except maybe a Sunday sermon."

"You're right, Brand. I do need to sit down while you sing." He eased his bulk onto the edge of the chaise. "Go on, entertain me some more."

"Listening in on this room alone, you could have gotten ribbed up about a certain flicker Patricia Metcalf made and wishes she hadn't. You would have heard her talking about it with VanderSaant, maybe even with Russell Cave present. If Cave wasn't, she would have told him about it when the Lemmerts tagged her for a shakedown. You would have heard her give Cave fifty large to buy back that film. You would have faced that rube down and cut yourself in on the Lemmert angle, then make

Cave fork over the scratch and the film. Then you could bleed Metcalf, through Cave, and she wouldn't get wise to any of it. A clean sneak for you and when the heat was off her, you could bump Cave to keep him from ever icing the deal. So you came up here just now expecting another payoff from her."

"You're gowed up, Brand."

"You pump the Nevada gas into the champagne that lit up the Lemmerts?"

He leaned back on an elbow and grinned at me. "What'd I just say?"

"It doesn't follow you'd trust Cave to do the job. My hunch is you went down to the *California* with him to make sure he didn't queer the deal. You wouldn't want to risk the chance that cake-eater would peach on you."

"If there was anything like the straight goods in that spiel, why the hell would I sic you on VanderSaant? I called you to come get him that night."

"You did, Beck. You heard all you needed and you wanted VanderSaant wrapped up and out of the hotel before he got too loud. Too bad for you Gallen wasn't home."

"It's a good yarn, Brand, but there's nothing to it."

"Russell Cave and Rachel Anne Maddon also took a room here. You took pains to tell me that, although you maybe didn't make her. I'm betting you wired that room too."

Nothing but hard lines creased Beck's face.

I grinned in return. "You would have heard them, among other things, discuss a certain film Rachel Anne also made for VanderSaant. She wanted that film, but didn't know how to go about getting it. Cave wanted it, too. That would give him two high-paid actresses to bleed. But neither one of them had the sand to face down VanderSaant. You got big ideas, too, Beck, so you went to see them. Me, if I was you, I'd have told them I could back down that gink and get the film for a price. And if I couldn't get it, they wouldn't owe me a cent."

"You're slicing that drivel mighty thin, Brand. The DA and the cops and everybody else would just laugh at you."

"You know where I'm going, Beck. You would have also meant to scare the Metcalf flickers from Vander-Saant, only you didn't know his son had it by then. You must have seen the gun Maddon had with her and got a better idea. At any rate, you sold her on the idea, and she gave you her key to VanderSaant's back door. You walked in on VanderSaant when he was upstairs. It was dark and you didn't want to turn on the lights. You propped open the kitchen door so you could see to get up the stairs. You meant to scare him. Get the drop on him and beat him till he talked. An ex-dick like you would rate a gink like VanderSaant an easy mark, but your easy mark went for a gun and you had to shoot him. He stumbled out of the bedroom and you heard a noise out back. Car doors, maybe. You didn't want to risk another shot, but you couldn't leave him alive to talk, so you tossed him over the rail. You wouldn't have wanted to leave the rod. The bulls could connect it to Rachel Anne Maddon, and that meant you might lose a good meal ticket if they pinched her. My hunch is VanderSaant knocked the gat out of your mitt when you tossed him and it fell over the rail and landed beside the body. It was dark and hard to see with only the light from the kitchen door and then you heard someone come in the back door. You didn't have time to pick up the gat. You hustled out the front door just as a fella named Charles Goriot came in the back. He spotted the body and recognized the gun and thought Rachel Anne had killed VanderSaant. He picked up the gun and got out of there."

"You're just beating your gums, Brand."

"Stick around. There's more."

"Break it up, Brand. That Goriot palooka copped to the fall, and Cave's too scared to tell you anything. He has too much to lose."

"There's the dame."

His eyes narrowed. "Rachel Anne? That sad little bunny won't get anybody to listen to her. You think Patricia Metcalf will beat her gums to anybody with all that she stands to lose?"

He stood. "I'm taking air now. And by the way, Brand, when that kitten pulled that gun on me I took it away from her while that Cave gink stood there pissing his pants. You're damned right I wouldn't let him go down to that boat alone."

I reached for my fedora and came up with the .45 pointed at McLain's belly.

He looked at it a hard second, smiled. "You won't use that."

"I know how."

"You won't shoot an unarmed man."

"You would."

"I ain't you."

"My wife is probably even happier about that than I am. A good story needs a finish, Beck. You'll like this one. It's a pill. The cops picked up Russell Cave a couple of hours ago. They like him for the Lemmerts, among other things. They're wise to the nudie flickers. A few brunos are giving Cave the works now, and how long do you think it'll take before that dewdropper falls apart like a paper baseball?"

"What's that to me?"

"You think he'll finger Metcalf instead of you?"

"My word against his."

"You might get somebody to buy a line, Beck, but

once the buttons start sniffing around you, what do you reckon they'll turn up? A large wad of dough? Leftover poison, maybe? Wires in every room? A missing button?"

McLain's face turned as cold as Harry York's heart. He started to say something, sucked in his breath when the horn blew. I answered on the first ring, keeping the Colt lined up with Beck's ample belly.

"Neil," Jimmy Gallen whispered. "Do you have Patricia?"

"Yes, she's expecting you to call. Where are you?"

"I'm in the lobby. I get you. Can't talk?"

"She wants four," I said, "delivered to the rear as soon as possible."

"What? She wants four? What do you mean?"

"That's correct, four. As soon as you can get to it."

"Wait a minute." After a pause, he asked, "You mean she's in room four?"

"Yeah, that's right."

"Is that in the back of the building?"

"She requests you make the delivery as soon as possible."

"Okay, Neil, I'll have her out of here in two minutes."

"Yes, be swift. That's a hot bundle and needs to be put on ice."

"I'll take her to Harry's place. He'll skin us if we don't wire him tonight. Get there as soon as you can. You know where it is?"

"I do."

The line went dead. McLain had eased his bulk to the edge of the chaise, poised, frantically trying to glom his chance for a break.

"What was that about?" he asked. "What's going on here?"

"Patience, dear Beck. Patience. Where were we? Oh,

yeah. Russell Cave's got a fancy yarn to spill to the buttons, Beck. They'll be here soon. They'll toss every room in the joint and they'll find your wires and they'll sniff out that fifty grand you squirreled somewhere, now they've got the scent. They'll believe Cave, some of it anyway, and maybe they'll have second thoughts about what Rachel Anne will have to say."

"I can sing my head off," McLain said smugly, "and where will that leave Patricia Metcalf and all those other York phonies I've been protecting."

"And bleeding? You should ask yourself, Beck, who's going to believe Chicken Little after the sky has crashed?"

A solid pounding rattled the door. Beck jumped to his feet and spun to face the door. A voice yelled to open up, but bulls on the prowl seldom show tolerance. The doorknob turned and Lieutenant Frank Harless and Sergeant Calvin Forrester strolled in, followed by Art Stiles and a couple of baby grands wearing plain clothes and fierce scowls.

I set the safety and put the Colt down beside my fedora, the barrel pointed toward the wall. Two uniformed bulls blocked the suite's exit. Forrester went straight to McLain, dragging nippers from the side pocket of his coat.

"Beck McLain, you're under arrest for suspicion of extortion and murder," Forrester growled. He spun Beck around and snapped the bracelets in place. Two uniformed bulls led McLain out of the room.

Harless stood in front of me, hands on hips, and shook his head. Stiles, slightly behind Frank, scowled at me.

"Where's Patricia Metcalf?" Frank asked me.

"You intend to arrest her?"

"That's police business, strictly."

I shrugged. "I hear Miss Metcalf likes to spend her

evenings alone, curled up with a good book and a bottle of Pluto Water."

"She isn't home, Brand. A little digging brought us here."

"This is her suite but imagine my surprise when I found McLain here and not her. I forgot, did you say she was wanted for something?"

Nothing about Frank's face softened. "For questioning," he said.

"Patricia Metcalf has no reason to avoid the buttons. She was saying the other day how much she enjoyed your visits. She won't be hard to find."

"No, she won't. And we'll round her up without your help."

"She might even cut you a piece of pie, Frank, and sign some photos."

"I'm sure she'll play nice." Harless looked at the Colt. "I won't even ask if you've got a ticket for that hardware. I hope you didn't plug anybody."

"I was showing it to Beck. He said it was a nifty gun."

"Take it and dangle. We have work to do in here and we're sorta in the mood to do it without your help."

I eased the clip out and dropped it into my coat pocket. I slid the Colt into the shoulder rig and picked up my fedora.

Forrester stepped up beside Harless, a tight smile on his hard pan. "You did do us a favor, Brand."

"How long did that gink stand it?" I asked him.

The tight smile widened. "He wet his britches before we even got warmed up. Took one hard slap to the kidneys and started spillin' so fast his teeth like to come out. Took three sets of ears to catch it all."

"All you need?"

"It's a start," Harless said coldly.

I nodded. "He cop to the Lemmerts or finger someone else for that job?"

"Finger who?"

"Patricia Metcalf, if he was looking for a patsy. Beck McLain, if he was scared enough to wire you the straight goods."

"He was plenty scared," Forrester said.

"You're free to take air." Harless jerked a thumb toward the door. "You make yourself scarce unless we ask for you."

"Frank, your boys find a burgundy button somewhere in VanderSaant's place?"

Harless regarded me warily. "Yeah. It was under the body. Why?"

"I think you'll find the blazer it goes to in Beck McLain's closet."

"How'd you know about that button? We didn't pass out that info."

"Saw it in an evidence bag."

Frank nodded. "Okay, we'll check McLain's closet. You can dust."

"One other thing. What you boys are looking for is behind the chaise, Frank. There's one in the other room, behind the bed."

Harless pulled out the chaise, grunted. He turned to a baby grand, who nodded and eased into the other room with his partner. They forced the bed's headboard out a few inches from the wall, and one of them knelt down. He quickly got to his feet and nodded again.

"McLain wired other rooms," I said. "My hunch is they're only on this floor. The hotel rents this floor to a lot of high-pillows who want to keep their faces hidden and their pleasures secret. And some of them have ripe secrets. You'll probably find a storage closet or something on this floor where McLain set up his stuff. He had a sweet little layout going for him."

"Not anymore." Frank stared at me several hard seconds. "Art, call down to the desk and see if Brand rented a room tonight."

Stiles made the call and we waited in silence. Stiles spoke a couple of words into the horn and then muffled the mouthpiece in his hand. "Clerk swears nobody rented a room tonight. He says the place is booked solid."

I considered those five Franklins a yard well spent.

Frank started to say something, stopped himself. "Go on, Brand, beat it. We won't need you anymore tonight."

"Boss, I think he knows where the Metcalf dame is," Stiles said.

"Damn straight he does, but we'd get nothing but a run-around from him. Send him on his way. Call headquarters and have as many squads sent over as they can spare. We're going to go through this joint room-by-room, including the closets."

I snapped my fedora in place. "You're going to make a lot of enemies, Frank. No telling who you might roust."

"What's another enemy?" Harless growled.

I made the door before Frank stopped me. "Neil, give my love to Alice. You two have a nice life."

CHAPTER 38

Harry York had magically managed to squeeze his underprivileged family into a two-story, four-teen-bedroom shack on North Carolwood Street, high up in Holmby Hills. York family members held down the long leg of the L-shaped manor, while the shorter leg housed guest rooms and servants' quarters and a solarium large enough for a herd of giraffes. A front yard about the size of Catalina Island stretched green and perfect along Carolwood, bordering several luxuriant trees, deep green head-high bushes and enough multi-colored flowers to overflow the Gardens of Versailles. The manicured lawn curved around the L and past the six-car garage, hiding the pool and pool house, the tennis court and the half-acre putting green.

A blindfolded pilot could have landed a Boeing 247 on the long roof had it not been for the cross hipped ga-bles and the dormers and towers.

A chiseled, white stone fence matching the big house surrounded the entire property, topping out about twice my height. The gated entrance had been left open and the tall uniformed gink standing there didn't try to stop me. He gave me a nod and a thumbs-up as I dashed past and up the circular driveway.

I squealed the Mercedes to a stop just behind Jimmy

Gallen's red-and-black Packard, just in front of a collection of Greek statues bordering a small pool. Water cascaded over a tall rock fountain in the corner of the pool. Curved stone steps led up to the imposing double doors, set off by long, narrow windows on each side.

York's squat butler opened the left door on my first knock. "Mr. Brand, sir. Mr. York is expecting you in the library. This way, sir."

I stepped into a large, nearly empty foyer, my heels clicking on the marble floor. More statues separated a few austere chairs only the desperate would sit in. Two large, matching tapestries decorated the cold white walls, one on the south and the other on the east. The butler held open the wide door between the tapestries that opened into York's library. The fractured Republican Party could have comfortably held its next national convention in Harry's library, but the three fractured people who looked up as I sauntered in did not appear at all comfortable.

Gallen had apparently been pacing the floor. When I entered, he stopped abruptly and leaned against a marble fireplace the size of an Army half-track. He eyed me with relief.

Patricia Metcalf sat stiffly in an overstuffed leather chair, a half-filled glass of amber fluid in her left hand. Her right hand shook slightly as she took a long drag on a gasper. Her sour smile held no humor. Her mink stole huddled on her lap. She had pulled the red evening gown's hem as far down to her ankles as it could get.

Harry York, puffing an ever-present Cuban, sat behind a dark-wood desk even bigger than the one in his studio office. The deep scowl on his flushed face might have started down in his toes, growing deeper red as it worked its way up. The heavy wooden library door closed behind me with a solid click that seemed to scare both Gallen and Patricia.

Nobody said a word for several seconds. Even the hands of the clock on Harry's desk seemed to freeze. Gallen and Metcalf were not going to pipe up until they were asked. I waited for Harry to break the silence, which he did with a sudden and lengthy stream of curse words that would have caused hard-crusted sailors to seek refuge.

When Harry's verbal barrage finally trailed off, all he had said boiled down to four simple words: "How bad is it?"

"Russell Cave spilled his guts tonight," I told him. "He copped to killing VanderSaant's ex-wife and their son, David. He would have wired the bulls about the nudie flickers VanderSaant shot. Cave knew about the ones of Patricia, and he knew about Rachel's. My hunch is he put Patricia on the spot for the Lemmerts, but the bulls wouldn't say. But they want to talk to her, and they'll pull the Rose Bowl off its foundation to do it."

Harry took a deep breath and scowled at Metcalf. I took the weight off my feet, thanks to an overstuffed chair by the door. I kept talking.

"You need to reach Patricia's lawyer tonight, Harry. Have Gallen write a statement for her—some hooey about how much she loved her sainted husband and that she had nothing to do with his death, or the deaths of his ex-wife and son. How the thought of their deaths prostrates her. Lay it on thick, Jimmy."

Gallen grinned. "My specialty."

"Call the DA, Harry, and tell him he can talk to Patricia sometime tomorrow. That'll get the immediate heat off. When she talks to the DA, don't let her answer any questions. She can read her statement—and make sure she turns on the faucets when she does—and then shut her yap permanently." I looked at Patricia. "Sister, I hope you can roll out a sad bunny act on cue."

She smiled and let tears stream down her reddened cheeks. "Perhaps I can convince the police of my innocence."

"It doesn't matter a damn what the buttons think, only what they can prove. It's a lead pipe cinch Cave fingered either you or Beck McLain for the Lemmerts, and those flickers give you motive. They've got Cave and McLain dead-to-rights and those two jobbies will sing plenty. Clam up and maybe the DA won't have enough to go after you."

"Beck McLain?" Those two words fouled Harry's mouth. His head popped up. "Isn't he that bum you brought—"

"That's right. He also killed VanderSaant, but I don't think the DA can prove that, not even if Cave tries to put him on that spot."

Harry's stogie rolled across his lips. He pulled it out and waved it around. "Didn't somebody confess to killing that pissant?"

I nodded. "Fella named Goriot, but that confession's got more plot holes in it than a Vincent Brothers picture. The DA will have to skirt that confession and try not to look like a sap. The press will roll him down Sunset on a hoop if he tries to go to court on it after tonight."

Harry nodded, turned to Patricia Metcalf. A strange light filtered through his dark eyes. His fingers began drumming the desktop.

"Patricia, you will appear before the DA tomorrow at the time of his choosing. I'll set it up for sometime around ten. I do not want you leaving this house, so he will come here. You will have your attorney present. You will read the peppered statement that Gallen will write and you will say nothing else. Is that amply clear?"

Patricia nodded. She ground out the half-smoked gasper in a crystal ashtray and reached for the red Farragamo shoes on the floor beside her feet.

"I'll set it up tonight," Harry growled, "and make that bastard promise no media will be here. I will not tolerate anybody getting wind about this and trying to smear me."

The glare returned to his eyes.

"As for you, my dear, I want you to pack your trunks the minute you get home tomorrow. As soon as we can make the arrangements after you see the DA, I'll have my studio pilot fly you up to San Francisco. On the cutie. I'll arrange that flight for you and I'll book passage for you on a boat to…to…who the hell cares?"

"Harry," I said. "QT or otherwise, the DA won't let her leave town."

"To hell with that lousy bum. I'll take care of that miserable grifter. And believe me, it won't come cheap."

"She can't go home, Harry," I said.

"Why not?"

"They're sitting all over her place tonight. Even after she talks to the DA they'll keep eyes on her place. She shows up tomorrow and then dusts, I'm betting she'll be shadowed. They'll also be watching your place to tail her if she leaves after she sees the DA."

York nodded. "All right then, Patricia, I'll send some-body to your place tonight to pack a couple of trunks for you. You have anyone there who can help?"

"My maid. She'll know what to pack."

"Send a studio truck over in the morning," I said. "Tell the driver to take her stuff to the lot. If the bulls tail it, you can bar them from the lot until they get a search war-rant." Harry snorted. I went on. "Transfer her stuff to an-other truck. Traffic flows in and out of the lot constantly and the bulls can't tail all of it. Tell the driver to haul her trunks to your airfield. Get a driver who's been around the block and can spot a tail."

"You said they'd be watching my place," Harry grunted.

I nodded. "They will. Get a makeup man over here and a hairdresser. Put Patricia in a man's suit, either cut or pin up her hair so it doesn't fall out from under a fedora, and cover her with a flogger. Bring over a bunch of studio people early tomorrow, long before the DA gets here. Say six or seven cars. Hide them out so the DA won't see them. When the DA leaves here tomorrow, send out three cars full of passengers and see if the bulls follow. Likely, they won't. If they don't, send out three more. Put Patricia in one of them and take her to the airfield. Tell the studio pilot—what's his name?"

Harry shook his head.

"Wells Mitchell," Gallen said.

"Phone Mitchell to have that plane gassed and running when she gets there and don't waste time getting in the air. Tell him to file two flight plans. San Francisco and San Diego. Bribe somebody to show the bulls the phony plan if they do show up."

"You think they will?" Gallen asked.

"It's just a precaution. If there's any heat, your guy can just say there was a last minute change in plans, and he got balled up and showed the bulls the wrong one. Harry can square that beef easy enough."

Harry nodded, looked at Metcalf. "I'll send someone along with you, a male companion."

His eyes turned to me. I wasn't going.

"Brand, you know Mack Sanger," Harry asked.

I nodded.

"Ring him up for me, will you? Tell him I acquire one of his boys for a long ocean cruise. He won't need any details."

I nodded again.

"But you'll also acquire a female traveling companion," he told Patricia. "Someone close to you. Got anyone who can do that?"

"My personal assistant will accompany me," Metcalf said. "Miss Constance McLemore. She is unattached and always travels with me."

"Good. Passage will be booked in her name."

"How long will I be gone?"

"A damned long time."

Harry leaned back in his chair. He puffed on the Cuban and found great interest in the massive chandelier.

"Gallen will fix up another statement from you announcing your retirement from motion pictures. You intend to live abroad. You need to get away from the dreadful memories of your husband's death. He'll pile that on thick, too."

"Retirement?" Patricia's eyes flared. "But I have a contract."

"I could remind you about the morals clause, my dear, but no matter what everyone says, I am not a painfully heartless bastard. I'll live up to the terms of your contract until it perspires. By then, maybe someone will have paid for the death of your husband, and maybe the rest of this mess will have flown away, and you can come back. We play our cards right, your public will tremor to see you in pictures again."

"Thank you, Harry. I will, of course, do exactly as you say."

"Damn right, you will. Is everything clearly understood?"

"What if the police want to take me with them tomorrow?" she asked.

Harry rolled his eyes at me.

"Not likely," I told her. "They'll ask their questions and then do a little digging. If that does happen, tell the bulls you're too busy baking a cake to go with them."

Patricia tried a brighter smile. "The last time I baked a cake, it would have been more suitable as the cornerstone of a building."

"See?" I said. "It wouldn't have worked out, you and me. I admire a woman who knows her way around the oven and knows when to keep her yap closed."

"You are so right, Neil."

"So, it's understood?" Harry asked again.

She nodded her head. "Perfectly."

"We're counting on that," Harry said.

"I shall be ready. I am quite anxious to leave."

"You should be. When the scandal breaks about that nudie flicker you made, you need to be far away from here and far out of touch. I do not think I should have to impress on you the importance of that."

"No, Harry. I quite understand."

"Tell your Miss Macklemore to write to me personally, at my home, with your address when you settle. She is not to mention your name. You will receive a monthly check that lives up to the terms of your contract. When the coast looks clear, I'll let you know and you can come back home and resume your career. Understood?"

"Completely."

York pressed a buzzer on his desk. The library door silently opened. The stoic butler stood stiffly waiting.

"Henley, Miss Metcalf will be our guest tonight. Please open a room for her and ask one of the maids to get her anything she needs."

"Sir."

The door closed solidly behind Henley, and York turned back to Patricia.

"Breakfast will be served at seven," he told her. "My lawyer will be here. After breakfast, you and he will go over the statement Mr. Gallen will have written, and you can discuss with him what needs to be done. I trust you have a pleasant night, and I am sorry for all this, but it seems you have brought it upon yourself. Please wait outside for Henley. He will see to your every need. Good night, Patricia."

When the door closed behind her, Harry leaned back in his big leather chair and rubbed his eyes with the heels of both hands.

"Making pictures would be a lot easier if it weren't for actors. Disney's got the right idea. Laminated pictures."

Gallen slowly shook his melon. I sucked in my breath and tried not to snicker. I wanted to tell Harry the word was animated but this wasn't the time.

"Disney?" I said. "Isn't he that Mickey Mouse guy?"

Harry nodded. "Yeah, my neighbor. He doesn't have any trouble with that mouse of his running around getting into jams that take money to fix. But look at me? I'm a dizzy patsy for that Metcalf dame. She's costing me plenty, but what can I do? I'm suckered. Do you think she killed those two people?"

"No, I don't. She was content to pay them off but Cave had other ideas. He wanted the fifty grand and he could have used that flickers to bleed Metcalf for a lot more. Then McLain got wind of the deal, and it all blew up."

"And Cave told all that to the cops?"

"He would have covered himself with soap," I said.

York's eyes searched my face. "And they'll be happy with Cave and that McLain bum?"

I shrugged. "I think the DA will come around to your way of thinking."

"The DA has a practical side. He knows he can't be in office forever and he has to look out for his future." Harry turned to Jimmy Gallen, still leaning against the massive fireplace. "Don't you have something to write?"

"Yes, sir."

"I'm not paying you to stand around here."

Gallen fled. Harry pointed to the chair Patricia Metcalf had vacated. "Sit down closer, Neil. That was good work on that *Inspector Cooper* picture. You gave me just what I wanted, and those pictures will play well. I want you to do four or five more. By that time, they'll be running out of steam, and I'll give them over to somebody else until they die off. Nine or ten pictures are all the public will put up with before they tire of the series. Keep up the good work on the ones you do, and I'll have something better for you."

I stood. "Is that all, Harry? It's late."

"Yeah, but I want you here first thing in the morning."

"Okay, but I'm through playing copper, Harry."

"Nobody asked you to in the first place."

CHAPTER 39

What I told Harry York, I meant. I was finished with playing copper, although I hadn't many fine-tuned skills left in me, anyway. I had blundered through this whole mess, beginning to end, costing Harry York a little goodwill in high places, a couple of actors, and some scratch, of which he had plenty. In the end, Harry's money and political pull turned the thing in his favor, and he had no reason to sweat over losing a few players. An ill wind blew in new actors daily, right along with the marine layer.

In the end, the affair cost me a treasured friendship, although I held out the hope it would someday be repaired.

Somehow, Harry thought I had done him another good turn, just like in the Johnny Cutter mess, and I got in even more solid with him.

Turns out the public took to *Inspector Cooper*. Maybe the death of Leviticus Bible had something to do with the first picture's popularity. Harry reworked the credits and the publicity and played up Bible's name. Leviticus got top billing on everything connected to the picture, although the great actor appeared in only one scene, and that lasted just slightly less than four minutes. The picture made three times more at the box office than it cost to produce, and studio big shots began to wink and nod at me.

I finished three more routine *Inspector Cooper* programmers, and they all made money, even without Leviticus Bible. Four was enough. I turned the reins over to a young and ambitious producer hell-bent for celluloid immortality, after showering him with the same welcoming speech Eban Browner had given me.

Rose and I moved into an even more spacious office and started producing A-list pictures. I sometimes got invited to the roof to bask in the sunshine with top executives while Harry wasted our time. I decided the basic job didn't change, A or B. I pretended the A pictures were simply *Inspector Cooper* knock-offs, but this time I worked with big budgets, meatier scripts, and top people all the way around. I saw it as a worthless job that, in the end, churned out worthless pictures that conned the gullible public into shelling out hard-earned sugar. It brought me a new deal for a ridiculous five thousand clams a week at a time when the average joes, working important and necessary jobs—if they could find a job at all—brought home, if they were lucky, sixteen hundred dollars a year.

That change of fortune likely would have sent most men into spirals of ecstasy. It made me feel grummy. I had started out to be an honest cop, working an honest job for honest pay, but the dirtiest bull I ever knew framed me for taking a bribe. While he pushed up daisies from a long forgotten hole in the dark ground, I turned into a big butter-and-egg man, settling in to an easy lifestyle, knowing well the picture business would keep spinning on axles greased by big money with or without me.

At some point in his short and meandering life, a man faces the awkward decision whether to cross over whatever moral line he has drawn for himself, and he faces that decision for a variety of reasons. Most of those reasons—good or bad—have to do with a woman. I had a good woman and now a baby son. Making worthless motion pictures meant I provided for lives that were worth plenty. In the end, I guess, the drumbeat really had nothing to do with me.

Alice and I set up a couple of worthwhile charities, and I hired help I didn't need and gave them salaries much too large, simply to help salve my conscience in some small way. I resolved to be the best husband and father I could be, make the best worthless motion pictures I could produce, try my best to make my unsettled spot in the world worthwhile—and to hell with the rest of it.

The day after Patricia Metcalf gave her statement to the district attorney, she set sail with her personal assistant and one of Mack Sanger's hard-edged trouble boys. Nobody followed her from Harry's place. Nobody followed the truck carrying her trunks. As far as I could tell, nobody followed anybody. Harry's former motion picture star shared a deluxe cabin with Constance McLemore, and the name Patricia Metcalf appeared nowhere on the passenger list. By the time the DA tracked her down, she was frolicking on the sunny French Riviera with an authentic Italian count, a high-pillow official in Mussolini's fascist government. She apparently did not mind the handsome count sweating on top of her. She let him handcuff her and the former Patricia Metcalf, now the Countess Something-or-other, moved into a forty-room villa arranged along a mountainside overlooking Lake Como. Harry immediately quit paying her.

The Los Angeles district attorney tried hard to rope her in, but he stood the same chance of getting the countess back to the States as he did of convincing Mae West to quit motion pictures and join a convent.

Without Metcalf, the DA couldn't get the nudie flicker introduced into evidence, but he didn't need it. He had Cave's confession. The fifty grand—along with nudie flickers of Metcalf—turned up in a safety deposit box traced back to Beck McLain. The bulls also found in the box a little more than two pounds of nose candy. A jury wasted no time in finding Cave and McLain guilty of the murders of Charlotte and David Lemmert, with an additional charge of cocaine possession added to the beef against Beck. Those two had tickets for a long bit and a short rope at a place called Folsom.

The DA passed the VanderSaant case down to the lowest assistant on the rung and ran it through a quick, mock court case at the end of a long docket late on a Wednesday evening. In a trial with no jury, a predisposed and retiring judge—first cousin to the DA's wife—pronounced Charles Goriot guilty of manslaughter and ordered his seven-year stretch reduced to probation, with the stipulation Goriot did not leave the court's jurisdiction. As the district attorney hoped, the newspaper boys never got wind of it.

The next day, I was at the port to wave farewell to Goriot as he sailed off to Rio, by way of Havana, on *California*. A gink from the district attorney's office stood beside me, along with one of the LAPD's finest. We watched the big boat head out to sea and then went our separate ways. I went home to nurse three fingers of Kentucky's finest while I watched Alice nurse and bathe our son. That's when she informed me she expected another addition to the family before I could finish my next picture.

Some men get a lot luckier than they have any right to be.

THE END

About the Author

Ray Dyson first took up eating in Evansville, IN, just long enough ago that, not only is the house he was born in no longer there, neither is the street. He attended The Ohio State University School of Journalism and spent several years as a newspaperman, covering crime and sports. He is a former sports editor and sports columnist, and now lives in Mansfield, OH, with his wife, Pamela, where he works as a freelance journalist. He has a particular interest in American history (especially the Civil War), the American West, and the American cinema.

Dyson is the author of three other books: a baseball story, *Smokey Joe*, a Western novel, *Bannon: The Scavenger Breed*, and the first Neil Brand crime story, set in Hollywood in 1931, *The Ice Cream Blonde* (Black Opal Books 2016).